NO LONGER PRETENDING

Lauren caught at his fingers when he started to unbutton her jacket. "I'll do that," she said nervously. Just the touch of his hand on her throat had her areolas puckering with desire. "You go on to your room. I'm tired and want to go to bed."

Flint slid her a lazy smile. "You're not as unmoved by me as you pretend, Lauren. Why did you act as though nothing happened between us in the woods?"

"I . . . I don't know what you mean," she stammered. What was it about Flint Mahone? When she was near him common sense flew out the window. She made no protest when he pushed the neckline of her blue velvet gown down over her shoulders.

She was like a small bird hypnotized by a cobra, unable to move as he untied the ribbons of her camisole and slowly pushed it down to her waist.

He gazed at the twin mounds of her breasts, surmounted by pink puckered tips. "You are a wonder," he breathed, then lowering his head, he opened his mouth and covered most of one.

The roughness of his coat pressing into her tender flesh, the working of his teeth and tongue on her breast brought Lauren near to fainting.

Flint

Norah Hess

LEISURE BOOKS NEW YORK CITY

To Tequila Rose and Miss Belle

A LEISURE BOOK®

March 2001

Published by

Dorchester Publishing Co., Inc.
276 Fifth Avenue
New York, NY 10001

ISBN 0-8439-4840-X

The name "Leisure Books" and the stylized "L" with design are trademarks of Dorchester Publishing Co., Inc.

Printed in the United States of America.

Visit us on the web at www.dorchesterpub.com.

He was a hard man,
bred of a hard and lonely land.

Chapter One

Wyoming 1867

He was a tall man and very good-looking in a rough kind of way. He wore a mustache, his hair was black, and his eyes were a dark gray. His shoulders were wide and his hips lean. He carried with him an air of readiness for trouble. His hard-bitten looks appealed to women.

Although Flint Mahone had been carousing for two days and one night when he weaved his way to the bat-wing doors of the Trail's End Saloon, there was the grace of a cat about him. The men at the bar watched him leave, a reluctant respect in their eyes. It was like an old mountain man put it. "His pa, old Jasper, was a wild one, and his get is the same."

Flint stepped down onto the dusty street and unwrapped the reins that tied his stallion to the hitching rack. He affectionately scratched the palamino's rough ears, thinking he must remember to tip the young man who had looked after Shadow while he raised hell with his friends.

He stuck his foot in its hand-tooled boot into the stirrup and, grabbing hold of the pommel, swung himself into the saddle. As he headed out of Jackson Hole, it was close to sunset and the land was still and lonely. There was a sharp tang of fir and pine coming down from the mountains, and the air was cold enough to make him pull the collar of his mackinaw up around his ears. He wondered if it might snow before morning. It was the last week in November, so it wouldn't be surprising if they got a dusting overnight.

Flint urged Shadow to step along a little faster. It was getting late. The sun had already dropped behind the mountains. Kate would have supper ready in another hour. When she clanged a striker around the inside of the angle iron, he'd better get his rump to the table, his face washed and his hair combed . . . and be sober.

His lips curved in a soft smile. Kate had been a part of his life as long as he could remember. When he was four years old his mother had died giving birth to a stillborn baby girl. His father had hired seventeen-year-old Kate Allen to come take care of his house and two young sons. He and Jake, two years older, had grown up loving and respecting Kate.

She had not spoiled them, never hesitating to give them a whack on the bottom if they deserved it. But she was just as free with hugs and kisses when they came to her with scraped knees.

When his father died, Kate had been the only person in the world besides his brother that he loved. A sadness came over his face. Kate was the only person he loved now. Brother Jake had not come home from the war.

He and Jake had joined up at the same time. He had felt that his brother only went to war to get away from his no-good nagging wife. But Jake had had very different feelings about leaving his three children, two boys and a little girl. There had been tears in his eyes when he said good-bye to them.

The brothers hadn't been able to stay together once they enlisted, and only saw each other occasionally. Jake had been sent with Grant to Virginia, and Flint had stayed in Ohio. The last time Flint saw his brother, Jake was concerned about his children. He had received a letter from a cousin of theirs who wrote that the children's mother was inviting different men to the house all the time and the children were being neglected.

When the war was finally over, Flint had gone looking for Jake. It had taken two weeks to learn that Jake had been taken prisoner by the Rebs and had been held in deplorable conditions for eighteen months.

He had learned this from another Yankee ex-prisoner. The man spoke of never having enough to eat, and said it had rained often during the winter. Since their quarters leaked, and the prisoners were wet most of the time, Jake, along with most of the camp, had contracted consumption. He had lasted only a few weeks. The man didn't know where Jake was buried.

How were the children faring? Flint wondered now. Who was supporting them now that their daddy was gone? Had their mother straightened out and taken responsibility for them?

He only wished he knew. As soon as he got home from the war he had gone to the small farm in Utah to learn how his two nephews and little niece were doing. But all he had found was an abandoned homestead. The neighbors said the family had disappeared in the middle of the night. No one knew where the had gone.

His conscience whispered, with some contempt, "And you've been drowning your sorrow in a bottle ever since."

He shook his head to dispel the gloomy thoughts as the ranch house came into sight.

Flint looked at the buildings with pride as the palamino broke into a gallop of his own volition. When he had arrived home from the war he had found the place run-down. He told himself that wasn't surprising, seeing as how it had been neglected for close to four years. To help dull his grief at the loss of Jake and the children, he had worked like a dog to bring everything back to its former condition. It had taken brutal labor combing the breaks for cattle that had grown as wild as deer.

But with the help of six of his cowhands who had made it through the war, he had rounded up two thousand head of longhorns to drive to market. He couldn't believe the amount of the check the buyer from New York handed him. It seemed that now the war was over, the whole world was starving for beef and was willing to pay a high price for it.

One of the boys in their teens who worked in the barn came out to take the stallion. He took one look at his boss's red-rimmed, bloodshot eyes and two days' growth of beard. The kid bit his tongue not to laugh, but Flint had seen the amused glint in his eyes.

"Say one word, you little bastard," he growled, "and I'll knock you on your rump."

"I wasn't going to say one word, Flint," the young man said most seriously. Then, when Flint got out of hearing, he added with laughter in his voice, "You'd better get that whore smell off of you before Kate sees you."

Flint stepped lightly onto the porch. He bent over then and removed his spurs. He hung them on a nail put there for that purpose. He grasped the doorknob and began to slowly turn it. When the door eased open he stepped inside the front room and began to silently slip past the kitchen.

He wanted to avoid Kate at all costs. He hadn't been home for two days and nights. He knew she would be waiting to give him a tongue-lashing that would flay his hide. If he could just get past her and wash up and change his clothes her tongue would be a little less sharp when he had to face her.

When he passed the kitchen door he saw Kate stirring something on the stove. He sighed a deep sigh of relief when he stepped into his room without her notice.

The water pitcher on the washstand was full, and he filled its matching basin almost to the rim. He dropped a bar of soap into the water, and after stripping off his clothes, he began scrubbing away the dirt and odor from his face and body. When he had washed and towel-dried his black hair, he pulled on clean clothes. He stropped his straight razor a couple times, then attacked the whiskers on his face.

The mantel clock in the front room struck the half hour as he finished rinsing the shaving soap off his face. He passed a comb through his hair and squared his shoulders as though preparing to do battle.

But it would be no battle, he told himself. He would stand quietly, taking the whiplash of Kate's tongue. He knew that every word she launched at him was motivated by love. To her he was wasting his life. Her dream for him was to see him married, settled down with a family.

Marriage and children weren't in the cards for him, he thought as he walked down the hall in his stocking feet and entered the kitchen.

Kate, her red hair pulled back from her narrow face and tied with a rawhide string, looked up from setting the table. She swept cool eyes over Flint's person and then remarked scorchingly, "Well, your looks have improved a little since you rode in."

When Flint seemed surprised that she'd been aware of when he came home, she said, "Oh, yes, I saw you sneak by the door hoping that I wouldn't see you. I not only saw you, I smelled you. You looked like a mangy dog that had been chasing bitches in heat. And I don't mind telling you, you smelled like one too.

"Thank God your sainted mother couldn't see you."

Flint silently heaved a sigh of relief. When Kate brought his mother into her chastising, she was running out of steam.

He was right. Kate placed a platter of fried chicken on the table, and said as she turned to pick up a bowl of mashed potatoes and a tureen of gravy, "Well, don't just stand there all night. Sit down and eat your supper. You look like a starved hound dog."

Flint had always claimed that Kate was the best cook in all of Wyoming, and when he bit into the crusty fried fowl he knew he was right in claiming that.

Flint recalled, though, that Kate hadn't always cooked so well. As a girl in her teens she had known very little about cooking. His father had taught her the rudiments of putting a meal together. She had experimented with the plain dishes she had learned from Jasper, and was soon turning out mouth-watering meals.

He remembered with a grin that all her culinary endeavors hadn't turned out so well. When he and Jake would have curled their noses and made unkind remarks, they'd received dark, warning looks from their dad.

Kate and he spoke together companionably now, speculating on whether they would have snow soon and if the men had cut enough hay to get the cattle through the winter. Kate asked if there was anything new in town.

"Not much," Flint answered. Polishing off a piece of pie, he pushed his chair back. He rose to his feet, his fingers fishing a little white muslin bag out of his shirt pocket. "Supper was good as usual, Kate. Thank you. I'm going to have a smoke, then hit the hay. The men and I will be up early in the morning. We are going to comb the breaks again for cattle that have gone wild. I suspect we missed a lot of them in our hurry to get a herd together for market."

"I'll have breakfast waiting for you." Kate rose and began gathering up the dirty dishes.

"No need for that, Kate. Just brew a pot of coffee before you go to bed. I'll reheat it in the morning."

When Kate said, "I'll see," he knew she would have a hot breakfast waiting for him the next morning. She was still taking care of Jasper's son.

"You make sure you watch out for them ornery longhorns. No matter what might happen, you stay in the saddle. Them devils will attack a man on foot at the blink of an eye."

"I'll be careful, Kate," Flint answered. As he left the kitchen he thought to himself that he was thirty-six years old and she was still treating him in the same manner as when he was four. Would she never realize that he was a grown man?

He sat down in one of the wicker rockers that graced the long porch, and pulled from his shirt pocket a packet of thin papers. As he rolled a smoke he was thinking how good his bed would feel and smell tonight. Whores' beds weren't very comfortable, and they certainly didn't smell very good.

And speaking of whores, he thought with a grin, here comes one now.

He lit his cigarette and peered through the fragrant smoke at the female rider approaching the house. He hoped that Kate hadn't seen Ruth Spencer coming to visit.

Coming to visit, that's a laugh. Ruth Spencer was not the kind of female who would come to visit a woman. She had no time for the weaker sex. He had heard her say many times that female talk bored the hell out of her.

No, Ruth Spencer was coming to visit *him*. And there would be few words spoken between them. He wondered, though, if he was up to Ruth tonight. He'd made pretty much a pig of himself in town.

Flint watched the rather plump, but attractive, woman climb out of the saddle. She was now in her late forties, but was hot stuff in bed, he was remembering as she climbed the steps to the porch.

He had learned that by accident a year before he went off to war. Ruth's husband, old man Clayton Spencer, had sent word that he would like Flint to ride over to his place, that he wanted to talk to him about buying one of his horses for his wife.

Ordinarily, if a man wanted to talk to Flint, he would ride out to the ranch to talk. But seeing as old Spencer was in his late seventies, Flint decided he would respect his age and ride out to his ranch.

Clayton wasn't home when he knocked on the Spencer door. His eyes had widened when it opened and a half-dressed woman smiled up at him. All she wore was a thin robe tied loosely at the waist. He didn't have to guess what lay beneath the flimsy material. Nothing was hidden from view. Not her pink nipples, nor the brown patch between her thighs.

"Well, cowboy," she purred, her eyes glued hungrily to his bulging crotch, "what can I do for you?"

Flint knew what she could do for him, and he also knew that she would. He pushed his way into the room and closed the door behind him. "I came to do business with old Spencer, but I'd rather do it with you." There was a shimmer in his hard eyes as he untied the ribbon belt and opened the robe.

"What kind of business would you want with me?" Ruth made no attempt to pull the material back in place.

"The kind that we're both good at. When will Clayton be home?"

"Not until late this afternoon." There was an avid light in Ruth's eyes.

"Let's get at it, woman," Flint growled, and taking her by the arm, he propelled her down a short hall, asking, "Where's your bed?"

Two hours later Flint felt wrung out. He could hardly climb into his clothes when Ruth told him it was time they left the bed, that Clayton would be coming home before long. "Could we sit on the porch and have a glass of whiskey before I leave?" Flint asked. "I don't think I can climb into the saddle yet."

When they sat on the porch sipping Clayton's ten-year-old bourbon, Flint looked at Ruth and asked with grin, "What are you going to do if Clayton wants to go to bed for a bit before supper? You've got to be as tired as I am."

Ruth gave a snort of laughter. "He's not going to want anything this afternoon . . . or tonight either." On a more serious note she added, "Clayton is a fine man and he treats me like a queen. But in bed he's as useless as one of his castrated bulls."

"That's a pretty rotten trick to pull on a healthy woman like yourself," Flint said, compassion in his voice.

"You don't know the whole story, Flint. Clayton was honest with me before we got married. He told me right out that he wouldn't be any good to me in bed. I could have refused to marry him then. The thing is, I'm no longer a young chicken. I wanted a husband and a home while I was young enough to attract a man. So when Clayton asked me to marry him, I jumped at the chance even though I knew he couldn't do his husbandly duty to me. He told me that he was lonely for a woman's company. He said he longed to talk to a female, to watch her move around his home.

"I will always be grateful to him and will never shame him by flirting openly with other men. But I'm only forty years old and I still need a man. A single man who will be discreet."

She flashed him a white smile. "Are you a discreet man, Flint?"

"I am a very prudent man, Ruth. What goes on between us stays between us. All right?"

"All right." She leaned over and squeezed his hand.

They had met twice a week after that until he went into the army. They were now well on their way to picking up where they had left off.

As Ruth climbed the steps to the porch and sat down beside him, he wondered who had taken his place while he was gone. He would probably never know.

"You look pretty rough, bucko," Ruth teased as she sat down in the chair next to him. "I hear that you and your friends tore up the town pretty good over the weekend."

"That's what they tell me. I don't remember it too well."

Ruth looked at Flint and shook her head. "Flint, don't you think it's time you stopped boozing and whoring and settled down? Why don't you court one of the ranchers' pretty little misses. Did you ever woo a nice young lady?"

Flint's laughter was long and loud. "Tell the truth, Ruth," he finally managed to gasp out, "can you see me wooing a pretty little innocent? My rough ways would scare the pants off her."

"You could tame your rough ways. You'd like acting the gentleman once you got used to it. I know that you know how. I've seen how you act with Kate. You're real nice and sweet."

"That's because Kate is like a mother to me." Flint paused, amusement in his eyes. "She'd clobber me one if I was disrespectful to her."

Ruth breathed a frustrated sigh. "I'm hoping that someday a young woman will clobber you one and that you'll fall in love with her. I hope she rocks your head real good, and I hope she won't have anything to do with you until you straighten out."

Flint's only answer was an amused smile. He let a few seconds go by, then asked, "Did you make a special trip over here just to give me a lesson in manners, and to tell me that I'm wasting my life?"

"No, I didn't. I don't know why I even brought up such a useless subject. I came to tell you that Clayton wants to sell the ranch. We'll be moving into town then."

Flint straightened up from his slouched position, and giving Ruth all his attention, said in surprise, "You don't mean it. Why does he want to leave the ranch? He's lived there all his life."

"Well, he is seventy-eight years old and his legs are so stove up it's hard for him to walk around very long. And though he won't admit it, I think he's doing it on my account. He's got it in his head that ranch life bores me."

"Does it . . . bore you?"

"Not at all. When I was young and empty-headed and my blood ran hot, I was bored on the small ranch where I grew up." She leaned her head on the back of the chair and closed her eyes. "That boredom got me into a lot of trouble. I became so wild I shamed my family. Finally my dad wouldn't put up with it anymore and kicked me out of the house. I don't have to tell you where I ended up.

"But today, I find ranch life very soothing.

However, what Clayton wants, that is what we'll do. I'd do anything in the world for him. I don't know where I'd be today if not for him."

"This move you're going to make, will it interfere with us?"

"I'm afraid so, friend. There won't be any more 'us.' It would be too chancy rendezvousing in town. I've got to act the lady from now on."

Flint gave Ruth a knowing smile. "You have yourself another man, don't you?"

Ruth grinned and nodded. "Yeah, I do."

Flint grinned back. "Do I know him?"

Ruth hesitated a minute, then admitted, "Yes, he's an acquaintance of yours."

"I'm going to miss our times together, Ruth," Flint said sincerely.

"Me too, Flint." Ruth rose and bent over to kiss him lightly on the lips. "But all things come to an end." As she went down the steps, she said, "I hope that by this time next year you'll be bouncing a baby boy on your knee."

"I'll see that it happens." Flint's ironic laughter followed Ruth as she mounted her mare and rode away.

Chapter Two

Weariness stole over Lauren Hart. For close to two weeks the team had pulled the wagon through cold winds, icy rain, thunder, and lightning. The badlands of the Dakatos were as bleak and lonely as death. It was November and she and old Dud were in a land she had never seen before. She would be thankful when it was all behind them.

She and old Dud wouldn't be bumping along on this excuse for a road if not for dire circumstances.

Lauren thought she had cried her eyes dry, but as she thought back over the last three weeks a tear slipped down her cheek. She was remembering her father, Big Red Hart.

Red Hart had been an outlaw, plain and simple. He and his four men had made their living by holding up banks and stagecoaches for as long as she could remember. But no child could ever have had a more loving father. He was a big, rough man, but always gentle with his delicate-looking little daughter.

As were his men. Every one of them would give his life for her if necessary. Especially Dud Carter. He had always treated her like she was his own. When the men went to pull off a job, he was left behind to watch out for Lauren. It was he who taught her to read and write and do her sums. And to play poker.

Lauren's mother, Maida, claimed she did not like the outlaw life, but when her child was two years old she ran off with one of the gang members. A year later they learned that she and the man had been shot and killed in a holdup they were attempting to pull off.

Her father had seen to it that Lauren grew up as innocent as possible. The men were careful about swearing and bathing in her presence.

Grown now, nineteen years old, she was not quite as innocent as Dud thought she was. She realized that there was much more to life and living than she knew. And she was very nervous about that. The only female she'd ever had a conversation with was an elderly woman who ran a shop in Pottersville catering to women only. Her father had taken her there once a year to purchase whatever she needed in the way of feminine clothing. It was Mrs. Stevens who had explained to her about a woman's monthly.

She was going to miss that old woman very much.

Yes, she thought, and I'm going to find it very hard to converse with other women, especially those of my own age. What did they talk about? she wondered. The single ones would have no husbands or babies to discuss. She somehow doubted that they talked about horses, hunting, or fishing. She wondered if any of them could shoot a gun or a rifle as well as she could. And she'd bet they couldn't play poker.

But what about the pretty dresses they wore, the dainty shoes. Lauren Hart had none of those. Ole Dud said she shouldn't worry about that; as soon as they got settled they would buy her some woman duds. When she asked him how they were going to do that when they had no money, he mumbled something about playing poker.

Lauren left off thinking about women and gave all her attention to the rough road they traveled. All day the rain had fallen heavily, the rivers and washes roaring with floodwaters. She hoped they wouldn't have to cross any rivers.

It was late afternoon when the rain slackened to a fine drizzle. At the same time they came to a level stretch of road that they followed until the sun was about ready to set.

"Turn off at the next bunch of trees you come to, Lauren," Dud said. "I want to make camp before dark."

When she came to a stand of cottonwoods she drove the team in among the trees. Dud jumped from the wagon. "You might as well stay in the wagon while I rig up something to keep the rain off of us."

Lauren watched him unlatch the wagon's tailgate and prop it up with a couple of sticks. He next stretched a heavy tarpaulin between four trees. With the tarp and the tailgate, they now had at least five feet of coverage.

Dud wasn't finished yet. He spread a canvas groundsheet beneath the makeshift roof. While Lauren wondered what he would do next, he searched around beneath the trees until he found enough dry wood to make a small fire at one side of the tailgate.

When it burned brightly he looked up at Lauren, and with a grin he said, "Your palace awaits you, Your Majesty."

Lauren chuckled as she bent her head to enter her new quarters. She sat cross-legged in front of the fire and watched as Dud set a pot of coffee to brewing. While it perked, he laid out some of the beef jerky they had brought from home. There was only enough meat left to last them a couple more days.

Lauren gratefully accepted the tin cup of coffee Dud handed her a short time later. She cupped her chilled fingers around the cup, its warmth traveling into her hands and up her arms. As her white teeth bit into the cured beef, she thought she had never tasted anything so good.

After Dud had finished eating and rolled a smoke, he unhitched the team and gave them and the two riding horses each a measure of oats in their feed bags. He had been careful to bring along food for the animals in case they found grass scarce. He liked to repeat his father's admonition, "If you don't take good care of your horse, he can't take care of you." While the animals munched their supper, he went further back in the trees to answer nature's call.

When he returned to the wagon he said, "If you need to relieve yourself there's a big boulder a few yards away in the trees. We'll go to bed when you get back. I'm hoping to reach Jackson Hole sometime tomorrow."

When Lauren returned to the fire a few minutes later, Dud had spread another ground-cover canvas beneath the wagon and pulled the straw mattress from the wagon for them to sleep on. It would be a little damp, but passable. Lauren knew this from experience. It had been a nightly routine for more nights than she cared to remember. She had almost given up hope of ever sleeping on a regular bed again. She tugged off her boots and with a tired sigh stretched out beside the already snoring Dud.

As tired as she was, though, Lauren couldn't get to sleep right away. Thoughts of her father came to mind. She kept remembering the last time she'd seen him. It had been a cold, fall day the morning her father and his men prepared to ride off to a small town in Nebraska where they planned to rob a bank. Her teeth had chattered as she stood saying good-bye to her father. She knew it wasn't completely because of the chilly air. She was nervous about this job Red Hart planned to do. The prickle on the back of her neck told her that he shouldn't go, that it would be a dangerous undertaking.

"I wish you would get out of this business, Dad." Lauren looked up at the big man as he settled himself in the saddle. "Can't you do something else to get money? I worry every time you ride out."

Red reached down and stroked her smooth head. "You mustn't worry, honey. You'll get wrinkles on your pretty face," he teased. "Besides, I don't know what else I could do at my age. I've lived too long on the wrong side of the law to change now. Maybe, when I get too old to outrun a posse, I'll settle down."

He gathered up the reins. "Don't fret about me, daughter. I'm always careful. I never forget that you're back here depending on me." He was gone then, riding away into the fog. It was the last time she ever saw him. Dud's old Indian friend, Long Hair, had brought them the news that her father and his men were dead. They had been cornered in a dead-end canyon by a posse somewhere in Nebraska. In the shoot-out

Red Hart and his men were shot to death. It had happened three hundred miles away, and the four of them had been buried in a boothill in a small town. Their wooden markers said only, "Unknown."

That she could not visit her father's grave was another sorrow.

She had been so distraught that day, she had only vaguely heard Dud making hurried plans to leave their hideout of several years. "I don't know for a fact, but the law might want me too and might come looking for me," he said, a worried frown on his wrinkled face. "If they took me in, that would leave you all on your own and you're not ready for that yet."

Lauren could remember Long Hair saying, "Don't worry about that, friend. It has been many years since you rode with the gang. Your picture is not with the others on the 'Wanted List' in the Post Office."

The old Indian's words calmed Dud, and he went about more methodically planning what they must do. "I've got about forty dollars, Lauren," he said. "Do you have any money?"

When she shook her head, he wondered out loud, "Do you suppose Red kept any money in that tin box under his bed?"

When he pried the lid off the rusty tin, he was disappointed to see only a folded sheet of paper and a key inside the box. Without much interest he spread out the yellowed sheet. When he saw that it was some kind of important document, he started reading avidly.

When he had finished reading he gave a whoop, so loud that Lauren and Long Hair let out a startled yip. "What is it? Dud?" Lauren asked, looking at him with wide eyes.

"Girl!" he exclaimed, tapping the paper with his gnarled finger, "we've got a place to go to. A place that belongs to you."

Lauren thought for a minute that the old man had lost his mind in the grief of losing a man he had looked on as a son. But the usual bright intelligence in his eyes made her ask, "What are you talking about, Dud?"

"Here, read it for yourself." He shoved the paper at her.

Lauren recognized at once that she was looking at something of importance. It was a deed. It was dated 1862, five years ago. A Mr. Claude Hayes had deeded a thousand-acre ranch to Mr. Arthur Hart and his daughter, Miss Lauren Hart. The house and outbuildings were situated in the area of Jackson Hole, Wyoming, near the Snake River, and included several hundred head of cattle.

Lauren, having read the document out loud, said in stunned tones, "I never knew Dad had enough money to buy a ranch."

"He didn't buy it, Lauren," Long Hair put in. "I was with him the night he won it off a rancher in a poker game. It was a high-stakes game. Red told me not to tell anyone. He said that the ranch would be a home for you, and for the men when they became too old to ride the owlhoot trail any longer."

Tears of relief and sadness swam in her and Dud's eyes as they gathered up the few things they would take with them. There were guns and ammunition, the few supplies they had on hand, a skillet, a coffeepot. There were also two pans and two tin plates and cups.

Their few clothes were folded into a wooden crate, covered with a blanket to keep the dust off them, and shoved under the wagon seat. Their saddles were shoved in a corner and covered with a piece of canvas.

The guns were kept handy to their reach. They would be traveling through the badlands of the Dakotas.

It was high noon when they were ready to leave the shack where Lauren had spent most of her life. "Long Hair, will you take care of Wolf?" Dud asked as he patted the head of Lauren's pet, which was part wolf, part dog.

Before the old Indian could answer him, Lauren jumped in front of Dud. With her fists on her hips she demanded hotly, "What do you mean, take care of Wolf? I'll take care of my dog like I always have. He is part of the family and he will go with us, or I will stay here with him!"

"But it will be a long trip for him, Lauren. He's gonna get awfully tired."

"When he gets tired he'll ride in the wagon."

34

"I hadn't thought of that." Dud looked sheepish.

And that was how it was as the wagon bumped across South Dakota and into Wyoming. When Wolf got tired of trotting alongside the horses or taking off after jackrabbits, he'd leap into the wagon. There he'd lay his big head between his stretched-out front paws and fall asleep.

Now Lauren sighed and turned over on her side. Dud said they should reach Jackson Hole tomorrow. She looked forward to it with excitement, but with a little uncertainty too. She was ever so grateful to have a home waiting for her, but how were she and Dud going to survive in it? They had little money and winter was coming on. Dud had said not to worry about it, that he had a plan that would see them through the cold months.

I can't imagine what it can be, she thought as she finally slipped into sleep.

It was mid-afternoon the next day when Dud told Lauren to rein in the team and set the brakes. "There it is!" he exclaimed excitedly, standing up in the wagon. "Jackson Hole!" Lauren stood up also, and together they gazed down at the rough little Western town.

"It looks like it's sitting in a bowl with the mountains surrounding it," Lauren said.

"Them's the Teton Mountains," Dud explained, "and that river runnin' through town is the Snake River. It's claimed that it never freezes."

"I bet it gets plenty cold here in the winter. I notice there's snow on the peaks already."

"Little cold ain't gonna bother us, huh, girl? It couldn't get any colder than Nebraska," Dud said as he jumped down from the wagon. "You stay here with the team while I go on down and scout around a little, find out from somebody where the Hayes ranch is located.

"I won't be gone long," he said as he saddled his sorrel.

Jackson Hole's main street was a quagmire of mud, and the stallion's hoofs made sucking sounds as he slowly walked along.

There were a few illuminated windows, they were the buildings doing the most business Dud guessed. He recognized one building as a saloon by its bat-wing doors. Across the alley from it was a bawdy house, with a red light over the door to advertise it. Next to it was a dance hall, where the sound of a piano drifted out onto the street.

Dud was interested in only one building, the saloon. He tied the sorrell to the hitching post in front of the long, narrow building, and as he went through the swinging doors he hoped it had a gambling hall attached to the barroom.

There were several people in the room, and Dud stood to one side making a slow survey of them. Most of the men looked ordinary and probably lived ordinary lives. But there were a few who were shifty-eyed and mean-looking. He'd bet his horse they were hiding from the law. These men would be dangerous. Dangerous because they were scared, not because they were handy with a gun. They were the worst kind. They would draw their guns and shoot into a roomful of innocent people.

There were several scantily clad saloon women moving around the room, cozying up to the men, soliciting drinks. They would ignore him, Dud thought. His worn clothes and down-at-the-heels boots said clearly that he had no money to buy them drinks. Not that he cared if they ignored him. He'd had no use for a woman in a physical sense for a long time.

The whirling of a roulette wheel caught Dud's attention. His pulse leaped as he heard the sound of the small ball whipping around in a shallow bowl.

Several of the men in the gambling hall were playing either monte, faro, or fortune. None of those games interested Dud. He walked over to a corner where poker was being played. The four men sitting at the table paid no attention to him. Their eyes were on the cards they held in their hands.

After some fifteen minutes of watching the players, he knew the weakness of each. He could predict the strength of their hands by little telltale signs that escaped them. He left the hall then and went back into the saloon. It was time now to learn the location of the Hayes ranch.

Dud made his way across the room and laid the price of a drink on the bar. He wanted the barkeep to know that he was paying for his drink and not panhandling. When the drink was put before him he nodded his thanks, then asked, "Can you tell me how to get to the Hayes ranch?"

The bartender gave him a curious look and said, "Ain't nobody living there. Ain't been for around five years."

"Yeah, I know," Dud said. "The new owner is moving in now. We don't know where it is exactly."

"Oh, yeah?" The fat man looked surprised. "What's his name, if you don't mind my askin'."

"Don't mind at all, seein' as how we'll be neighbors for a good long while. The owner goes by the name of Hart."

"I remember there was a man by the name of Hart was here for a couple weeks several years back. He liked to play poker. One day he just up and left. Never heard from him again. He was a big friendly feller.

"Now about the Hayes ranch," the bartender said, coming back to Dud's question. "It ain't hard to find. You just hit the river trail at the end of town and follow it for about five miles. You can see the ranch house and buildings then. Old Man Hayes built them about two hundred yards up in the treeline of the Tetons."

"Much obliged, mister," Dud said, and finishing his drink, he left the saloon. He had the information he had come for. Now all he had to do was set the wheels in motion.

Chapter Three

When Dud mounted his horse and guided him
down the street, heading out of Jackson Hole,
Flint was entering town. They nodded at each
other as they passed. Flint rode on up the street,
pulling his mare in when came to Richards'
Mercantile.

Flint hadn't planned on coming to town tonight. But when he rolled his after-supper
smoke this evening and reached for his little
white muslin bag, he found it empty. With a
resigned sigh he went to the stables and saddled
the first horse he came to. Like it or not, he had
to ride to town and pick up some tobacco. He
couldn't sponge off the men all day tomorrow.

As he went through the door of the mercantile, he wondered about the man he had just passed on the street. The old fellow looked awfully down at the heels to be riding such a fine piece of horseflesh. That stallion looked as good as any Flint owned, and he had the best around Jackson Hole. If the man wasn't careful, one of the riffraff that hung around Trail's End Saloon would make off with the animal.

"Well, Flint, what brings you back to town so soon?" Florence Richards leaned against the counter, smiling at him. Flint thought to himself that her long face and stained teeth made her look like a horse. He did not like the woman. She was the biggest gossip in all of Jackson Hole. She was also a mean gossip. She had no scruples about telling outright lies about people. She had ruined the reputations of some young women in town with the wagging of her vicious tongue.

She'd do well to keep her mouth shut, Flint thought, considering that her own two daughters were the biggest whores in three counties. Of course, Florence didn't know this, or if she did, she wouldn't admit it. Even to herself.

"Did you want to buy something, Flint, or did you just come in to see me?" She gave him a coy look.

"I've run out of makins'. Better give me a couple bags. I don't want to come to town again this week."

"You know, Flint—" Florence handed him

the tobacco—"you should stop your wild ways and settle down. All your drinking and messing around with whores is going to shorten your life."

"Could be, Mrs. Richards, but I'll be happy on the way." He gave her a devilish grin, then hurried from the store before she could start on him about her daughters.

It was still early in the evening when Flint left the mercantile. He stood a moment on its long narrow porch. He was still thinking of the old man and his handsome sorrel. He wanted to talk to him, maybe buy the animal from him. He wondered if he could learn anything about him at the Trail's End. He decided he'd go buy a drink and ask a few questions.

Flint stepped into the saloon early in the evening. The place was busy, as usual, with men and women milling about. He elbowed his way to the bar and found a place where he could squeeze in.

"Howdy, Flint, didn't expect to see you in town for a while." The bartender grinned at him.

Flint shook his head when Hank Jones uncorked a bottle of whiskey. "I don't want anything to drink." He shuddered. "I had to come to town to pick up some tobacco. I stopped here to ask what you know about that raggedy-looking old stranger that just left here a few minutes ago."

"Not much." Hank poured a drink for the

man sitting next to Flint. "He was pretty close-mouthed. He spent most of his time in the gambling hall watching the men play poker. After he had a drink he asked the way to the Hayes ranch. When I said nobody lives there, he said he knew that, but a new owner was moving in. I told him how to get there, but before I could question him he downed his drink, said thank you, and left the saloon."

"Do you think he's the new owner?" Flint looked doubtful even as he asked the question.

Hank shook his head. "I don't think so. He didn't look to me like he could own a kerchief for his neck, let alone a spread as big as the Hayes place."

"What about that stallion he rides?" Flint said. "That horse is worth a lot of money."

"I know. Them three fellers at the end of the bar was eyeing it. I hope the old man gets home all right."

"I'm going to go watch the poker players for a while. If they leave and you think they're going to follow to the old gent, come let me know. I'll tail them a bit, keep them honest."

When Dud rode up to where he had left Lauren and the wagon, she was sitting pretty much where he had left her, with Wolf by her side. "It's about time you got back," she complained as she slid off the boulder she was perched on. "I was beginning to get worried about you."

"When are you going to stop worrying about

me?" Dud sounded a little testy. "I can take care of myself. You forget that I've been looking after you for nineteen years."

"I can't help it, Dud. Dad always told me that, but he left and he won't be coming back."

Lauren's voice trembled, and Dud was immediately sorry for his gruffness to her. Putting his arm around her shoulder, he said, "I'm not mad at you. I'm mad at myself for not taking better care of you since Red died."

"We don't have to worry about that anymore." Lauren rubbed the heels of her palms across her wet eyes. "This winter we'll have a roof over our heads, and according to the deed, we can kill a beef once in a while, so we won't go hungry."

"I have plans for us to eat better than that." Dud chuckled.

"I don't mean to belittle your forty dollars, Dud, but you've got to admit it won't buy us much grub for the long winter months coming up.

"Did you find out the directions to our ranch?" Lauren asked, changing the subject. "I'm anxious to see it and to sleep under a roof again."

"Yes, a bartender told me how to get there. It's only a few miles from Jackson Hole. He said to just follow the Snake River about four miles and we'll see the ranch house."

"Well, let's get going." Lauren started to walk toward the wagon.

"Hold on a minute," Dud said. "We're going back to town first. There's a poker game going on in the gambling hall attached to the saloon. They're playing big-stakes. I figure you can win enough to buy our winter supplies. So stick your hair up under your hat and put on that big loose shirt that your dad used to have you wear when we was on the run. You know the one. The one that hides the fact that you're a woman."

"I don't know, Dud. What if I can't beat these men? And if it's high-stakes they're playing, your forty dollars wouldn't get me in the game."

"Number one, you'll have no problem beating them. I watched them play. I know all the little things that give them away when they have a good hand or a bad one. I'll tell you about them as we ride along. I never said anything before, but I've got a hundred dollars saved up. I've been keeping it for an emergency. I figure we're in an emergency now."

"Shame on you, you old reprobate," Lauren said with an affectionate smile as she buttoned up the heavy shirt that hid her femininity, "holding out on me all this time."

"Ain't you glad now that I did?" Dud smiled back as he saddled her horse, a match to his sorrel. He cinched the saddle and said, "Come on, let's go fleece some of them there poker players."

Lauren pulled the floppy, worn hat down on her head, made sure that none of her hair was showing, then mounted up. When Wolf wagged his tail and ran around the horses' legs, she ordered, "You have to stay here, Wolf, and take care of the team."

The dog whined as she and Dud rode away, but went and lay down in front of the wagon.

Flint was thinking that he would leave as soon as the poker hand was finished. He hadn't planned on staying this long, but the game was a close one. He figured there was at least a couple hundred dollars lying on the table.

The man on his right won the hand and Flint started to rise, then sat back down. The old man with the handsome sorrel was back. There was a tall, skinny boy in his teens with him. What were they doing in a gambling hall? he asked himself. He'd bet his new boots that they didn't have two coins between them to rub together.

His lips curled in amusement when the pair walked up to the table and the old man asked, "You fellers got room for a couple more players?"

The four men sitting around the table looked up, stared a moment, then laughed uproariously. "This ain't no two-bit-ante game, old-timer," one man explained when he stopped laughing.

"I reckon I know that," Dud snapped, pride in his voice. "Me and the kid's got enough money to sit in the game . . . and take *your* money away from you."

A couple of the men snickered at his boast, but one man asked on a serious note, "Do you want the kid to sit in too?"

"Yeah, I do. He can hold his own. I taught him how to play."

After a sardonic laugh the man said, "I'm sure he knows how to play then. Take a seat, both of you."

Flint watched the kid move forward and slide into a vacant chair, and thought that he was surprisingly graceful for a kid. He moved like a female. When the old fellow sat down across from his companion, the spokesman of the group shuffled a deck of cards. He offered them to Dud to cut. When Dud only tapped the top with his fingers, the man picked them up and began to deal.

"Five-card stud, men. Jacks or better to open. Five dollars to get in the game. After that the sky is the limit." He looked at Dud and gave him a sly smile.

The kid opened and the game began. Silver dollars clinked as all six men joined the game. The players in turn threw down the cards they wanted to exchange for new ones. When the kid asked for two cards, Flint quietly switched his seat to an empty seat behind him. Flint leaned forward to see his hand. What was he hoping to build to? he wondered.

The kid held three of a kind. He wanted to draw a pair, but to Flint's mind it was unlikely that he would. He was wrong. The kid had drawn a pair of tens.

The cards were dealt again. Again the kid won with three of a kind. He looked at the elderly man he called Dud and gave him a quick wink. Dud's lips twisted in a hint of a grin. Flint wondered what that was all about. It was as if they were signaling each other.

Dud won occasionally, as did a couple of other players, but the elderly man's young friend seemed to win every other hand. The players were beginning to direct suspicious looks at him.

But Flint knew the kid hadn't been cheating. He was just an extraordinarily good poker player. Flint suspected that he knew how to count cards.

The deck was passed to the young winner to deal. Flint watched the long, slender fingers neatly shuffle the cards, and thought that the kid had hands like a woman.

When the cards were dealt and everyone had anted up, Dud said as he picked up his cards, "Son, we'd better get over to the mercantile after this hand and get some supplies before they close."

The kid was dealt three kings and drew a fourth. Flint couldn't believe it when he tossed in his cards after betting a couple times. Why had the damn fool done that? Flint frowned. It was almost certain he would have won this hand.

It came to him then why the skinny kid had folded up. He was wise enough to know that there wouldn't be too many hard feelings toward him when he left the game after losing a couple of heavy hands.

Dud gathered up his winnings, along with those of his young companion. They pushed away from the table and stood up. Flint sucked in his breath and felt a jolt to his loins. The kid's shirttail had caught on the back of his chair. It hung there long enough for Flint to catch sight of the prettiest little rounded butt he'd ever seen. What a waste for a neat little bottom like that to be put on a gangly kid in his teens, Flint thought.

When the bat-wing doors slapped behind the pair, one of the men at the table complained, "That kid was uncommonly lucky. Do you reckon he was cheating?"

Before anyone could answer, Flint spoke up. "I thought that at first, but after watching him real close for a while, I'd say he didn't cheat once. He's just a damn good player. I think he counts cards."

"I'll tell you one thing," one of the men said, "I'm not anxious to play with him again. He cleaned me out."

Most of the men said the same thing, and the game came to an end. Flint figured that between the man and the kid, they had won a little over three hundred dollars.

Most of the men left the saloon, and Flint followed them. He was untying his stallion from the picket rope when he heard his name called. He grinned and dropped his hands. He knew that voice. He had spent all of one day and part of a night with the owner of the voice. When she came up to him he smiled at the brassy blonde with the painted face and said, "Hiya, Tillie. You look all bushy-tailed and ready for a romp."

"That I am, big man. Are you ready for a couple hours of play?"

Flint grinned down at the buxom woman. "I don't think so, Tillie. You wrung me out the other night."

"Aw, come on, Flint," coaxed the whore, her hips swaying. "You know you could. Especially if I gave you a little help." She plastered herself against him and planted a passionate kiss on his lips.

"You crazy woman, what are you doing?" he said half laughing and half chastising. "Someone is going to walk by and see us."

"I don't care," Tillie giggled.

In the mercantile Lauren and Dud had completed purchasing a winter's supply of grub. There was assembled on the counter a hundred pounds of beans, the same amount of potatoes, fifty pounds of coffee beans, and the same amount of sugar. There was a hundred pounds of flour and two five-pound pails of lard.

In smaller bags were salt, pepper, and

yeast. There was also about twenty-five gallons of kerosene and three boxes of matches.

Then, pushed to one side, were the air-tights. Ten cans of milk, the same of peaches and of tomatoes. There were several bars of lye soap, and despite Lauren's protest, Dud tossed some bars of scented soap on the counter.

"You oughtn't to be goin' round smellin' like scrub soap all the time," he said. "Did you pick out a heavy jacket and hat and a pair of boots?"

"Yes, I did. Did you do the same?"

Dud nodded, then looked from the pile of their purchases to Tom Richards, who owned the store. "Mister, after we pay for this, would you see to it that it's delivered to the Hayes ranch?"

"Sure thing," Tom answered after almost swallowing his Adam's apple. "Are you folks gonna live there now?"

"Yeah, we're the new owners. Figure up our tab. We want to get home," Dud said, cutting the store owner off before he could ask more questions.

Lauren went through the packages and set aside a slab of salt pork, a can of beans, and four potatoes. "Take enough coffee beans for tonight and tomorrow morning," Dud advised.

Tom Richards handed her a small bag. "You can put them in this," he said, smiling at her. She smiled back, thinking he was a nice man.

Dud had only about fifty dollars left after he paid for the supplies. He wasn't worried, though. He could always take Lauren to the gambling hall in Jackson Hole again.

"Let's go, kid," he said, and with a lift of his hand to Tom, they left the store.

Lauren took one step down from the store porch, then stopped so short that Dud almost knocked her down. "What's wrong with you?" he started to say, then saw what had stopped her so abruptly. The man who had sat behind Lauren and watched her play poker was standing in the street. Plastered up against him was painted hussy with her hands all over him.

"Howdy, pleasant evenin', ain't it?" Dud gave the cowboy a devilish grin.

Flint only grunted, and refused to make eye contact with the old man. He was furious with himself for blushing like a fool. So what if an old man and a fresh-faced kid would think he was a willing participant in Tillie's outrageous behavior?

In the dim light coming from the store he saw the kid's lips curl in cool contempt when Tillie linked her arm in his. He jerked his arm free of her clutching fingers so fast, she gave him a cross look of surprise.

Lauren was very disappointed in Flint. She had noticed him the moment she and Dud stepped into the gambling hall. She had been very aware of him sitting so close behind her. She'd thought he was the handsomest man she had ever seen, and had been hard put to keep her mind on her cards. Only the dire need of winter supplies had enabled her to concentrate on the cards. She told herself now that she was glad she had found out that he was a whore-monger, because otherwise, if he had asked her to step out with him, she would have said yes.

She knew now there was no danger of him asking her to do anything. He liked full-bodied women with big breasts.

With her chin in the air and looking very feminine, she went down the steps and walked to her stallion. Dud caught himself just in time to prevent himself from helping her mount. That big man who was watching every move she made would think it mighty strange if he helped a tall kid climb onto his horse.

Flint thought how graceful the kid sat the saddle as he watched the two magnificent horses move down the street. There was a mystery about that pair, he thought, and before he realized what he was doing, he had mounted his mare and was following them at a distance.

When the two were about three miles out of town, they came to where the road forked. Flint was surprised to see them turn their horses onto a narrow, seldom-used road overgrown with grass. Where were they going? he wondered.

He turned the mare's head to follow them. The animal took two more steps, then stopped short, snorting uneasily. "What's wrong, girl?" He patted the quivering neck. He saw then what had spooked his mare. At the edge of the timber stood a wolf, looking straight at him. It was the biggest lobo he'd ever seen. He and the big gray stared at each other a moment; then the wolf turned and silently vanished into the night.

Flint felt so shaken by the experience that he turned the mare's head in the direction of home. He felt as if the wolf had warned him to stay away from the kid.

Chapter Four

The gray of the fog that had crept around the horses' feet was rising and deepening. Soon, with the oncoming night, the dim road would be almost obscure.

It seemed that in a matter of minutes the sky was totally black. Lauren gripped the side of the wagon nervously as far off in the distance came the rumble of thunder. "It feels like it might rain," Lauren said. "But it's too cold for that, don't you think?"

"It happens sometimes, but I think it will more likely sleet instead of rain. In any case, I hope we come to the place pretty soon. I don't know about you, but I'm danged tired and hungry."

Lauren was about to ask if he was sure he'd gotten the directions right, when the team came to a stop. Dud peered through the darkness and made out what had once been a white picket fence. Half of it now lay on the ground.

"I think we've arrived, girl," Dud said with relief and gladness in his voice. "There's a fence here, but be careful. A part of it is on the ground and may have nails in it. They'll be rusty, and we don't want the horses stepping on one and getting lockjaw. Let's get out of the wagon and explore on foot."

They didn't take many steps before they could go no farther. "I think we've come to the house!" Dud shouted over a deafening crack of thunder. "And just in time. There's a set of steps here. I don't know how many, so climb carefully. I'll go ahead and see if I can find a lamp or a lantern in the house."

Lauren had just stubbed her toe, and stumbled on what she supposed was a porch, when a dim light suddenly shone through a dingy windowpane. Such a rush of relief passed through Lauren that it left her weak. What was she going to find inside? she wondered as she opened the heavy door.

Dud stood at a kitchen table, his lips spread in a wide grin. "Welcome home, honey," he said softly.

"I can't believe that we're finally going to have

a place we can call home." Lauren shook her head in bemusement.

"You sure can, girl. What should we do first? Look the place over or fix us some grub?"

"I don't know, Dud. I want to do it all at the same time," Lauren laughed.

"Well, since you can't do that, how about if I make some supper and you take a quick walk through the house. There's a wall lamp beside the stove. You take the table lamp and go see what you can find."

Holding the lamp high to light her way, Lauren went from room to room. Besides the kitchen there were three bedrooms, a dining room, and a large sitting room. One wall was dominated by a huge fieldstone fireplace. It had a raised hearth about a foot and a half high. A perfect place to sit on a cold winter's night. She decided that the reason the kitchen was off by itself was to keep the heat from the rest of the house in the summer when meals were being cooked.

Nothing seemed out of place, but dust was thick on everything. The house would get a thorough cleaning tomorrow, she promised herself, and walked back into the kitchen.

Dud looked up from the stove, whose top was dusty also, and slid a pot of coffee to the rear of the black range. "The coffee is done. Pour us some, will you?"

"It sure smells good in here." Lauren sniffed the air as she opened a cupboard and took out two white china mugs. "The rest of the house smells musty and unlived in."

"It's probably been shut up for five years," Dud said as he stirred a skillet of fries. "Maybe we should open the windows and air the place out." He took a long swallow of coffee from the cup Lauren handed him.

"I'll do it now." Lauren set her cup down and walked into the sitting room. Clouds of dust lifted from the heavy drapes when she pulled them apart in order to open the window. A gust of air swept into the room, quite cool but very refreshing. She opened the windows in the other rooms, then returned to the kitchen.

In her absence Dud had filled a basin with water from a small sink pump and had wiped the dust off the table. Two plates, knives, and forks were in place. He was in the act of forking salt pork out of a frying pan and onto a platter. When he placed the meat on the table, he lifted some fried Indian bread from another pan.

"I hope the flour I found in the cupboard didn't have any bugs in it." He gave Lauren a teasing grin.

"I don't care what it might have," Lauren said and, sitting down at the table, attacked her plate of food like a starving animal. Wolf thumped her leg with his heavy tail so hard, she stopped eating long enough to feed him as well.

Lauren and Dud sat back from the table minutes later, wide smiles on their faces as they rubbed full stomachs. "That hit the spot, Dud."

Lauren stood. "I'm going to have another cup of coffee. What about you?"

"Yeah, you can pour me some more. Then I've got to take care of the horses and bring in some firewood. It's gonna get real cold tonight."

Later, when Dud stepped out of the house, he was hit by a cold, wet breeze. By the time he unhitched the team and led all the horses fifty yards to the barn, it was raining. It was not a hard rain, but one that quickly soaked a person.

The barn was warm and dry, and the four horses whinnied softly in appreciation of the gray blankets Dud found and spread over their backs. When he returned to the house, running through the rain, he felt the same sentiments as the horses. Lauren had a large fire going in the fireplace. "Where did you find the wood?" he asked, holding his hands over the flames and rubbing them together.

"There's a lean-to shed attached to the back of the kitchen. It's full of wood. Some short pieces for the cookstove and bigger ones for the fireplace."

"That's good news." Dud picked up the poker lying on the hearth and pushed some burning wood together. "I won't be at all surprised to see snow on the ground in the morning. It's getting colder by the hour."

"You know," Lauren said, sitting down in a rocker and stretching her stockinged feet out to the fire, "I'd kinda like for it to snow. For the first time in my memory there would be enough food for our bellies and a warm house to live in. I'll be able to walk in the snow without it getting through holes in my boots and freezing my feet."

She yawned and stretched her arms up over her head. "Yes," she said with a nod of her head, "I look forward to a good heavy snow."

"You'll get plenty of snow here, but not right away, I don't think. There might be a light skimming on the ground in the morning, but the real stuff won't come for a few more weeks."

"What do you plan for us to do tomorrow?" Lauren asked at the end of another yawn.

"First off, I want to ride around, see if that deed is telling the truth, that several hundred head of cattle come with the place. I kinda doubt that we'll find very many. It's been over five years since your dad won the place. Rustlers could have made off with all of them by now."

"Would you really care if they were all gone? You've always claimed that cattle are the dumbest animals alive."

"They are dumb. They can stand on a patch of dry grass that is covered with only six inches of snow and are not smart enough to dig down to it. But I'd like to have a few head to drive to market next spring to get some money together. I want to buy some good blood mares to put to our horses. If we could build up a herd of our stallions' get, men from all over the country would be clamoring to buy them."

"Where do you expect to get mares with bloodlines equal to Cyclone's and Silky's? I don't think you'll find any running wild on the plains."

"Do you recall that young feller who sat behind you in the poker game?" Dud asked. Lauren nodded. "He was ridin' a fine-lookin' mare. We might be able to do business with him."

Lauren didn't say what she was thinking. She didn't want to do any kind of business with a man like him. She said instead with a laugh, "You'll be years building up a herd with just one mare." She pulled her feet down from the hearth and stood. "I made up a couple beds while you were tending to the horses. I think I'll turn in."

"Me too. It's gonna feel real good, sleepin' in a bed for a change."

"The sheets and blankets are clean. I found them in a linen closet. They just smell a little musty."

In the room she had chosen for herself Lauren pulled a nightgown out of her saddlebag. It took her but a moment to undress and get into the long flannel. The room was cold and she hurried into bed. As she stretched out, she hoped that Dud's bed was as comfortable as hers.

She pulled the covers up over her shoulders, and as she lay listening to the rain pounding on the roof, her thoughts went to the tall man they'd seen in town. There was something about him that was reckless, dangerous, and she wished she wasn't so drawn to him. She didn't want to have anything to do with him. He meant trouble, she was thinking as she fell asleep.

However, off and on during the night, his handsome face would float before her as she slept, his devilish eyes telling her naughty things.

The first thing Lauren became aware of the next morning when she awakened was that she was cold and that there was a strong aroma of frying meat and brewing coffee. The sun was well up and was trying its best to penetrate the grimy window glass opposite her bed.

She lay there a moment, gathering her courage to leave the warmth of the bed and dash to the kitchen. Wolf entered her room and nudged his wet nose against her cheek. She scratched his rough ears, wishing that she had his fur coat or at least a robe of her own.

And while I'm wishing, I might as well wish for a pair of fur-lined house slippers, she thought. Firming her lips, she jumped out of bed and dashed into the kitchen.

"Good mornin', Dud," she said through chattering teeth as he let Wolf out the door.

"Mornin', Lauren." Dud handed her a pair of his woolen socks to put on her bare feet. "Take a look out the window."

Lauren walked to the window and gave a little

cry of surprise. Sometime during the night the rain had turned to snow. Everything wore a glittering coat of white.

"Don't get too excited about it," Dud said, placing breakfast on the table and pouring their coffee. "It won't last. It will all be melted by noon."

"I'm sure there will be plenty more later on," Lauren said as she washed her face and hands in a basin of water Dud had heated for her. As she dried off with a towel he had unearthed from someplace, she glanced out the window.

"There goes Wolf," she said, a smile on her face. "I bet he's hunting some breakfast."

"More likely looking for the local dogs to fight," Dud grunted as he seated himself at the table.

Chapter Five

Flint awoke soon after dawn began coloring the eastern sky. He lay in the warmth of his bed a moment, listening to Kate singing an Irish ballad as she prepared their breakfast. When the aroma of coffee drifted into his room, he knew it was time to get out of bed. Any minute now she would come hurrying into the room and jerk the covers off the bed, never mind that he was stark naked beneath them.

He flung back the covers and rushed to the chest of drawers, and yanked out fresh underclothing and socks. Shivering, he pulled them on, then yanked on his denims.

He went to the window then and parted the

drapes. He let out a yelp that Kate heard in the kitchen. She grinned. She knew what that yelp meant. Snow covered everything. The conditions were perfect for tracking deer. But he had to get out there early, he thought as he pulled on his boots. Once the sun came up the snow would soon melt.

"Got no time to eat, Kate," he said in a rush as he pumped water into a washbasin. He splashed cold water over his face, and his voice was muffled as he rubbed a towel over his face. "I'll take a cup of coffee, though."

Kate had already poured his coffee, and was just now wrapping a thick beef sandwich in a cloth napkin. "You got home kinda late last night," she said.

"I ran into some newcomers in town. Rumor has it they're taking over the old Hayes ranch."

"My goodness, it's about time someone moved in there. It's been empty for five years."

"I happened to ride past the house a couple weeks ago. There are repairs to be made, but it looks pretty sound. We chased cattle with the Hayes brand on them out of the bush. We didn't take them to Abilene, though. They're still running around wild. I counted around four hundred head."

"That will be a pretty good start for whoever is taking over the place."

"Yeah," Flint answered as she handed him the sandwich. "Thanks, Kate," he said, giving her a peck on the cheek before putting the meat and bread in the pocket of the mackinaw he had shrugged into. He emptied the coffee cup with two long swallows, then picked up the rifle that always leaned beside the kitchen door.

"Wish me luck," he said as he stepped outside. Kate walked to the door to close it behind him, and stood a moment watching him walk away. He was six feet two inches tall and his stride was light and graceful, like that of an Indian. The Indians called him Long Tall Man.

She wished he would meet a nice woman, marry her, and settle down. She longed to hear the happy squeals of children as they ran in and out of the house. It didn't look like she would, she thought, sighing and closing the door. He had been too wild, too long.

Flint rode one of his sturdy mountain-bred horses, the kind that could navigate the rough terrain of the mountainous country. They were surefooted traveling through ice and snow.

The forest was somber and hushed as Flint rode along, his eyes steady on the ground. He was looking for deer tracks. When he heard the long yowl of hounds on the trail of an animal, he swore under his breath. He knew the dogs belonged to Jonas Kile. The ranchers in the area hated the man as much as they did his hounds. The dogs ran down and killed cattle and sheep, and maimed horses. Most of the ranchers had lost pets to them. Only cats were safe from them, thanks to their ability to climb trees.

Flint remembered, though, that one day one

of the hounds had cornered a large tomcat. When he rushed in for the kill, however, the big tom sprang at his face and scratched out one of his eyes. The hound ran off yelling in pain.

The cat had still had a sad ending. That night the owner of the big yellow gave a barbecue in its honor. While everyone was eating steak and spare ribs, Jonas Kile rode up to the gathering, his eyes spitting hate and venom. When he saw his neighbors celebrating the cat's action, he jabbed spurs into his horse and sent it racing for home.

Two days later the rancher stepped outside and found his big tom lying on the porch, its head missing. They never knew which of the Kiles killed the cat: the father, Jonas, or one of his sons, Herbert, thirty-three years old; John Henry, thirty-two; or Froggie, thirty-one. Froggie had bulging eyes, hence the nickname. No one knew his real name.

All four men were short and pudgy, dirty and ugly. Their mother had died giving birth to Froggie. It was said by the midwife who attended the mother that there were signs on her body of recent beatings. Jonas's wife hemorrhaged to death giving birth to the baby boy.

The midwife told everyone that it was Jonas's fault that his wife was dead and why. The enraged neighbor women tried to have him arrested and sent to jail for murder.

The law said no. A wife was a man's property and he could do as he pleased with her. A week later the woman who had led the charge against Jonas found her milch cow lying in a pool of blood. Someone had cut her throat. Everyone knew who the culprit was, but no one had the courage to say so. The Kiles might kill a human next.

An hour after Mrs. Kile was laid to rest, Jonas went to the orphanage thirty miles away and married a fourteen-year-old girl. She was pretty, with rosy cheeks and a lush body. She lost her beauty and her fresh looks within a week.

It was said, by those who knew what they were talking about, that Jonas used her night and day, even interrupted his work on the ranch a couple times a day to ride in and take the girl to bed. She was expected to cook and wash clothes and take care of the two motherless toddlers. She soon learned that to complain of the treatment she received was to provoke an unmerciful beating. The girl went around all the time with black eyes and numerous bruises on her face, arms, and legs. One day the neighboring ranchers realized they hadn't seen the new Mrs. Kile around for some time. When Kile was asked if his wife was ill, his answer was short and gruff.

"I took the no-account back to the orphanage. All she wanted to do was lie in bed and sleep."

Nobody credited his story. It was their belief that his beating of her had gotten out of hand and that he had killed her, that she was buried in one of the deep ravines. At any rate, Kile hadn't married any other unsuspecting woman.

Someday I'll kill all four of the bastards, Flint thought, then drew the horse in when he heard a racket going on at the bottom of the ridge he was traveling. It sounded like a vicious dogfight. He dismounted and peered down at the bottom of the ridge. He saw three hounds circling around what he first thought was a wolf. They were darting in at the big fellow, nipping at his hips, legs, and neck.

Flint soon saw that the animal was more dog than wolf. He also realized that the big fellow was no stranger to battle. As Flint watched, the dog flung a painfully yipping hound six or seven feet into a ditch. He turned on the other two dogs then, his teeth pulled back in a snarl as he charged the largest one. He soon had it on its back, whimpering in pain from the grip of fangs on its throat.

"Kill the bastard!" Flint encouraged the wolf, or whatever it was. "And look to your back, here comes the other one."

Flint knew the wolf-dog couldn't understand him, but it spun around to meet the charge of the last dog as though he had. He had the hound on its back, his teeth sunk into its throat, when Flint heard the click of a hammer being cocked. He spun around and saw Froggie Kile aiming his rifle at the big dog.

He grabbed his Colt from its holster and

called out, "You squeeze that hammer and you're a dead man!"

"Dammit, Flint, that wolf is gonna kill my hound!"

Flint aimed his Colt at the sky. "You know how to stop the fight," he said, and squeezed the trigger. The fight came to an immediate end. The winning combatant released his grip on the hound's throat and shot off through the trees.

"I'll kill the bastard the next time I see him," Froggie threatened as he examined his dog. "I'll gut-shoot him so he'll be a long time dyin'."

"If I ever hear of it, I'll give you the same medicine. A brave dog like that deserves a better death. So you'd better pray that animal lives a long time. And you can bet I'll be watching my back."

Flint struck out in the direction the wolf had gone. He felt pretty certain the animal was the same one he had encountered last night on his way home. It belonged to someone in the area.

He was surprised when the tracks led to the old Hayes place. How long, he wondered, had the lobo been hiding out here? He might have dug himself a lair beneath the abandoned house.

Flint pulled the horse in when he smelled wood smoke. He sniffed harder, and was sure he smelled brewing coffee also. Had the new owners moved in already?

He decided to investigate, and nudged the horse with his heel. He stepped up on the porch and knocked on the door. He was wondering just what he should say when the door opened.

His eyes opened wide at the beauty of the young woman who stood looking inquiringly at him. He was throughly tongue-tied. He could only stand and gaze at her slender willowly frame, her face of fragile beauty. Her rumpled curly hair reached her shoulders, and was so blond it was almost white. Her eyes were dark blue, heavily fringed with thick lashes.

He was just becoming aware that her gown covered very little of her body, the material was so worn and thin. He could see clearly the outlines of her firm breasts with their pink areolas.

He had just dropped his gaze to the dark blond smudge in the vee of her thighs when she asked coolly, "Are you looking for someone?"

He had to swallow twice before he could stutter, "I was . . . was tracking a . . . wolf and his tracks led here."

"So? What had he done to you? What did you plan on doing to him if you found him? Were you going to shoot him?"

Flint flinched at the contempt in her voice and explained, "Three coon hounds jumped him. And though he was getting the best of the fight, I had to interfere when the hounds' owner was about to shoot the wolf."

The girl raised a sardonic eyebrow. "Are you, a rancher, trying to tell me that you're a friend of wolves?"

Flint was becoming more and more irritated

at the young woman's attitude. His eyes took on an angry glint. "I'm not trying to tell you anything. Whether it be human or animal, I'm always for the underdog."

Usually, Flint talked easily with women, but with this young lady he felt awkward, could find no easy words to say.

He was spared that necessity when the wolf he had been tracking came bounding around the house, snarling and growling. "Get inside, miss," he ordered, jerking his feet out of the stirrups and drawing them out of reach of the lunging animal.

"Wolf!" The girl came down the steps. "Stop it. He's a friend."

The dog skidded to a halt, looked Flint over, then sat down, his wagging tail brushing the snow.

Flint felt like a fool with his legs drawn up to the seat of his saddle. I must look like a young button, he thought angrily.

"I take it he belongs to you," he griped. He eased his legs down, his feet fumbling for the stirrups. "Is he a wolf or a dog?"

"He's a mix." Lauren bent over and patted the dog's large head. "His mother was a full-blood Arctic husky and his father was a wolf."

"He certainly is a handsome fellow. If he should ever have any offspring, I would sure like to have one of his pups."

"He's not going to have any," Dud said from the doorway, his voice rough, "Lauren, get in the house and get dressed." He bent cold eyes on Flint then. "Are you looking for somebody in particular?"

"No, I'm not." Flint's voice was equally cold. "I saw your dog fighting off three hounds. He was holding his own, but then the owner of the dogs came along and was going to shoot him. I stopped him. I followed the dog here because I was curious whether he was a dog or a wolf."

"I expect Lauren straightened that out for you."

"Yes, she did," Flint answered; then after a pause he said, "I heard you called Dud in the gambling hall. Was the young man with you your grandson? I've never seen anyone play poker as well as he can."

The wrinkles around Dud's lips twitched a bit. "I'm sort of an uncle to that young player, and he's not a he. He's a she. Her name is Lauren."

Flint's eyes flew to the door through which Lauren had disappeared. "You mean that beautiful young woman is the same person who emptied the players' pockets of money?"

"That's right," Dud said proudly. "I learned her how to play when she was just a little bit of a girl."

"How have you managed to keep some young fellow from taking her away from you?"

"That won't happen until I find the right man. And let me tell you, I've set my sights high. No fast-talking, two-timing cowboy will do for that little gal. I want a hard-working family man."

"Does Lauren know of your plan for her? Does she approve?"

"Of course she approves. She knows how hard a woman has it when she's married to a wastrel."

Dud nailed Flint with cold eyes. "You can pass the word around among your wild friends that they'll be wasting their time to come around here with courtin' on their minds."

We'll see about that, you old bastard, Flint was thinking as a heavily loaded wagon pulled into the weed-choked yard.

"Looks like our supplies have arrived," Dud said, jumping off the porch. When the door behind him opened, he ordered, "Stay in the house, Lauren, and make room for everything as it's brought in."

"Can I give you a hand?" Flint started to dismount.

"Go on about your business," Dud ordered sharply. "Me and the driver can handle it."

Flint gave one longing look at the house before turning the horse around and heading it toward home. He had a smile on his face as he departed. Old Dud would have a fit if he knew the beautiful Lauren had sneaked Flint a smile and a wave from the kitchen window. Maybe Dud's plans for her wouldn't turn out as he hoped.

Chapter Six

The sun was melting the thin covering of snow as Flint rode toward home. He was unmindful of that fact as the horse plodded along. Thoughts of Lauren hadn't left his mind for a minute. Over and over he pictured the soft, shadowy mounds of her breasts under the threadbare gown, the pink nipples pushing against the material. Never in his adult life had he ached so to sink his growing hardness inside the warmth of a female the way he wanted to do to her. He wanted to rock in and out of her until they were both exhausted.

He was imagining the feel of her soft breasts in his mouth, his tongue wrapped around a nipple, when he neared his ranch house and saw a familiar horse tied to the hitching rope. It belonged to his friend Asher Davis. He grinned and rode on to the barn. He would exchange the mountain horse for his stallion. He and Asher would be going to town. His grin widened as he thought that maybe he and his longtime friend might have missed a couple whores when they were in town the other night.

Asher Davis, slim like all cowboys, looked up from the cup of coffee Kate had just poured for him when Flint walked into the kitchen. He gave Flint a crooked grin. "Kate said you went out to kill a deer. Where is it?"

Flint sat down at the table, removed his hat, and laid it on the floor beside his chair. "I got distracted by a fight between a wolf-dog and three of Jonas Kile's hounds."

"I hope the wolf won," Asher grunted. "I bet my life it's those varmints that tried to take my horse down. If I ever catch them, there'll be some hounds shot through their heads."

"The wolf-dog was going after them pretty good. He maimed one and had another one on the ground, with a good grip on his throat. Then Froggie Kile rode up. He was about to shoot the dog until I stepped in."

"I wish you wouldn't tangle with those low-lifes," Kate said as she poured Flint a cup of coffee. "You know how they sneak around and back-shoot a man."

"I know that, Kate, and you can bet I'll be

careful from now on. I just couldn't let him kill that dog. He had been fighting so bravely. He's so magnificent-looking I just felt it would be a sin to let a mangy cur like Kile kill him."

"Does the animal belong to anyone, or is he wild?" Asher asked.

"You'd never believe who he belongs to. Last night I met a stranger and a kid in his teens in the gambling hall. The kid cleaned everyone out."

"You don't say?"

"Yeah, the old fellow is a rough-looking character. The kid called him Dud."

"Does the dog belong to him?"

Flint nodded. "I tracked the dog to see if he had been hurt. He went straight to the old Hayes ranch."

"Don't tell me this Dud person is the owner of the ranch now?"

"I guess he is. He and the kid have moved in lock, stock, and barrel. The man who works for Tom Richards at the mercantile drove a wagon load of supplies up to the place while I was there. I know there was at least a winter's supply of grub in the wagon."

"What's this Dud person like?"

"He's a crusty one. Not very friendly. He didn't even invite me in for a cup of coffee. He didn't offer any information about himself, and I didn't ask."

Asher Davis finished his coffee and pushed the cup away. "You want to take a ride into town with me?" he asked Flint. "My horse has a loose shoe that needs looking at."

"I might as well." Flint finished drinking his coffee. "I've got nothing else to do. I'll go change my shirt and we'll be off."

When Flint left the kitchen, Kate gave Asher a stern look. "Seems to me you two could find something better to do than whorin' around all the time."

"Now, Kate, I didn't say anything about whorin'. My horse needs his shoe looked at."

"In a pig's eye. You had that same excuse three weeks ago."

Caught in his lie, Asher blushed and muttered, "It was a different shoe that was loose."

"I'm sure," Kate said stiffly. "You just try to keep Flint out of trouble while I'm away for the next few weeks."

When Flint and Asher came to the place where the river road split, they reined their horses. One trail went east to Jackson Hole, and the other one followed the river to a fur post a few miles further on.

"What do you think?" Flint looked at Asher. "Should we go to the post? We haven't been there for a while."

Asher's teeth flashed in a crooked grin. "And I remember why. Do you?"

"Kind of." Flint looked a little sheepish. "I think we sort of tore the place up a little."

"Sort of doesn't begin to describe what that

place looked like when Old Johnson threw us out and ordered us never to come back."

"Yeah, but we didn't start it. That tall, skinny mountain man pulled a knife on me," Flint explained irritably.

"And why did he do that, Flint? Do you think he did it just to while away the time?"

"Hell, I don't know. I was pretty drunk by then."

"You weren't too drunk to coax his woman away from him and take her into one of the back rooms at the post."

"It wasn't like she was married to him."

"They were betrothed, which is the next best thing to those mountain people."

"I didn't know, and I feel sorry about that. If she'd said she was promised, I wouldn't have touched her. You know that."

"I know," Asher agreed. "Which trail are we taking?"

"Do you suppose Old Johnson is over his mad fit yet? I remember handing him a fistful of money to pay for our share of whatever was broken."

"I guess we'll have to go and find out." Asher headed his horse down the river trail. "If he doesn't shoot us, then we'll know he's over his mad."

As they rode single file along the narrow, gravel trail, Flint fell to reminiscing about his friendship with Asher. They had met during a drunken brawl in the Trail's End Saloon in

Jackson Hole when they were both in their early twenties. Neither had known what the fight was about, who was in the wrong. They only knew that here was a chance to throw a fist into someone's face.

They had finished the evening drinking, then escorting a couple of whores upstairs to their rooms.

That one evening had created a friendship that would last forever. Asher had nothing of his own but a pair of guns, a horse, and a saddle. But that fact didn't seem to bother the genial, easygoing man. It was as if he knew that when the time came that he was too old to punch cattle anymore, he would always have a home with his friend Flint Mahone.

Flint caught sight of Old Dud riding toward them on his magnificent sorrel stallion. He raised his hand in greeting, and the old man rode up to them.

"What brings you out this way again?" Dud asked suspiciously.

"My friend Asher and I are headed for the fur post, just a couple miles further on. Care to join us?" Flint said with a devilish grin.

Dud shook his head. "I'm checking to see if we've got any stock left on the place. Got no time for carousing," he said gruffly, riding on.

Laughing, Flint and Asher kicked their horses into a lope. Within ten minutes the crude building of the post emerged through the heavy fog that was rising from the river.

Flint looked at the large number of horses tied to the picket line. "Looks like Johnson has a full house."

As he dismounted Asher said, a little nervous, "Do you think we should go in? Them mountain men don't have much love for us after our run-in with them."

"Hell, Asher, are you afraid of them possum-eating ignoramuses?" Flint said as he tied his stallion far back in the trees.

"The thing I don't like about fightin' them is they use big knives. I hate knives."

"There's nothing to handling those men and their knives. When you see one coming at you, just bop him on the head with your fist."

"That works?" Asher tied his horse a few feet away from Flint's stallion, Shadow.

"It works every time. Just make sure you whack him real hard." Flint straightened his jacket and smoothed down his denims. "I wonder if Johnson has gotten in any new girls since we were here last."

"You just have to wonder about one thing, Flint. If that mountain man is in there with his woman, or his wife by now. You stay clear of her."

"Don't worry about it. I wouldn't poke her in a fit. Come on, let's go."

Flint pushed the door open, and was met with a raucous sound. A skinny man was pounding piano keys that were badly out of tune, and the men and women in the place were trying to talk over its noise. The long room was filled with the smoke of home-grown tobacco.

Asher closed the door behind them, and they stood to one side and let their gazes drift over the room. Most were familiar faces, not men that they were acquainted with, just men they saw every time they stopped by. When Johnson looked up from behind the bar and lifted a hand in greeting, they knew everything was forgiven. They made their way around the dancers and bellied up to the makeshift bar of rough planks laid on top of empty barrels.

"I take it you fellers are gonna behave yourselves," Johnson said as he filled a couple glasses with moonshine.

Flint looked at him and grinned. "Are there any wives here tonight?"

The bartender grinned back. "None that I know of." After a moment he added, "That gal you fought over is married now. She married the man you half killed. He don't bring her around here anymore."

Flint downed his drink, then started looking around the room, sizing up the women. He was disappointed that there were no new faces. Somehow he kept looking for a tall, slim girl with rumpled blonde hair.

"What do you think, Flint?" Asher asked. "Do you see anything that interests you?"

"Naw, not really. I'm not drunk enough yet.

Let's have a few more drinks. If we're blind drunk, they might look a little better."

Kate balanced the pie she had taken from the oven twenty minutes ago in the crook of her left arm while she held the reins with her right. It was the custom in the area that when you called on a new neighbor the first time, you brought a pie, a cake, or some cookies. She figured that since there were only two men in the household, her new neighbors would appreciate something sweet.

As the horse plodded along at its own pace, Kate thought about her upcoming visit to her parents' home.

Every autumn, after roundup, she went to visit her parents and brother for several weeks. She looked forward to these times spent with her mother. She caught up on news of her aunts and uncles and cousins, what they had been doing since the last time she'd visited the old home place. Her parents and friends there had stopped asking when was she going to get married and have some children. Her answer had always been the same. There was still enough child in Flint for her to keep an eye on.

A deep warning growl brought Kate to the realization that she had reached her destination, and that a wolf stood in her path. She froze. From the way the animal's lips were pulled back, his fangs exposed, she was afraid to move, too afraid even to call for help.

She was trying to get up the nerve to turn her horse around and race it home as fast as it could run when a man's voice ordered, "Go lie down, Wolf. It's all right."

The wolf immediately jumped up on the porch and stretched out, his huge head resting between his paws. "You can get down now, miss," the man said. "He won't bother you."

"How do you know what a wolf will do?" Kate's voice was quivery from fright.

"He's half dog. That part of him will obey me."

"Are you called Dud?" Kate asked as he came to help her dismount.

"What makes you ask me that?" He watched her closely.

"The man I work for, Flint Mahone, said that a man called Dud had bought the Hayes ranch. I just assumed you were the new owner."

"You're partly right. Dud is my handle. But the ranch is owned by a Hart."

"That would be the boy in his teens Flint saw you with?"

"You're partly right again." Dud looked at Kate with dry amusement as he descended the two steps of the porch. "That boy is a girl. Miss Lauren Hart."

Kate stopped and stared at him. "Does Flint know she's a girl?"

"Yeah, that long tall galoot found out when he tracked the dog here. He had seen him fightin' off three hounds and trailed Wolf to see if he was hurt."

When Kate chuckled, Dud asked, "What do you find so funny?"

"The Indians call Flint Long Tall Man."

"It's a good name for him." Dud chuckled too. "Come on in the house and meet Lauren. She'll be glad that another woman lives close by."

Well, I'll be blasted, Kate thought when she stepped into the kitchen and saw a beautiful girl down on her hands and knees scrubbing the floor. The young woman looked up and blushed at being caught in a raggedy pair of denims and a shirt with the elbows out.

She's a proud one, Kate thought, noticing that the girl didn't apologize for her appearance, merely stood and gave Kate a friendly smile.

"Lauren," Dud said, "this is our neighbor—"

"Kate Allen." Kate held out her hand. "I'm the housekeeper for Flint Mahone. Actually I've raised him since he was four years old and his mother passed away. His ranch is just a couple miles from here."

"You met him," Dud said to Lauren. "He's the feller who tracked Wolf here to see if he was all right."

"Oh, yes, I remember him," Lauren said, and Kate wondered why the girl blushed. Had that rapscallion Flint made improper advances to her?

Somehow, Kate doubted that. This girl was

different from any Flint had ever seen before. Why hadn't he mentioned her to Asher? she wondered.

Kate was hard put not to show her amusement. She guessed what Flint was thinking. If he could court Miss Hart first, he would have an advantage over Asher.

Lauren invited Kate to come in and have some coffee with her. As she seated herself at the table, Kate was thinking that this coming winter might not be so dull. It would be interesting to see which of the two-legged wolves Lauren would choose.

Dud followed Kate into the kitchen. When he sat down at the the head of the table, he said bluntly, "What about having a piece of that pie Kate brought?"

Lauren gave him a glaring look, then said to Kate, "He's too old to be taught any manners."

"I don't mind." Kate grinned at Dud. "I live with a man who has no manners at all."

"Do you mean that Flint feller?" Dud watched Lauren slice pie, practically smacking his lips.

"He's the one. He wouldn't even wait for a fork and a pie plate. He'd just pick it up in his hands and shove it in his mouth."

"He seemed mannerly when he was here," Dud said, reaching eagerly for the piece of pie offered him.

"Oh, he knows how to behave when he wants to. I managed to pound a few manners into him when he was young and was afraid I might whack him one if he acted out."

Kate's voice grew soft. "He was the sweetest little thing. He loved for me to rock and sing to him. Missed his mama, I guess."

"Jake, his older brother, was a handful, though. He was always polite, never sassed me. But that young'un could get into more trouble than a rattler with two heads."

Kate's smile faded. "When Jake was twenty-four or five, he fell in love with a no-account woman, married her, and moved away. Unfortunately, when he stopped carousing around, Flint took up where his brother left off. Flint and Asher Davis are the worst hellions in the country."

A sadness came into Kate's eyes. "War broke out and both brothers joined up. I wrote to Jake not to go. By then he had three young children. But he insisted on enlisting. He wrote that if he didn't get away from his cheating wife, he might kill her."

"Where do Flint's brother and his family live?" Lauren asked.

"Jake didn't come home. He died of pneumonia in a prison camp."

"I take it Flint has the children now," Lauren said.

"It's so sad"—Kate stared out the window—"but Flint doesn't even know where his niece and two nephews are. After the war he went to his brother's homestead, but they'd disappeared. No one knows what's become of Jake's wife or children."

Dud broke up the conversation by saying, "This is the best pie I ever et. Could I have another piece, and could you learn Lauren how to cook?"

"I would love to if Lauren would like me to."

"I'd appreciate it." Lauren's face glowed eagerly. "I'm not much of a hand in the kitchen. I only know how to cook plain dishes."

"She didn't have anyone to learn her except me and her daddy," Dud said. "He always said that I was the worst cook that ever came out of Missouri."

When Kate gave him a questioning look, he said quickly, "She lost her maw when she was two years old. Me and her dad raised her."

"You did a good job of it." Kate smiled at Lauren and asked, "When will your father be joining you?"

"He won't," Dud said gruffly. "He was shot and killed a couple weeks ago."

Dud's statement was so short and sharp, Kate knew he didn't want to answer any more questions. She dropped the subject after saying, "I'm sorry to hear that."

Although she was curious how Lauren had come to own the Hayes ranch, she didn't ask. She was sure she would learn in time. Private affairs weren't kept private very long in Jackson Hole. Someone would nose out the details of how the Hayes ranch passed into the hands of Lauren Hart.

"I guess I'd better be getting home," Kate said after looking out the window and seeing that the sun had moved a good distance westward. "I want to make something for Flint's supper before I leave this afternoon."

Dud and Lauren walked outside with her. As Dud helped her to mount, Kate reminded them that she'd be back in a couple weeks. "So come visit me then."

"I will, and you come back to visit me," Lauren said, her voice warm.

"Seams like a nice woman," Dud said as Kate rode out of sight.

"Yes, I like her. I think she's an honest, sincere person and will make a good neighbor."

Chapter Seven

Kate had already left for her parents' home when a rented buggy from Jackson Hole livery rolled into the Mahone yard. No sound disturbed the clear air as the woman who handled the reins pulled the horse to a halt.

"Don't you young'uns move," the sharp-featured woman ordered as she climbed to the ground and smoothed down her skirt. She untied the ribbons of her black bonnet and tucked some pale brown straggly hair into the small, tight bun at her nape. Her narrow face puckered in a frown as it became evident to her that there was no one around the place.

"You shut up, Mercy," she threatened a little

six-year-old who was sobbing, curled up against a boy of around ten.

"She's thirsty," the other boy explained, "and hungry too."

"You hush up too, Henry, or you'll get clobbered."

"Nasty old bitch," Henry said under his breath as the skinny woman climbed the steps to the porch. "I wish a snake would crawl out of a hole and bite her."

The words were hardly out of Henry's mouth when the sharp-faced woman let out a loud scream and ran for the buggy. The children looked alarmed also when they saw a large wolf stalking after her. The animal sat down and watched the frightened woman scramble into the buggy and grab up the reins. She popped them over the horse's back and it took off at a gallop.

"Miss James," the oldest boy cautioned, "you'd better pull the horse in a little. Otherwise the buggy is going to turn over."

"I'm trying to, Tommy," she panted, "but the horse is too strong."

Tommy pushed his little sister into Henry's lap, and standing, grabbed the reins out of the now hysterical woman's hands. "You're pulling too hard on the reins," he said impatiently. "The bits are biting into his mouth."

With the reins loosened and soft words crooned to him, the horse soon calmed down.

"I ought to take a whip to him," the woman screeched, reaching for the whip.

When she had it in her grip, Tommy snatched it out of her hand. "So help me, I'll lay this whip on you if you don't settle down," he said grimly.

The old maid knew by his tone that he meant every word. "Well, Mr. Know It All"—Miss James jerked the lines from his hands—"what do we do now? I've got to get rid of you young'uns and get back to Jackson Hole in time to catch the coach back to the orphanage."

"I guess the best thing to do is to follow the wagon road. I imagine we'll find another ranch. They can probably tell us where my uncle is."

"Are you sure the people at the orphanage sent him a letter saying we would arrive today?"

"Yes, I'm sure," Miss James snapped, sending the horse down the country road. The children didn't open their mouths as the wheels whirred along, eating up the miles at a fast clip. The look on the woman's face said that she might put them out of the buggy and go off, leaving them sitting with the longhorn cattle they could see at a distance.

It was shortly before sundown when the Hart ranch appeared at the bottom of a short hill. Everyone sat forward eagerly. The children were tired and hungry, and Miss James was eager to be rid of them.

When they arrived at the big house and she reined the horse in, a gruff-looking man stepped off the porch and walked up to them.

"Are you lookin' for somebody, miss?" He flicked his gaze over the children.

The little girl looked all right, he thought, but the younger boy had a lot of the devil dancing in his eyes. And the older one. There was anger and bitterness in his eyes. Life hadn't treated him very well.

Dud shifted his gaze back to the woman. That one was raised on sour milk, he thought, studying her thin, narrow face and black gimlet eyes. If the children angered her, she wouldn't hesitate to hit them.

Miss James blushed at Dud's close scrutiny. She did not like being stared at for such a long time. Her thin lips became thinner. "I'm looking for a Mr. Flint Mahone," she said sharply. "These are his orphaned niece and nephews. He was supposed to meet our coach in Jackson Hole, but he did not. Nor could I find him at his ranch. Do you know where I might find him?"

Dud didn't want to make anything easy for this sour-faced woman. But there was a pathos about the children that made him say reluctantly, "Earlier on I saw him and another man riding along the river road. They told me there's a fur post a couple miles down. I expect you'll find him there."

Lauren had walked down the steps as Dud and Miss James talked. She smiled into the little girl's tear-stained face, and received a shy smile in return. "You've been crying, honey," she said softly. "Are you tired?"

The little one knuckled the tears out of her eyes and whispered, "I need to go to the privy real bad."

When Lauren reached up to take the little one from her brother, he jumped to the ground with his sister still in his arms. "I think we all could use that facility, miss."

He put Mercy down on her feet and said, "The lady will take you in and help you with your bloomers and all."

When Lauren had helped Mercy, she and the little one went outside and sat on a rock while Tommy and Henry took turns in the outhouse.

When everyone had answered nature's call, Lauren slid off the rock and reached up to Mercy, saying, "Come on, honey."

She had never before held such a small hand, and a softness welled up inside her. The child was so little, so helpless. Would Flint Mahone be kind to her? She felt that he would do the best he could, but he probably didn't know any more about children than she did.

It was Lauren's opinion that what the children needed most right now was a lot of love. They hadn't had nearly enough of that in their young lives.

At the sound of a sharp crack, Lauren gave a start and ran around to the front of the house. The bony woman was laying the whip on the horse, sending him away at a fast gallop. "Good Lord," she muttered, "is she leaving the children here with me and Dud?"

The boys, having heard the buggy wheels, came bolting around the corner of the house. Lauren and Dud blinked when Tommy exclaimed angrily, "Has that ugly bitch gone off and left us?"

When Lauren got over her shock that one so young could talk so rough, she looked at Dud. "Did you tell her to leave?"

"Hell, no. As soon as you and the young'uns walked behind the house she asked me for a glass of water. While I was inside getting it for her, she whipped up the horse and went tearing down the road toward town. I think she just wanted to get rid of Mahone's young relatives."

"We sure are glad to be rid of her," Tommy said. "If she had slapped Mercy one more time, I'd have hit her back."

"Well," Dud said, "I'll go hitch up the wagon and we'll go to the fur post. I'm sure that's where we'll find your uncle."

"Miss"—Tommy tugged at Lauren's skirt when she started to go into the house to get a shawl—"could you please let Mercy have a slice of bread? She's hungry. We haven't eaten since early this morning."

"Of course she can," Lauren answered promptly. "And you and Henry can also."

When the children seated themselves at the table, Lauren stood in a state of uncertainty. What with Kate visiting, then Miss James bringing the children, she hadn't started supper yet, and she didn't have a crust of bread in the house.

Her gaze rested on the half-eaten pie. She took three small plates out of the cupboard, then sliced the pie into three equal parts. She placed a fork beside each helping and smilingly said, "Dig in, kids."

The pie disappeared so fast, Lauren knew the children were still hungry.

"What's holding you up?" Dud asked from the doorway.

"The children were hungry, so we stopped long enough to have some pie."

Dud looked so sad when he saw the empty pie tin, Lauren said, "I'll bake you a pie tomorrow."

"You don't know how to bake a pie," Dud snorted. "You can't cook worth spit."

"You can't either then, because you're the one who taught me."

"Tommy can help you bake a pie, Miss," Henry said. "He had to help the cook in the orphanage. He knows a lot about cooking, don't you, Tommy?"

"I reckon I know a little bit," Tommy said, blushing at his brother's praise.

"I sure would appreciate it if you would teach me what you know," Lauren said sincerely.

"I'd he happy to." Tommy looked directly at her for the first time and smiled.

"If we're gonna go lookin' for Mahone, let's get started," Dud grumbled.

* * *

"What do you think, Flint, are you drunk enough to poke one of them gals that are makin' eyes at us?" Asher leaned an elbow on the rough bar.

"Hell, I don't know." Flint peered with bleary eyes through the smoke. "Tell you the truth, I can't even see them. If ole Dolly is free I'll take her," he said, though he didn't sound too enthusiastic.

Asher straightened up and motioned to a long-legged whore sitting at a table. She hurried over to the bar. "What can I do for you, Asher?" She gave him a coy smile.

"You can't do anything for me, Dolly. It's Flint here who wants your company."

Dolly turned her smile on Flint, and wrapping an arm around his waist, she shoved her hand down the front of his denims.

That was how Lauren and the children saw him when they walked into the fur post.

Lauren's eyes widened when she saw what was going on between Flint and Dolly. She pressed Mercy's face against her side so that the child couldn't see her uncle and what the woman was doing to him.

She took the boys' arms and whispered, "Let's go outside and send Dud in to speak to your uncle."

Tommy started to follow Lauren to the door, but Henry recognized Flint and dashed across the floor to him. He jerked on Flint's arm for attention. When Flint stared down at him, muttering, "What in the hell is a kid doing in this hell-hole," Henry grew nervous and half afraid. When he tried to speak a couple times and failed, Flint said irritably, "Spit it out, boy, before you step on your tongue."

Something snapped inside Lauren when she saw Henry's woeful little face. He had been so anxious to see his Uncle Flint, to have a relative again. It was as if that relative had slapped him in the face instead of giving him a welcoming hug.

Without fully realizing what she was doing, Lauren pushed Mercy into Tommy's arms, then flew across the saloon floor. Everyone but Flint saw her coming. They all, including Asher, stepped aside at the fury in her eyes. Only the whore stood her ground. She kept her arm around Flint's waist and her hand down his pants, smugly possessive.

Her brave stance didn't last long. Lauren grabbed her by the elbow and jerked her hand out of Flint's pants. Dolly let out a screech. "What do you think you're doin'?"

"I'll show you what I'm doing, whore," Lauren gritted. She tore Dolly's arm from around Flint's waist, spun her around a couple times, then sent her staggering toward the door, which a grinning Tommy was holding open.

Flint pushed away from the bar and stared down into a pair of eyes so full of contempt, they froze his blood. Flustered, he stuttered,

"What's . . . what's wrong, what did I do?"

"You shamed your little nephew, that's what you did, you whorin' drunk."

"Shamed my nephew? I haven't seen those kids in years!"

"Well, those children have been living terrible lives while you've been living in your big ranch, drinking and carousing."

"You seem to know an awful lot about them." Flint was becoming embarrassed, and was angry because of it, so his voice was sharp.

"The orphanage woman who brought the children to your ranch couldn't find you. She brought them to my place and told Dud some of their history. She said their mother abandoned them when the war ended. Seems she ran off with some man. The little ones claimed they had an uncle in Wyoming, so the orphanage sent them here in her care. She said you'd been sent a letter."

Flint could only stare for a moment. "A letter?" he repeated. "I never got any letter." Lauren's sharp tongue had sobered him up. He looked down at freckle-faced Henry pressed against Lauren's legs and felt his heart twist. The boy looked just like his Grandpa Mahone. Flint laid his hand on the blond head and said softly, "Welcome, nephew."

Henry gave him a gap-toothed smile and put his skinny arms around Flint's waist.

His eyes wet, Flint asked, "Where are your brother and sister?"

Henry pointed them out, and Flint looked across the room and into Tommy's eyes. He was a carbon copy of his father. With a lump in his throat, Flint walked toward his dead brother's firstborn. When he held out his hand to the tall, thin boy, it was ignored.

"I'm your Uncle Flint," he said gently.

"I know who you are. I remember you."

When Tommy's face remained hard and tight, Flint looked down at the little girl gripping her brother's hand. Flint hunkered down beside her, and smoothing his hand over her curls, he smiled and said, "I'm sure you can't remember me. You were just a baby when I saw you last."

Big brown eyes looked up at him, and pink baby lips parted in a smile so sweet, Flint thought his heart would melt. He was ready to hug her to his chest when she replied innocently, "I know who you are, though. You're my bastard uncle."

Shocked, Flint looked up at Tommy. "Have you been telling her that?"

"I have not!" Tommy denied vehemently. "She heard it all the time from the people who run the orphanage." He flung the words at Flint bitterly.

"She don't know any better, Uncle Flint." Henry put his arm around Mercy's small shoulder.

"I don't know any betta, Uncle Fint." Mercy smiled at him again.

I've got to get out of here before I break down and blubber like a baby, Flint thought. "You kids must be hungry," Flint said, picking Mercy up and holding her on his hip. He got up the nerve to look at Lauren and say, "Thank you for bringing the children to me. How did you know I was here?"

"Dud said he'd met you and your friend riding down the river road that leads here. We thought it best to get them to you as soon as possible. Mercy is sleepy and all three are hungry. I didn't feed them because I hadn't made supper yet when the orphanage lady ran off and left them with us."

"And Lauren can't cook worth spit," Mercy piped up. "I don't think I'd like spit for supper. Would you, Unca Fint?"

"Mercy, we're going to have to teach you to curb your tongue a little. Lauren wouldn't serve you spit for supper. Whoever said that meant that she can't cook very well."

"Dud said it," Mercy explained. "I think he was mad that we ate all the pie."

Flint looked at Lauren and shook his head. One never knew what might roll off Mercy's tongue.

"Your housekeeper, Kate, brought us the pie. She rode over to call on us before leaving to visit her parents," Lauren explained.

Flint nodded vaguely. He didn't tell Lauren that he had forgotten all about Kate's trip. It hit him like a whack on the head that it would be up to him to take care of three youngsters for two weeks. Other than his horse, he had never taken care of anything in his life. He wondered if his neighbor might lend him a hand. One look at her cold features told him to give up that hope.

"Hey, Lauren, did you find Mahone?" Dud appeared in the doorway. "The team is getting restless."

Flint stepped in front of Lauren. "She found me. We were just leaving. Did you all come in a wagon?"

"Yeah, we did."

"I wonder if I could use the wagon to take the children home, and you and Lauren could ride our horses to your ranch."

"It's up to Lauren." Dud looked at her for confirmation.

"I expect that's the best thing to do. Mercy is almost asleep on her feet."

"Dud, Lauren, meet my friend Asher Davis." Flint introduced them just before they walked outside.

Asher looked at Flint and barely contained a chuckle. You wolf, he thought, you didn't want me to meet her yet.

A mischievous glimmer appeared in Asher's eyes. Giving Lauren a wide attractive smile, he said softly as he took her arm to help her down the step, "I'm real pleased to meet you, ma'am."

Before Lauren could answer, Henry put his foot between Asher's feet, sending him tumbling down the step to land awkwardly on his rump. Everyone but Lauren guffawed loudly.

When no one was looking Flint fondly gave Henry's head a rub and said loudly, "Nephew, go help the old man up."

He earned himself a look from Asher that said, I'll take care of you later, *old man*.

Flint grinned and climbed into the wagon, and Tommy handed Mercy up to him. As he settled her in his lap, Tommy and Henry climbed into the wagon and stood, holding onto the back of the seat. Flint turned his head to see what was keeping Asher, and swore under his breath. Friend Asher had helped Lauren to mount his horse, and was taking his time adjusting the stirrups for her shorter legs.

"You snake in the grass," he muttered, "you can walk home." He snapped the reins over the team's backs and they moved out.

"Hey, Flint, hold up!" Asher came running after the wagon.

It appeared that Asher would be walking home until Tommy reached his hand down and helped him climb into the wagon.

"Thanks, kid." Asher smiled at Tommy. "I guess your uncle didn't know that I was running after you."

"I expect he doesn't know a lot of things if he doesn't want to," Tommy said in a low, dry voice.

Flint wasn't sure what Tommy had said to Asher that made his friend laugh, so he let it pass. He felt pretty sure, though, that whatever it was, it wasn't anything very complimentary to him. The kid didn't like his only uncle, and Flint would have to work on that. Tommy was older and wiser than his siblings, and would see through adult pretense.

Flint was still hoping that he could live up to what an uncle should be as the lights of the ranch cookhouse came into view.

"We're just in time for supper, kids," Flint said, bringing the team to a halt. "Wait here while I go in the house and light some lamps so that you can see where to walk."

"Why can't we wait in the cookhouse where it's warm?" Asher asked, already lifting Mercy out of the wagon.

Why hadn't he thought of that? Flint asked himself with contempt. He'd better get hold of himself, stop thinking of that long-legged beauty who curled her nose every time she looked at him. Would she ever forget seeing him standing drunk at a bar, a whore's hand down his pants?

"Go on in the cookhouse then," Flint barked. "I just thought it would be a good idea to get some heat and light going in the house as soon as possible."

"You take the kids into the cookhouse and I'll see to warming up the house," Asher said.

"No, you take them on in. I want to check the bedrooms, see if the beds are made up."

Asher nodded, and with Mercy on his hip, he ushered the boys into the warm cookhouse.

Chapter Eight

By the time Flint unhitched the team and forked some hay into their troughs, a fine drizzle was falling. Would it turn into a full-fledged rainstorm or become snow? he wondered as he hopped up on the porch and entered the house.

The kitchen was still warm from the red coals that remained in the stove, thanks to Kate baking pies and sourdough before she left to visit her parents.

After he had added more wood to the big black stove, Flint walked into the front room and built a roaring fire in the fieldstone fireplace that took up one end of it. It had been built so that heat from the hearth would travel down the hall that led to the four bedrooms.

He took off his jacket and went to inspect the bedrooms. Ever since his father's death, the only one used was the one he slept in. Kate had her own small quarters behind the kitchen.

The three doors squeaked from disuse as Flint opened them. The rooms were clean, the beds made up. His nose twitched. Everything smelled musty. That was to be expected after being closed up for so long. He wished that he could open a window, but that was out of the question. A full-blown rainstorm was now beating against the glass panes. However, he thought as he pulled the bedcovers to the foot of the bed, once the heat reached the rooms, much of the staleness would disappear.

As Flint went from room to room, he lit a lamp in each one. He left them burning and pulled on his slicker to dash to the cookhouse. Before he left he swung his gaze around. He liked the cozy look the lamplight gave to the big place. He couldn't remember ever seeing it look so warm and friendly. Kate kept the kitchen that way, but the other rooms in the house had always seemed a little lonesome once his father and brother were gone.

When Flint entered the warm cookhouse he was surprised to see Asher and the children sitting at a table off by itself. There was an empty chair at the head of the table. It was for him, he knew, and a warm feeling came over him. I reckon I'm a family man now, he thought, and was surprised at how well he liked the idea. He took off his jacket and shook the rain off it before approaching the table. Asher saw him first and gave him a crooked grin before saying, "We'd have waited for you but the young'uns were hungry."

"The way you're shoving that stew into your mouth, I'd say the oldster is hungry too," Flint said dryly as he drew out his chair and sat down. "Well, what about it, kids, is the stew any good?" he asked as he helped himself to a heaping plate of meat and vegetables.

"It's the best stew I ever ate," Henry declared.

Mercy echoed her brother's declaration, but her brother Tommy didn't respond one way or the other. Flint looked at him and said, "I haven't heard from you, Tommy. What's your opinion of supper?"

When the older brother only shook his shoulders indifferently, Henry piped up, "Don't pay any attention to him, Uncle Flint. He's just being ornery. He's had three helpings already and he'd ask for another, only it would embarass him."

"You just hush up, Henry, before I give you what for." Tommy glared at his younger sibling.

"I ain't afraid of you, *Thomas*," Henry said with a devilish look in his eyes.

Flint hid a smile. The little imp knew that Tommy hated to be called Thomas. Tommy was a serious-minded youngster, deeply hurt at losing his father to the war and being abandoned by their mother. The boy was bitter, and it would take careful handling before he would trust anyone.

Flint helped himself to another plate of stew and said, "It's not at all unusual for men to ask for four helpings around here."

Henry wouldn't let it go. "Maybe for men, but Tommy is just a skinny little kid."

"You're wrong, Henry," Flint said quietly. "Tommy was forced into being a man a long time ago."

"No, he wasn't. He just started bossing me and Mercy because he wanted to."

"I imagine the reason he did that, Henry, was because he knew somebody had to be head of the Mahones. Since he was the eldest, it should be him." Flint paused a moment before continuing. "But things are different now. You're with your uncle now and he's the oldest, and as such I'll be calling the shots from here on. However, when I'm not around, you're to look after each other. Especially look out for Mercy."

He passed a grave look around the table. "Is that clear to all of you?" he asked. "There's to be no hitting each other."

Mercy, her little face stern, said solemnly, "I won't hit the boys unless they are really bad."

When her brothers would have burst out laughing, Flint shook his head at them. Asher had to turn his head to hide his amusement.

Flint rose from his chair, and picking Mercy

out of hers, said, "I think it's time we all went to bed. You boys will want to get up early and look over the ranch, your new home, maybe pick yourself out a horse."

"We sure will, Uncle Flint," Henry readily agreed. "Our own horse! Can you imagine, Tommy?"

When Flint looked at Tommy, he received a wide grin from the youngster.

So with Mercy on his hip, asking when she could have a horsie, and Asher and the boys following him, Flint walked toward the welcoming lights of the ranch house.

"Don't it all look nice and warm?" Henry whispered to Tommy. "All them lights burning? Not like the gloomy old orphanage with only one lamp burning in the whole big room."

Tommy's answer was to gently squeeze his brother's shoulders.

Flint let the children sit with him and Asher in front of the dancing flames in the fireplace for a while, the men answering eager questions put to them by the boys. Mercy was content mostly to sit curled up on her uncle's lap. The one time she did ask a question, Flint was hard put to answer her.

"Uncle Flint," she asked, "where do cows get their calves?"

While Flint stuttered and stammered, searching for words that would satisfy his niece, Asher spoke up. "They scratch them out from under rocks and stumps, Mercy."

When Mercy nodded that she understood, her brothers burst into fits of giggling. Flint gave them a stern look, and they bit their tongues to squash their mirth.

When the mantel clock struck nine, Flint announced it was time the children washed up and went to bed. "Did you kids bring in your duds?" He looked at Tommy.

Tommy blushed an embarrassed red. Dropping his head he muttered, "We weren't given any clothes except what we've got on."

Flint held back the curses he wanted to let loose on the people who ran the orphanage. Instead he looked beseechingly at Asher. The children couldn't sleep in the dirty clothes they had arrived in; neither could they sleep naked.

Asher's face showed that he was just as confused as Flint. His face brightened then with an idea. "The boys can sleep in your underwear tops, and little sister can sleep in something of Kate's," he suggested.

"I guess that can work for tonight," Flint agreed. "But tomorrow, early, I've got to go to town and get these young'uns some clothes. They can't run around in my underwear all the time."

"I can't go with you tomorrow," Asher said. "There's going to be a full day of branding at the ranch tomorrow, but I'll help you bring in the tubs from the porch and fill them with warm water from the reservoir before I leave."

The big wooden tub that Flint bathed in was

brought into the kitchen and filled with water, and a smaller tub that Kate washed clothes in was set up for Mercy.

"Put it in the front room in front of the fire," Flint ordered. "I don't want her catching a chill."

When the boys had shucked off their clothes and climbed into their bath, Flint went looking for nightclothes they could sleep in.

He knew exactly where to find the woolen tops, and as he took them from the chest of drawers he took out one for himself. The clouds tonight were low, heavy with moisture despite the earlier storm. Rain or snow, it was going to be quite cool tomorrow.

As he walked down the long hall to the kitchen, he paused at the linen cupboard at one end and took out some towels and washcloths.

There was water all over the floor when Flint stepped into the kitchen. "Stop the splashing!" he ordered sternly. "This is your home, not a stable in the barn." He glared at Asher. "Why didn't you stop them?"

"Hell, I don't know. I didn't see anything wrong with it."

"You wouldn't," Flint snapped. "If you're going to hang around, will you see to it that they finish washing up in a civilized manner while I go find something for Mercy to sleep in?"

Asher mumbled something that Flint didn't catch, but the boys did and they couldn't stifle their laughter. As he walked into Kate's room, he wondered if it was a good idea to let the boys be around Asher very often. He would be a bad influence on them with his tomfoolery.

Flint hadn't been in Kate's room since he was a youngster. It looked the same, neat and homey, and smelled of her rose scent. He hated opening her dresser drawers, but he needed something to cover up his little niece's nakedness.

He breathed a sigh of relief when the first drawer he opened revealed a woman's short-sleeved blouse. He picked it up, whispering, "I sure wish you were here, Kate."

He left Kate's room, closing the door behind him and hiding a smile when he walked into the kitchen and saw his nephews. After they had bathed, Asher had dressed them in the woolen underwear. The upper part of the two-piece underwear came down to their ankles.

Flint looked beyond their garb, and knew a sense of pride as he gazed at their clean, shiny faces and damp curly hair. Each boy looked very much a Mahone.

"Off to bed with you, fellows." Flint gave each one an affectionate pat on the rump. "Choose any room you want except mine and the room next to it. That one is for your sister. You'll know my room by my belongings. The other two rooms are alike, so I don't want to hear you two scrabbling over who gets what."

Flint and Asher received sleepy smiles and

good nights from the brothers as they followed each other from the room.

"They're nice young'uns, ain't they?" Asher said. "Do you think we can raise them right?"

"That's a good question, friend," Flint said, a twinkle in his eyes. It amused him that Asher, wild as a March hare, had included himself in the raising of his two nephews. He was barely housebroken himself.

Flint blew out the light in the kitchen and went to the front room to bathe Mercy. A tender smile curved his lips when he saw her curled up on the leather couch, sound asleep. The little one had had a long day. He hadn't the heart to pick her up and sit her in a tub of water that by now was probably getting cold.

He gathered up the washcloth and bar of soap that lay in the bottom of the basin, and began to wash her small hands, making sure he got all the dirt from between her tiny fingers.

Her face didn't look too bad, he decided. Asher had washed it before they sat down to supper. He carefully eased the dress over her curly, blond head, then sat and stared, shocked to his core. The little one wasn't wearing any bloomers. Seeing the little round bare bottom made him want to cry more than seeing the small feet encrusted with dirt, more than the fact that she had been so hungry at supper time.

Clenching his hands into fists, Flint silently swore that if it was in his power his little niece would never again experience the indignity of not having underwear to cover herself.

He eased the little body into Kate's blouse and gently gathered her into his arms. He had never before felt a soft, small body in his arms, and he was overwhelmed by a feeling of tenderness and responsibility. He carried her into the room next to his and tucked her into bed. She smiled and sighed contentedly as she slept on.

Flint gave a weary sigh as he stretched out in his own bed and pulled the covers over his shoulders. It was a good feeling that at last he had his brother's children safe under his roof. He would do his best for them, but he wondered if his best would be good enough. He had never been around children, didn't know the least thing about them. Henry was a little scamp, he thought, his lips twisting in a grin. No doubt he would keep things jumping around the ranch. He worried some about Tommy, though. The boy was so grave, so wary of people. He guessed the poor kid couldn't be blamed for being suspicious of adults. Who knows what he had experienced since losing both parents.

But little Mercy . . . Flint's eyes grew soft. He felt that she was going to fill an empty space in his life, that maybe from now on he would no longer sometimes get what Kate called "the dismals."

Sleep didn't come right away to Flint. He had much on his mind. He had to purchase the children some clothes first thing in the morning, and he hadn't the faintest idea how to go about it. Asher coundn't help him. He'd be rounding up cattle tomorrow.

His thoughts kept returning to his new neighbor, Lauren. Would she help him? He doubted that she would. He still flinched every time he remembered how her eyes filled with contempt when she looked at him.

But maybe she had a softness for children. For their sake maybe she would give him a hand choosing some clothing.

With that hope, he fell asleep.

Gusts of wind battered at the shutters and rain slashed at the roof. Lauren, listening to nature's rampage, snuggled into the covers. Had she still been living with her father and his outlaw gang, she would have been shivering hard enough to rattle her bones. The old shack had so many cracks in it, and there was always the fear that the flimsy roof might blow off every time there was a storm.

She snuggled deeper into the covers. She had no fear of anything like that happening in this sturdy old building. She knew without being told that it had weathered many blizzards and summer storms. For the first time in her life she felt completely safe.

And so did old Dud, she knew. He was more relaxed now, more at ease. She noticed also that his hands didn't shake as much as they used to when he was worried.

Unbidden, there popped into her mind the

image of a tall man with unruly black hair and dark gray eyes. Even as he had an arm thrown carelessly across the bare shoulders of a tavern whore, his stormy eyes had swept over her person suggestively. She was still mad at herself for having lent him her wagon. She had done it only because the children were so pathetic-looking.

But was that completely true? she asked herself, afraid that Flint Malone might be able to talk her into anything.

As Lauren feel asleep, she wondered what kind of guardian Flint would make for his niece and nephews. She wouldn't want to leave any children of hers in his care.

Chapter Nine

Flint stood before a small mirror attached to the kitchen wall. In the sun shining through the window he carefully stropped a razor. He wanted to make sure he shaved close this morning. He was going to ask Miss Lauren Hart to accompany him to town to help choose clothes for his young charges. He must look better than he had yesterday, or she'd slam the door in his face before he could utter a word.

When he had scraped the top layer of whiskers off his face, he raked the blade down his jaw again to make sure his face was smooth. He looked fairly good, he thought after he rinsed away the lather. He toweled his hair almost dry, then ran a comb through it.

He walked down the hall quietly, careful not to awaken Mercy, and entered his bedroom. He pulled open a drawer and took from it one of his best flannel shirts and a pair of denims that had only been worn a few times. When he had buttoned himself into the clean clothes, he pulled on his boots and left the house.

When he entered the cookhouse and sat down at the long table, Stubby, the cook, placed a large platter of flapjacks on the table and remarked, "You're lookin' pretty spiffy this morning, Boss. I don't suppose you got all gussied up just for the cows to look at you."

Flint helped himself to breakfast, determined not to pay any attention to the cook's razzing. He did fine until one of the hands said slyly, "Maybe he wants a special little heifer to notice him. I saw him eyeing a little one early last evening at the fur post. She sure was a little beauty."

"I don't think she took a liking to him, though," Asher said, walking into the cookhouse. "She gave him a lot of cold looks."

"I thought you went home last night," Flint said, glowering at his longtime friend.

"I was going to but I was too tired to make the ride, so I bedded down in the bunkhouse with your hands. I hope you don't mind that I used one of your bunk beds." Asher pulled a hurt look to his face even as merriment sparked his eyes.

"Go to hell, you long-legged coyote," Flint growled, "and pass me the syrup jug if you ever finish with it."

"How come you're out of sorts this morning?" Asher passed the stone container to him. "Since you're wearin' your second-best clothes, I bet you expect to see your new neighbor today."

"Since you'll hound me until I tell you, I'm going to town to buy the kids some clothes, just like I told you last night."

Flint looked up at his cook. "Can I leave them with you a few hours this morning, Stubby?"

"Sure. I ain't been around young folks for a while, but I expect they don't change much. There was eight of us kids at home." Stubby said in an aside to Flint, "I hope they're better behaved than me and my brothers wuz."

"They'll be all right. Just make sure you keep an eye on Mercy. Don't let her wander off."

"I'll keep her by my side all the time," Stubby said, and meant it. It was plain that already the little girl meant a lot to his boss.

"They'll be coming in for breakfast pretty soon, I expect," Flint remarked, pushing away from the table.

"I'll feed them real good, Boss. They don't look like they've been eatin' very high on the hog."

"You're right there," Flint said, anger in his voice. As he shrugged into his jacket and slapped the black Stetson on his head, his cook wondered if the anger he displayed was directed at the orphanage.

The morning was brisk and bright as Flint lifted the gelding he was riding into a gallop. He dreaded what lay ahead of him. There was a dignity and calmness about Lauren Hart that intrigued him and also scared him. He didn't know how to respond to her stately manner. He had never been around a woman like her before. He stuttered and stammered, and of all things, he blushed. He hadn't done that since he was eight years old when little Janie Cragie yanked his pants down.

He grinned, remembering how he had chased her down and pounded her until she cried. He continued to smile as he wondered if she was doing that to men now. He doubted it. She was married, and at last count she had eight children. But as for that, maybe she was still pulling men's pants down.

Naw, Flint thought, he had seen her towheaded brood and they all looked alike . . . just like Buck Crandon, their dad.

The gelding followed the path around a hill until the Hayes ranch—he guessed he should call it the Hart ranch now—lay spread out before him. He pulled the horse in beneath a pine and sat a while looking at Lauren, who had just stepped off the porch and was gazing up at the sky. Flint followed her gaze and saw an eagle ready to swoop down on a rabbit. He heard her cry out, "Oh, you poor little thing," as the big bird swept away toward the mountains, the young hare's legs dangling from its claws.

Lauren wheeled around when Flint said softly behind her, "Don't feel bad, Miss Hart. The weak is always eaten by the strong. The big bird is most likely a mother who has young ones to feed. So who is to say what is right and what is wrong?"

Lauren tilted her head at a stubborn angle. "Right or wrong," she snapped, "if I'd had my my rifle I would have shot that buzzard."

Flint lowered his lashes to hide his amusement. It wasn't a buzzard that had taken the rabbit, but an eagle. He wasn't about to argue with her, however. He needed her help. He doubted that she would have been able to hit the bird anyhow.

Flint swallowed a couple times and lit a cigarette. He managed not to stutter when he asked, "Are you going to be busy this morning, Miss Hart?"

Lauren squinted her eyes against the morning sun. "I suppose I will. God knows there's enough to be done around here. Why do you ask?"

"I'm on my way to buy some clothes for my nephews and niece. I haven't the slightest idea how to go about it. As you know, my housekeeper is visiting her parents now, and I hoped that maybe you would help me choose the proper clothes for them."

Lauren gave a short laugh. "I'm sure that I know less than you do about children and the clothes they wear."

Flint didn't believe that. If she didn't have young brothers or sisters, she must have little cousins.

"Are you sure about that?" he questioned. "I can't believe that you don't have any young relatives."

"Yes, I'm sure." Her eyes sparked as she lost her temper. "What about you? You must have young sisters and brothers, or cousins . . . maybe some children of your own running around."

Flint narrowed his eyes at Lauren through the curl of smoke from his cigarette. Should he respond to her insult or let it pass? If he snapped back at her, a shouting match would erupt and he didn't want that. He needed her help.

He pinched out his cigarette butt and flipped it into a patch of grass, then said, "The answer is no to all three of your questions. I shouldn't have taken it for granted that you had young relatives. I guess I could manage dressing the boys, but I haven't got the slighest idea what to buy for Mercy. I was hoping you could help me there."

Lauren was becoming aware of Flint much more than she wanted. Everything about him appealed to her. He looked so different from the way he had last night. He was clean-shaven and neatly dressed. He smelled of horse and leather, of sage and wood smoke. There was something about him that reminded her of a big rangy tomcat looking for a female in heat. Don't be that cat, she reminded herself.

Still, when he asked her again to accompany him to the mercantile, she said, "Let me get my jacket and hat."

While Flint waited for Lauren to come back outside, Dud came from behind the house. The dog, Wolf, trotted along beside him, his ruff raised. He growled low in his throat, but he didn't bark. Nevertheless, Flint kicked his feet free from the stirrups in case the animal decided to lunge at him.

But Wolf only looked at him, then hopped up on the porch and stretched out in the sun. Flint decided he wanted to make friends with the animal as soon as possible.

"You're up early, Mahone," Dud said. "Did you want something from us?"

Flint didn't back away from the older man's gruff question. "Yes, I did," he answered shortly. "I came to ask Lauren if she would ride into town with me to help me choose some clothing for my nephews and niece. She said she would. I'm waiting for her to get her jacket and hat."

"Are you sure she said she would go with you? You might as well know you're not one of her favorite people."

Flint shook his head. These two people didn't

hold back from speaking their minds. They could hurl insults around like spit in the wind. He hoped that Lauren wouldn't use her sharp tongue on Kate. Kate was a very nice lady, and he wouldn't want her to get her feelings hurt.

"I'm well aware of her feelings for me, old man"—Flint bent a dark look on Dud—"but as neighbors I think she could put aside her dislike for me long enough to help pick out a few clothes for three little young'uns."

Dud nodded agreement. "She would do that. Lauren has a kind heart. She wouldn't refuse to help a child. But as for you—"

"I know," Flint interrupted Dud. "She wouldn't give me a crust of bread if she had a whole loaf."

"Yeah, that's about the size of it." Dud gave him a snaggle-toothed grin. "She ain't got no time for drunks and them that associate with whores."

"Are you trying to tell me that you never take a drink, nor have ever bedded a whore?" Flint demanded.

"No, I'm not saying that, but I am saying that any time I lay with a woman, it was in a bed and not in an alley."

Flint bit back a sharp retort as Lauren stepped out on the porch. "If you'll hold your dog back, I'll go saddle your horse," he said, his voice irritable because of Dud's remarks.

"Don't bother," Lauren said stiffly and walked

off toward the barn, her heels kicking up little clumps of mud.

"She ain't used to being waited on," Dud explained. "Her daddy taught her not to depend on anybody unless it was absolutely necessary."

"There's nothing wrong with that," Flint said, "but she is a female and she should act like one. A man likes doing for the weaker sex."

"I know that. I used to argue with her dad about that same thing. But he felt strongly that if she didn't have to depend on a man, she wouldn't owe him anything."

Flint sighed. It was going to be hard to court this young woman. Her father had planted some crazy ideas in his daughter's head.

The subject was dropped when Lauren rode her horse out of the barn. "That's a fine-looking animal." Flint ran his gaze over the sorrel stallion whose hide shone like polished silk.

"Yes, he is." Dud gave the stallion an affectionate pat on the rump. "Lauren caught and tamed it herself. The animal is surprisingly gentle for a stallion."

"If we're going to town, we'd better get going," Lauren called, easing the stallion up alongside the buckskin Flint was riding today. "We're in for bad weather later on."

Flint started to say that she was mistaken, but a glance at the sky changed his mind. In the last fifteen minutes its appearance had changed. The sky was now filled with large masses of dark clouds. It was going to rain before the day was over. He jabbed the buckskin lightly with a spur and led off toward Jackson Hole.

The trail was wide enough for them to ride side by side, but Lauren followed behind. Was that more of her father's work, Flint wondered, or did she dislike him so much she didn't even want to ride beside him?

This mode of riding didn't lend itself to conversation. But Lauren found she wasn't all that happy riding behind Flint. She tried not to look at his broad shoulders and narrow waist, or the way his leg muscles strained his pants.

Her eyes constantly strayed back to him. A heavy sigh of relief rushed through her lips when she finally looked down on Jackson Hole.

When they hit the main street, Flint headed straight for the mercantile. Lauren steered her sorrel ahead of him now and she had dismounted, looped the reins around the hitching post, and was ready to open the store door before Flint stepped out of the saddle.

Flint swore under his breath. He was getting a little fed up with her rude behavior. He tied the buckskin alongside four other horses and followed her inside. As he stepped into the store, the thought hit him that maybe she didn't want anyone to know she was with him.

That idea riled him all the more. Who in the hell did she think she was, the Queen of Sheba?

He found Lauren standing in the middle of the room, an uncertain look in her eyes. Well,

Miss Smarty, he thought, what are you going to do now?

Besides Mrs. Florence Richards, the owner's wife, who stood behind the counter, there were four other women in the store. A Mrs. Scot Brady and her three daughters in their teens. They were all staring at Lauren until they spotted Flint. The young women were on him in a rush.

Disbelief widened Lauren's eyes. The three looked like well-brought-up girls. Didn't the mother know what kind of man Flint Mahone was? Evidently not, the way she was smiling at the way her daughters were clinging to his arms, smiling up at him, all the time chattering like a bunch of magpies.

She frowned when she saw that Flint was leading the young ladies toward her. She became very conscious of her worn denims and jacket and run-down boots; she hadn't bothered to change into the new clothes she'd bought.

Her chin came up when she saw the well-dressed young ladies giving her person a close scrutiny. Her eyes narrowed angrily as she thought, Just let them say anything about my appearance and they'll feel my fist in their eyes.

They were standing in front of her then and Flint was saying, "Miss Lauren Hart, meet some of your neighbors."

Embarrassed by her faded and worn apparel, and having never had a conversation with females her own age before, Lauren was too flustered to pay attention to the names Flint gave each girl. She knew she would never remember them.

She smile stiffly at her new neighbors and received the same in return. When she turned abruptly away from them, they looked at each other with raised eyebrows.

Flint, observing the little byplay, untangled himself from the girls. Lauren didn't deserve to be saved from her unfriendliness, but he had a feeling she didn't know how to act around people, especially those of her own gender.

"Ladies," he said, "Lauren and I have some shopping to do, so if you'll excuse us . . . ?"

"Certainly, Flint," they chorused, white teeth flashing in smiles. "Don't forget, there's a barn dance planned a few Saturdays from now."

"I'll be there with my best dancing boots on. Make sure you girls save a dance for me." As he turned away from them, he knew the whispering that started immediately was about Lauren. Although he didn't like it that the girls talked about her, Miss Hart had brought it on herself. If she wanted to fit into the community, she would have to change her attitudes towards its people.

In the meantime Lauren had noticed a pleasant-looking woman enter the store. In her hurry to escape the disapproving girls, she hurried toward the smiling woman. She would naturally know about children's clothing, having a little girl and two sons with her.

The woman nodded when Lauren approached her. Lauren offered her hand and said, "My name is Lauren Hart and I'm here to help a neighbor buy clothing for his niece and nephews. I hate to admit it, but neither one of us knows a thing about young'uns' garb. I'm hoping that maybe you could give us a hand."

"I'd be happy to," the woman said, giving Lauren's hand a warm squeeze. "I'm Janice Summers. You're with Flint Mahone, aren't you?" When Lauren nodded, Janice added, "Flint is an old friend of ours. My husband, Ty, used to run around with Flint and Asher Davis." She laughed softly. "That was until I tamed him down and married him. All three are good men," she added on a serious note. "They're just a little rough around the edges."

Lauren didn't say so, but she thought that "a little rough around the edges" was too polite a term for Flint Mahone.

"Now," Janice said, "where shall we start, with Flint's niece or his nephews?"

"The little girl, I think."

As Janice and Lauren walked over to the table holding small articles of feminine clothing, Flint moved to lean against the store's counter. One glance at Florence Richards's sour-looking face told him she had her nose out of joint about something.

He didn't have to wait long to discover what the problem was. "The girl didn't have to ask Janice Summers to help her," Florence complained "I know just as much, or more, than Janice does."

So that's what's caught in your craw, Flint thought with amusement. You won't be able to pawn off any of your old goods that have been lying around gathering dust for the past three or four years.

"That girl should buy herself some clothes too," Florence snorted. "She looks like a ragamuffin."

"A beautiful ragamuffin, though, don't you think?" He gave Florence a thin smile. "And her name is Lauren, in case nobody has told you."

"I think I heard that old mountain man call her that when they were in here." Florence sniffed. "He bought her some new duds. I wonder why she's not wearing them."

"If you were smart, you'd think less about satisfying your curiosity and more about treating them in a civilized manner. They'll be needing a lot more merchandise, lumber and supplies, before the year is out. I don't think your husband Tom would like it if the Harts went across the street to trade at McCrackle's store."

Florence knew that her husband Tom wouldn't like it at all if she drove business away. She snapped her mouth shut, stamped off to the other end of the counter, and pretended to be busy, but all the while had her ears tuned to what Lauren and Janice were saying.

She was still pouting an hour later when the counter was stacked high with youngster's underwear, nightshirts and nightgowns, alongside denims and shirts, petticoats and little bloomers.

Flint had chosen those, ones with lacy ruffles at the knees. He had also chosen Mercy a doll.

Janice laughingly said, "I see that you are going to spoil your little niece. When can we meet the children?"

"Anytime you want to stop by. When Kate gets home I'll have her cook us up one of her Sunday dinners, and then you and Ty and the kids can come over to eat with us." He looked at Lauren and added, "You too."

Lauren didn't answer yes or no. Janice gave her a puzzled look. Why didn't the girl like Flint? she wondered. Every girl within fifty miles liked Flint Mahone.

Had he been dumb enough to step out of line with her? Janice somehow doubted that. Flint was very careful how he acted and talked around the girl. She shrugged. She'd learn why in time.

"Come on, Flint," Janice said as they left the mercantile "make yourself useful. Help us tie all these packages on the horses."

"It's lucky your boys rode into town with you," Flint said as Janice lifted her little daughter onto the back of the mare she had ridden into town. "They can double up on one of their horses and we'll make a packhorse out of the other one."

As they rode out of town, with Florence Richards glaring at them through her flyspecked window, Flint looked up at the sky and frowned. It was darker than before, and a cool wind was blowing down from the mountains.

"Ladies," he called over the thudding of the hooves, "let's pick it up a little. I think we're in for some rain."

Janice agreed. "I think the children and I can make it home before the storm gets here. We don't live far away, but I'm afraid you and Lauren will get wet. Maybe you'd better cover the packages with your tarpaulin, Flint. Some of the things wrapped in paper could be ruined if they got rained on."

Flint agreed, pulling his gelding to a halt and dismounting. As he tucked the large piece of water-repellent material over the packages and boxes and bundles, Janice called to Lauren, "I'll drop by one day this week."

She and the children disappeared down a fork in the road that would shortly bring them home.

The wind was flopping the tarpaulin around, making the horses skittish, and Lauren dismounted and hurried to help Flint tie it down. It was fastened finally and they were remounting when a roll of thunder sounded and they felt a sprinkle of rain.

"Make that stallion move, Lauren," Flint called. "There's a deserted homesteader's cabin a mile off the trail. Maybe we can make it there in time to stay dry."

That was a vain hope on Flint's part. Ten minutes later the rain broke with a thundering roar and a flash of lightning that made Lauren jump. Flint turned the buckskin off the trail and Lauren blindly followed him, wet branches slapping her in the face.

She had never seen anything that looked more inviting than the homesteader's old delapidated log cabin when it loomed up in front of them.

"Go on inside," Flint shouted over the roar of the rain. "I'm going to put the horses in the lean-to back of the cabin."

Lauren bolted for the open door of the shelter. As she bounced inside, several doves flapped through the opening, brushing against her face. She squealed and brushed them aside.

Wet and shivering, she looked around the room. With the exception of a thin, narrow mattress with tufts of straw poking out of the corners, the room was bare.

There was a rude fireplace and a stack of wood on the floor near the hearth. At least, she thought, they could have a fire while they waited out the storm. As she walked across the floor to close the shutters on the single window in the room, she hoped that Janice and her children had made it home before the weather broke.

Lauren was ready to close the door, to shut out the sheets of water blowing into the room, when Flint almost knocked her over in his rush to get inside. He grabbed her by the elbows to steady her. In the gloom he could make out her white face staring up at him. He so wanted to lower his head and kiss her, but Lauren pulled away from his grip.

"If you have matches, we can light a fire," she said, her voice trembling a little.

Flint closed the door, and squatting down beside the fireplace, said, "Take your wet jacket off and spread it on the hearth."

The wood was old and dry and caught immediately from the match Flint struck and held to it. Lauren held her hands out to the leaping flames, welcoming the warmth.

Flint peeled his own jacket off and laid it out in front of the fire beside Lauren's. He then dragged the mattress over to the hearth and said, "Sit down and stretch your feet out to the fire. You'll feel warmer if they aren't so cold." He sat down beside her and stretched out his long legs.

Lauren only gave Flint half her attention as he talked. There were two things she had a dreadful fear of. Snakes and lightning storms.

She was giving thanks that this was mainly a rain and wind storm when a streak of lightning splintered the trunk of a nearby cottonwood. She gave a frightened cry and went stone still, awaiting the crash of thunder that was bound to follow. When it came, she threw herself against Flint. He almost fell sideways from the unexpected thrust of her body, and caught her just in time to keep them both from falling over. She clung so tightly to him, it was as if she was trying to crawl inside his skin.

Flint knew she was scared half out of her mind; otherwise she wouldn't come near him. A devilish grin twisted his lips. He was not one to pass up the opportunity to hold a woman's soft body next to his. He couldn't help feeling this was the only chance he would ever have of holding Miss Lauren Hart in his arms.

His heart thundering, he pulled Lauren across his lap so that her breasts pressed against his chest. When she didn't pull away, he put his arms around her and nestled her head in the crook of his shoulder and chin. She responded by moving closer to him.

The pain in his loins increased.

The rain continued roaring upon the roof and the lightning continued to streak across the sky. By now Lauren's arms had reached up to embrace Flint's shoulders. He blessed each crackle of lightning and dammed it at the same time. He was in so much pain he didn't know how much longer he could bear it.

Finally, he could no longer control himself. He started by gently stroking her cheek, then slowly moving his fingers down her smooth throat. He paused when he came to a shirt button. It took but a second to flip it open, and he beheld the beauty of her firm, round breasts. He had seen a lot of bare flesh in his many years of chasing after women, but never had he seen such perfection as he gazed on now.

He waited until lightning struck again, and when the thunder followed and she pushed up against him, he fitted his palm against one of the snowy white mounds. Lauren moaned, but not in objection. He slowly moved his palm over the pink peak, then lowered his head and opened his mouth over half the breast.

He was tugging gently on the pebble-hard nipple when he heard a dog bark. He jerked his head up and put Lauren away from him. The wolf-dog was out there and the old man wouldn't be far behind.

Lauren looked at Flint in bewilderment as he fumbled with her shirt buttons. "What are you doing?" she demanded.

"I'm just making sure you're all buttoned up," he explained, straightening out the shoulders of her shirt. "I think the storm is almost over."

To make a liar out of him, there was another loud clap of thunder, followed by Dud calling, "Lauren, are you in there?"

Flint gave Lauren a fast glance to make sure all her buttons were straight, then leaped to his feet and opened the door. "We're in here, Dud," he called as the dog rushed past him and went to Lauren. "Come on in out of the storm. We've been trying to dry out a little."

Dud gave him a suspicious look as he went and knelt down beside Lauren. "Are you all right, girl?" he asked. When she answered weakly, he looked up at Flint. "Lauren is scared to death of storms. She has been ever since she was a young'un and lightning struck a tree right outside her bedroom."

Dud looked back at Lauren and hugged her shoulders when thunder crashed again. "It's all right, honey," he soothed. "I started out looking for you as soon as I realized it was going to storm. Being new around here, I didn't know about this place. And of course Wolf couldn't track you through this downpour."

"The storm broke fast and luckily I remembered this old settler's cabin," Flint said. "We weren't out in the rain long, but we still got soaked. I see you're wet through also. Why don't you take off your jacket and spread it before the fire to dry."

Dud shook his head. "No need for that. The storm is letting up. I want to get home while we can."

To validate his claim, the next rumble of thunder was weaker and more distant and the lightning was no longer streaking, but only flashing.

"Come on, girl." Dud took Lauren by the arm and pulled her to her feet. "Let's go home now."

Chapter Ten

The rain had stopped when the three left the
cabin, Flint leading the way. However, an icy
wind blew down from the mountains and the
thick mud of the trail was already freezing in
deep ruts.

Flint and Dud exchanged some conversation,
their voices muffled in their jacket collars. But
Lauren had nothing to say. In a confused way
she was trying to figure out what had happened
during the storm. The overpowering fear had
blocked most of her memories of those moments in the cabin. But a vague recollection of
something pleasant happening to her kept
creeping into her mind.

Also, she was puzzled why it was that every time Flint looked at her in the shack when they were preparing to leave, she blushed like a twelve-year-old schoolgirl and her breasts tingled.

A faint smell of wood smoke drifted on the cold night air. When they rode out of a small stand of pine, Lauren felt a glow of happiness and safety. There sat her home. No one could come along and chase her away as had happened so many times in her young life. She had a deed to the ranch and she was going to live here the rest of her life.

They pulled the horses up alongside the porch, and Lauren was the first to dismount. Flint looked at her expectantly, but she didn't thank him for helping her to the porch. She didn't acknowledge him in any way. Flint stared after her as her boot heels clicked on the porch, then faded when she entered the house.

Anger glinted in his eyes. "Couldn't she at least say a measly thank you?"

Flint followed Dud into the house, although he was nervous doing it. The wolf-dog kept sniffing at his heels. Finally, he said irritably, "Dud, can't you make that hound go lie down somewhere? I'm going to step on his tail if he doesn't get out of my way."

"Don't you ever call him a hound again," Lauren said, hurrying into the kitchen. "The big dumb beast is only trying to be friendly to you. Why, I can't imagine."

Dud tittered. Flint gave him a look that wiped his face clean.

"Will you have a drink before you leave?" Dud asked, pulling a bottle of whiskey out of a cupboard.

Flint was about to say that sounded real good, for he was chilled to the bone. He happened then to glance at Lauren and changed his mind. She was glaring at him, her eyes daring him to take a drink with Dud.

But though Flint knew that Lauren wanted him to leave, still he lingered. He wasn't ready to leave her yet. There was no telling when he would see her again.

When he could think of no excuse to stay longer, he hit upon an idea that Dud, at least, would like. "Dud," he began, "we're all caught up on work at my place. I'm planning to drive two-thousand head of cattle to Kansas come spring, but there's not much to do on a ranch in the wintertime. What if some of my men and I ride over one day and help you drive your wild cattle out of the brush? When we were gathering up my strays, we saw two or three hundred back in the brakes with your brand on them."

"Hey, Lauren, ain't that good news?" Dud's face glowed. "Come spring we'll have a nice little herd to drive to market." Lauren couldn't help the happy tilt of her lips. This was indeed good news. For the first time she felt completely satisfied that she and Dud were going to have a safe and sound future.

Though she knew it would be the gracious thing to do, she didn't thank Flint for his offer.

But Dud thanked him wholeheartedly, pumping his hand vigorously. Flint expected to receive thanks for his offer, but not so much enthusiasm. It appeared the old man wasn't used to receiving favors from people. Flint wondered again what kind of life Dud and Lauren had led before coming to Jackson Hole. What kind of neighbors had they had? Or did they have any neighbors at all? Dud and Lauren weren't the friendliest people in the world. They weren't actually unfriendly, just a little standoffish.

One thing Flint did know. He'd be making a big fool of himself if he stood around much longer.

He settled his hat on his head and walked toward the door. "My men and I will be over one of these days to chase your cattle back on the range." At the door he looked at Lauren and said, "Thank you, Lauren, for helping me with the children's clothing."

Her only response was a stiff nod of her head.

Frustration and anger filled him as he jerked the door open. "To hell with the little witch," he muttered as he swung onto the buckskin's back. "She'll never get the chance to cut me again."

He nudged the gelding with his heels, urging him out into the gathering darkness. The rain had begun again, and it was beginning to freeze, hitting his face like grains of sand. He pulled up his collar, pulled his hat down to his eyebrows, and let his horse have its head.

Almost half an hour passed before Flint spotted the lamplight of his home sending out its welcoming beam through the curtain of rain. He also made out the small shapes of three children peering out into the darkness. Could they be looking for him? he wondered.

It gave him a warm feeling that maybe the children would be anxious for his return. He liked the little shavers, especially Mercy. She was so small and helpless.

Flint reined in the two horses alongside the porch and dismounted. He began trying to untie the rope that held the tarpaulin over the packages. His half-frozen fingers refused to do his bidding. He took a knife from his pocket and cut the heavy twine. Packages and bundles spilled onto the porch. He gathered up as many as he could hold and stumbled up the steps.

He took but one step on the porch before the door flew open. In another moment his young relatives were upon him.

To his surprise, it wasn't what he carried in his arms that made them give glad cries. The way they hugged him around the waist said they were happy to see that he hadn't deserted them. He wanted to drop everything on the spot and gather them up in his arms and promise he would never leave them except for short periods of time.

He didn't dare do that. It was unthinkable

that a grown man would cry with heartfelt thanks that someone loved and depended on him. And he would cry, he knew, for already his eyes were damp.

When he looked up and saw Stubby holding Mercy in his arms, his eyes grew wetter. She was leaning away from the cook, her thin little arms reaching out to her uncle. When he took her from the old man, her arms went around his neck, almost squeezing the breath from him. He buried his face in her tangled hair, and kept it there until he could control his voice.

Gently removing her arms, he laughingly said, "I believe you buttons are happy to see me."

"That's hardly the word for it," Stubby groused. "They've been standing in front of that window ever since you left. They've asked me every fifteen minutes if I thought you would come back. That's why I decided we'd eat in the kitchen tonight. The cookhouse window looks down on the barn. I couldn't have them running out in the rain looking for you."

"Of course I'd come back. I'll always come back to you. Don't fret about it anymore," Flint said, edging his way to the fireplace, which wasn't an easy feat considering how the children still clung to his legs.

When he eased himself into a chair and stretched his feet to the fire, he lifted Mercy to his lap. He looked at his nephews then and said soberly, "I want you children to understand that this is your home now. You will never have to leave it unless you want to. I'm hoping that you will want to stay here and help me run the ranch until you're men and want to get married and have a place of your own."

The boys leaned against his legs and whooped with laughter. It was hilarious to them that they would ever want to take a wife. They laughed louder when Mercy said with a wide smile, "When I get big, Unca Flint, I'm going to marry you."

When the laughter settled down, Stubby said, "I'll go take care of the horses, then put supper on the table. Can I get you a drink before I leave?"

"I think a glass of whiskey is just what I need to get the ice out of my veins. Thank you, Stubby."

When the cook left the house, hurriedly closing the door behind him to keep out the wind, Flint said to the children, "Shall we open some of these bundles and packages and see what's in them?"

The levis, shirts, jackets, and boots were met with glad cries, but when Flint unwrapped a long, narrow bundle that held a red painted sled, the house rang with joyous laughter. The ice skates were greeted in the same manner.

Flint reached down beside his chair then and took from the floor a bulky package. When he unwrapped the paper and revealed the doll he had bought for Mercy, the little one could only stare in awe.

"Go ahead, honey," he urged, "pick her up. She's yours."

Ever so gently Mercy picked up the pink-cheeked doll with long blond hair. She cradled it in her arms and stroked its smooth cheeks. They all looked surprised when she started softly humming a little lullaby. Was she remembering a tune her father had sung to her before going off to war? The children's mother had certainly never bothered to sing to her.

With the heat from the fire and the whiskey in his veins, Flint was pretty well thawed out when he heard Stubby stamping the snow off his boots out on the porch.

"It's colder than a whore's heart out there," the cook said, entering the family room and holding his hands over the dancing flames in the fireplace. He shrugged out of his jacket and took off his hat. "I'll go put supper on the table now."

Flint, with the boys at his heels, followed the cook into the kitchen, and set the table while Stubby put the pot of stew he had made that day on the table, and Tommy sliced a loaf of sourdough.

When it came time to eat, the boys argued over which of them would sit next to Flint. Since Mercy had already climbed into the chair on his right, Flint ended the hot debate by saying they would take turns sitting next to him.

He decided that Henry, being the youngest, would sit beside him tonight.

The stew was passed around and Flint ladled some into Mercy's plate. He helped her to bread as well. Everyone was hungry, and very few words were spoken at the beginning of the meal. Tongues loosened up when Stubby took the coffeepot off the stove and filled his and Flint's cups with the dark liquid.

When he sat back down at the table, he said, "A man and woman stopped by here today. The woman said she was looking for her niece, Lauren Hart, and asked if I knew whether she lived around here. I didn't know if Lauren would want her to know where she lived, so I told the woman to ride to Jackson Hole and make some inquiries there."

"What did the couple look like?" Flint set his cup down.

"They looked respectable enough. I'd say the woman was in her mid-forties, a good looker with neat blond hair. The man was in his mid-twenties, I'd say. A real handsome fellow. Almost as good-lookin' as you, Boss." Stubby grinned at Flint.

Lillie King's teeth chattered as an icy wind blew down from the mountains. As she sat in the rented surrey staring at the dim shape of a rustic ranch house, she fidgeted nervously with the ring on her finger.

Was her niece going to accept her? Chances

were the girl didn't know she even existed. It would be just like her stubborn brother, Arthur, not to ever mention he had a sister.

Lillie frowned when her stepson, Colly, raised his fist to rap on the door again for the second time. Why didn't anyone answer his knock? She knew someone was in there. She had seen shadowy movements inside the cabin.

Finally the door opened and a shaft of lamplight spilled out onto the porch. Someone was being mighty cautious, she thought, then wondered if Dud Carter was living with Lauren. She frowned. She hoped not. She and Dud had had a falling-out nearly twenty years ago. It would be just like him to try to turn Lauren against her.

She peered at the male figure who kept a tight grip on the door, straining her ears to make out what was being said between the two men.

When Lillie grew tired of waiting, she pulled the heavy shawl up around her shoulders and let her mind drift.

She was more than ready for the long trek to be over. She and her stepson had ridden three separate coach lines since leaving St. Louis, Missouri. Every bone and muscle in her body was crying out for rest. And why not? She was no longer in her twenties, but in her mid-forties.

However, it had been a necessary journey. Two weeks ago she had read in a newspaper that her brother, Arthur Hart, had been shot and killed as an outlaw. She had immediately thought of his daughter Lauren, her niece.

How old was the girl now? She thought back over the years. She would be around nineteen, Lillie decided. She had lived with Arthur and his gang when Lauren was just a baby. But circumstances had forced her to leave, and both being stubborn, they had never seen each other since.

Lillie had gone to St. Louis, where she soon got a job dealing poker in a gambling hall. There she had met a well-to-do widower raising a five-year-old son. When John King proposed marriage to her, she lost no time accepting him. She wasn't crazy in love with the man, who was ten years older than she, but he was a good and gentle man and her marriage had been satisfactory. She grew to love the little boy, Colly, and in time looked upon him as her true son.

She and John had been married for two years when the man who owned the the saloon decided he wanted to retire. Lillie coaxed her husband into buying the business from him.

What with Lillie's blond good looks and her husband's business acumen, the saloon and gambling hall, the Pink Lady, became profitable. With strangers passing through St. Louis all the time, she was able to keep track of her brother, who still rode the outlaw trail.

The saloon had been in operation ten years when John King was accidentally shot and killed in a barroom brawl. Lillie and her stepson, Colly, continued to run the business for seven more years. Lillie kept her blond good looks, and Colly had grown into a very handsome young man and had the pick of the dancers and other female help in the Pink Lady. Lillie, however, laughed and flirted with the men who tried to court her, but always turned them down. She liked being her own boss. She knew also that they were interested in her business and thought she was well off. Unfortunately, that wasn't true. No matter how hard she worked, the saloon barely made a profit when her husband was no longer there to run it. Colly often teased her, saying that money was her only concern.

"You're still young enough to want a man in your bed once in a while. Don't you get cold, sleeping all alone in that big fancy bed of yours?"

One day she answered him with a remark that left him stunned and staring at her.

"I'm going to sell the Pink Lady," she remarked in a quiet, calm voice, almost as if she had said, I'm going to sell one of my horses.

"What put that in your head?" Colly asked after he got over his shock.

"You've heard me speak of my brother Red Hart, the outlaw." When Colly nodded, she continued. "I read in a newspaper that he had been shot and killed by a posse that was chasing him. He wrote to me about five years back, telling me he'd won a ranch in a poker game. The property was near Jackson Hole, Wyoming. He wanted me to make sure his daughter Lauren inherited the place in case anything happened to him. I feel it's my duty to look after her now, so I'm selling the saloon and going there to find her."

"What if she doesn't want to be found? What will you do then?"

Lillie shrugged. "Then we'll open a saloon in Jackson Hole. I don't think I'd like living on a ranch anyway."

"I know I wouldn't." Colly slapped one of the serving girls on the rear as she walked past their table. The girl gave him a coy look and would have joined them, but Lillie waved her away with a dark frown.

"Why do you encourage the saloon help?" she complained to her stepson. "Aren't the dancers and singers enough for you?"

"Ma, don't be such a prude. The saloon girls like a little attention too."

Lillie's retort to that remark was an unladylike snort.

"Seriously, though, Ma, do you really think it's a good idea to sell a business that is providing well for you?"

"The Pink Lady hasn't made much profit since your father died," she admitted. "Besides, I've been thinking, Colly. It's time you got married and settled down. I'd like to see some little ones running around. I've been thinking how nice it would be if you and Lauren would take to each other . . . maybe get married."

Colly looked at her as if he couldn't believe

what he had heard. "Don't go making wedding plans for me, Ma," he said. "Especially to a female I've never met. I might not like her, nor she me. For all you know, she's as ugly as a mud fence."

"I doubt that she is unattractive. Her mother was very pretty and my brother was a good-looking man. Just keep an open mind when you meet her."

Lillie was beginning to think they would never meet her niece as Colly continued to be kept waiting on the porch. "Damn you, Dud," she said impatiently, "you're being your usual ornery self." She gathered up the reins and flicked a short whip over the horse. The surrey moved forward, and Lillie steered it up alongside the cabin's porch. When the wheels rolled to a stop, she jumped to the ground.

"Damn you, Dud, you old reprobate, you haven't changed with the years," she snapped. "You're just as stubborn as ever. How long do you plan on keeping my stepson standing out here in the dampness?"

"I don't know the young man and I don't have any intention of inviting him in."

"I suppose next you'll say you don't know who I am." Lillie stepped upon the porch and stood face-to-face with him.

"Oh, I know who you are," Dud said, a note of exasperation in his voice. "You're the same troublesome female you always were. What do you want now, after all these years?"

"I read in the paper that Arthur had been killed by a posse. I have come to get acquainted with my niece."

"She doesn't even know that you exist. I doubt that she would want to meet you."

"I think that decision should be left up to her. Either let us in or call her out here. One way or the other, I'm going to see her before I leave here."

Lillie took a threatening step toward Dud and the partially open door, then paused. Colly was staring over the older man's shoulder, awe in his eyes. She followed the direction of his intent look, and her lips spread in a wide smile. No wonder Colly looked stunned. Her niece was the most beautiful female she had ever seen. He would be changing his mind about marriage, she felt sure about that.

"Do we have company, Dud?" Lauren asked as she smiled at Lillie.

When Dud made no answer to her question, Lillie stepped forward and gave the door a hard push, almost knocking Dud over. "In a manner of speaking, Lauren, we're company. We're also relatives."

"Relatives?" Lauren asked as she took Dud's arm, helping him to steady himself.

"Yes, dear," Lillie said kindly. "I am your Aunt Lillie, your father's sister."

Lauren stared at the pretty woman, her lips slightly parted in surprise. "I wasn't aware that

I had an aunt," she finally managed to say. She looked at Dud questioningly.

When it looked as though Dud wasn't going to say yes or no, Lillie took a threatening step toward him. "Tell her, you cantankerous old goat. Tell her who I am or I'll punch you good."

"Aw, shut up, you troublemakin' woman," Dud said, and lowered himself into a rocking chair with a sigh. He looked up at Lauren and said, "God help us, she's your aunt."

"I don't understand." Lauren clutched at a chair back, bewilderment in her voice and on her face. "Why haven't I known I had an aunt all these years?"

Lillie sat down in a chair beside her, and taking Lauren's hand, said gently, "Your father was my brother. I left home when you were just a baby. I don't know why he chose not to tell you about me."

A vein throbbing in Dud's forehead looked ready to burst, he was so furious. "Damn your lying hide, you know damn well why he never told Lauren about you. You have a nerve showing your face around here after he wrote to you, begging you to come back and help raise Lauren when her mother ran off. But me and him managed to bring her up, and we don't need you comin' round now she's grown."

Lillie, who still held Lauren's hand, squeezed it and said gently, "Please don't believe his ranting, Lauren. When Arthur wrote to me, I had already married. I had a young stepson to raise and couldn't leave St. Louis. It is my deepest wish that you and I can get to know each other at last."

"You can just forget your deepest wish," Dud said bristling. "We don't—"

Lauren reached out and laid a silencing hand on his arm. "We can discuss that later. Right now let's have some coffee. Aunt Lillie and her companion look chilled to the bone."

"It is cold out there," Lillie said, removing her coat and handing it toward Dud. He turned away, pretending he didn't see the garment. Lillie gave him a look that would have singed the curly hair that circled his bald head.

"Thank you, Colly," she said when her stepson hurried forward and took the coat from her. She looked at Lauren. "Colly is my stepson. I married his father when he was just five years old."

When neither man made a motion to shake hands, Lillie said, "Lauren and Colly, I hope you two will be friends."

"I'm sure we will." Colly flashed his white teeth in a warm smile as he took Lauren's hand and held it a little longer than necessary, stroking his thumb across the inner side of her wrist. She blushed and lowered her lashes.

Dud had missed none of this, and his voice was rough as he said, "Lauren, if you're gonna give them some coffee, do it before it gets too late for them to find their way back to Jackson Hole."

Lauren jerked her hand free, saying in embarrassment, "But Dud, it's so cold and wet out."

"It's not raining. Besides, we got no place for them to sleep. We've only got two narrow bunk beds."

Lillie's face was almost purple with rage. "Damn you, you bastard," she cried. "I wouldn't sleep in your house if you begged me on your bended knees."

"Well, I'm not likely to do that, am I, Lil?"

Her eyes snapping and her chin in the air, Lillie stood abruptly and went to her stepson. As he held her coat for her to slip into, Lauren grabbed her aunt's hand.

"Will I see you again?" she asked, her voice wavering a bit.

"Of course you'll see me again, child. I wouldn't let that polecat keep us apart. When Colly and I get settled in somewhere, I'll send you a note." She leaned over and kissed Lauren on the cheek. "Don't you worry. We're going to spend a lot of time together."

"Oh, I hope so." Lauren followed Lillie and Colly to the door. Before they stepped outside, Colly said, "I am happy to have met you, Mr. Carter."

Dud only grunted a response, and Lauren wheeled on him the moment she closed the door. "Dud," she began, "I have never seen you be so rude to a person, and to a relative of mine. I can't tell you how happy I am to know that I have an aunt. Why do you dislike her so?"

"I have my reasons, and they're good ones. You must take my word for it. Whenever that woman comes around, trouble is not far behind her. We will rue the day she found us. I haven't figured out yet why she wanted to."

"What has she done that has made you dislike her so?" Lauren sat down in the room's other chair.

"I would have to talk the rest of the night to tell you all about Lillie Hart. Isn't it enough that your father never mentioned her name to you?"

It grew quiet in the room, the only sound the squeaking of the rocking chairs and the crackling of the fire.

"I miss Dad so much," Lauren whispered, breaking the silence after a while.

"I know you do, girl. I miss him too. We must never let anyone make us forget him."

"I would never let that happen, Dud, no matter who tried to do it."

Chapter Eleven

Flint frowned as he peered through the window at the clouds scudding across the moon. The rain had stopped, but a cold wind was whipping down off the mountain. It wasn't a night to be out, but he felt too restless to stay home. He had put the children to bed and kissed Mercy good night, and there was no light in the bunkhouse. His help had gone to town. He might as well do the same thing, he decided.

Stubby was still in the kitchen washing the dishes and putting everything away. He would ask the cook to stay in the house in case one of the kids woke up. A wry smile twisted his lips. Already he was learning that it took time and care to watch after children properly.

He walked into the kitchen just as the cook was taking off his apron. "Stubby," he said, "I'd like to mosey into town for a while if you'd agree to stay here while I'm gone. If the kids woke up and found me gone they might be frightened."

"No problem." Stubby yawned. "I'll stretch out on the couch and catch some shut-eye until you get back."

"Why don't you bunk in with Henry? He's so skinny he won't crowd you."

"Well, that's a notion. Maybe I'll just do that."

A few minutes later Flint stepped out on the porch, and a blast of cold air hit him like a blow. "I'm a damn fool to go out on a night like this," he said with a low muttered curse.

The stallion whinnied his disapproval when Flint entered his stall, carrying the saddle. It was evident that he too thought it a damn fool thing to venture out on a night like this.

Clouds of breath billowed from the stallion's nostrils when Flint rode him out of the barn. Flint kept him at a brisk pace, anxious to get to town as soon as possible.

Flint sighed his relief when he detected the faint smell of wood smoke on the cold night air. In another five minutes he would be in the Trail's End Saloon having a glass of whiskey.

The stallion also realized that warmth was near, and broke into a full gallop. His big hoofs hit the fork in the road at the same time a small surrey swung alongside them. Shadow snorted and rose up on his hind legs. The horse pulling the lightweight vehicle did the same. A woman gave a frightened squeal and a man cursed loudly as he fought to soothe the animal.

At last calm was restored and the horses stood quietly, their sides quivering. Both men were at fault and they knew it. It was no night to be speeding along.

"I guess haste does make waste," said the driver of the vehicle with a wry smile. "I was in a hurry to get my stepmother in out of the cold." He reached out his hand. "The name is Colly King. And the half-frozen lady beside me is Lillie King."

"I'm Flint Mahone." Flint shook the soft hand offered to him. He thought to himself, I bet this one never roped a steer.

"Could you direct us to a boardinghouse or a hotel?" Colly asked, releasing Flint's hand. "We'd like to get into some dry clothes and get something to eat."

"There's the boardinghouse a street down, but she closes her kitchen around seven o'clock. Your best bet is to go to the Jackson Hole Hotel. They'll still be serving supper."

"Thank you," Colly said with friendly warmth. "I'd like to buy you a drink the next time we run into each other."

Flint merely nodded and touched Shadow with his spurs. As the stallion moved on down the muddy road, his hooves sucking mud, Flint wondered why he had taken an instant dislike to the man. He hoped he wasn't judging the fellow by the softness of his palms. Colly King could be an educated man, a doctor or a lawyer.

Flint wouldn't admit to the thought that sneaked into his brain: Colly King was a threat to him in regard to Lauren Hart. The stranger had polished manners, and he made an impressive appearance in his broadcloth suit, black stetson, and hand-tooled boots.

Were Colly and Lillie King the man and woman Stubby had mentioned earlier.

Flint dismissed the handsome man from his mind when he saw the dim light of the saloon. He didn't have a ghost of a chance of courting Lauren Hart, so why dislike a man who might be welcomed to call on her?

When Flint arrived at the saloon, he turned down the alley to a line of stalls built there for the establishment's customers. There were only three empty stalls left, signaling that the weather hadn't deterred the regular vistors to the Trail's End.

He lifted the saddle off Shadow's back and rubbed him dry with a gray woolen blanket he took from a shelf. There was also a feed bag of oats, which the stallion lost no time in munching eagerly when it was slipped over his head. Flint then sprinted alongside the false-fronted building, his head lowered against the wind battering at his face.

Inside the saloon Flint took off his hat and

unbuttoned his coat. It was dry and warm in the long room, and as he had suspected, a number of men had gathered there.

He spoke to several on his way to the bar, and shrugged as many saloon women off his arm. This surprised him as much as it did the women. In his memory he had never done that before. He told himself he was just anxious to get a glass of whiskey under his belt, get the chill out of his body.

The bartender poured him a glass of red-eye, and he took a long drink of the tea-colored drink, set the glass on the bar, and turned around to hang his coat on one of the coat hooks on the wall. He stopped in mid-stride. Coming through the door were the man and woman he had talked to earlier. Flint hurriedly turned back to the bar, hoping that they hadn't seen him. He didn't feel like talking to them again so soon. He didn't rightly know why he felt this way about the pair. They had been pleasant enough. Maybe that was what bothered him. They had been too warm and friendly, considering they had just met him. Strangers were usually a little cautious when meeting someone for the first time.

Flint sighed in relief when the Kings didn't linger in the barroom, but went straight into the gambling room. Maybe the ladylike, well-dressed woman was going to play monte or faro while her stepson played poker.

When Flint finished his whiskey, curiosity got

the best of him. He made his way to the wide doorway of the gambling hall and looked in at the people playing the various games of chance. He was surprised not to see Mrs. King at any of the games. Where had she gone? It didn't seem possible that she had left the building without his seeing her.

He spotted the lady then. She was sitting at one of the poker tables, of all places. The way she held her cards, the way she squinted at them, said she was no stranger to the game. Colly King sat directly across from her. Flint said to a neighbor who stepped up beside him, "That woman looks more like someone's aunt than a poker player."

"I was thinking she looks like a preacher's wife," the man said with a laugh. "She must be new around here. I've never seen her before."

"She and her stepson came in on the late coach today. The man, the one sitting across from her, almost ran Shadow down on the river road. He was driving much too fast in the dark."

"Where are they from?"

"I didn't ask them where they came from. I just wanted to get out of the wind. They asked me where they could find a restaurant and a hotel. I told them and took off. They must have found accommodations quickly, considering I left them a scant half hour ago."

"They look like moneyed people. The man probably flashed a handful of greenbacks and got the best room in the hotel," the neighbor said. "I think I'll go sit in at their table, maybe win some of their wealth." He grinned at Flint. "You want to try your luck?"

Flint shook his head. "I'm gonna head for home." A proud grin lifted the corners of his lips. "I don't know if you've heard, but I'm a family man now."

"Yeah, I heard. Your friend Asher told me. Your dead brother's kids, right?"

"That's right. They're real nice youngsters. Two boys and a little girl."

"I guess you'll have to break down and get married now," his neighbor joked. "You'll need help raising three young children."

"I wouldn't do anything that rash. Kate will help me. Besides," he added, amusement twinkling in his eyes, "I have Asher to help me too."

"Asher?" the man hooted. "I wouldn't let that wild one get near your young relatives if I was you. There's no telling what he might teach them." This was said in good humor.

"You're probably right, but it would be done with good intentions. Asher was raised by an uncle, an old mountain man who was kind to him, but didn't teach him much in the way of manners and such. Still, he's a good man."

"You won't hear me say different," the rancher said, then added, "I've changed my mind about joining that game. I'm gonna head for home. There's bad weather brewing out there."

Flint agreed, and a few minutes later he

stepped out into the night. The wind was gusting, almost sucking the air out of his lungs. As he made his way alongside the building, he cursed himself for coming to town on such a night.

The street was slippery with mud as Flint, astride Shadow, rode away from the stables. The only illuminated windows were the saloon and the whorehouse. The good citizens of Jackson Hole had gone to bed a long time ago.

Flint couldn't remember it taking so long to ride from town. It seemed ages before he made out the dim light of the kitchen window. With his hat pulled low on his forehead, he battled the fierce wind to the barn.

It was dry and warm in the big building, and he thanked God for that as he stripped the saddle off Shadow and turned him into his stall. He hurriedly rubbed the horse down, covered him with a blanket, then ran to the house. He couldn't wait to sit by the fire and thaw out a bit.

He thrust open the door, and remembered just in time to close it quietly so as not to wake the children. "Did everything go all right?" he asked the shadowy figure sitting inside the blazing fireplace.

"Everything has been fine," a familiar feminine voice answered.

"Kate!" Flint exclaimed, and rushed over to the woman he loved like a mother. "What happened? Why aren't you in Utah?" He picked her off the chair and swung her around in circles.

"Put me down, you long-legged galoot," Kate said with a laugh, out of breath, "and I'll tell you." Flint set her back in the rocker and she began to explain. "The stagecoach broke down yesterday and we had to spend the night at some godforsaken way station. I've been traveling all day just to get back to Jackson Hole. This evening when we arrived, I got my horse from the livery and headed right out to the ranch." She looked up at Flint with a warm smile. "An hour ago, when I spotted the light coming out of the kitchen, it was the prettiest sight I ever saw. Stubby had to help me dismount and lead me into the house. I didn't think I would ever be warm again, but Stubby dug a couple stones from the fireplace and wrapped them in a cloth to put them on my feet. I was soon warm as toast."

Kate gave Flint a teasing, quizzical look. "Do you have any news to tell me?"

Flint grinned and nodded. "I expect Stubby has already told you. I am now a family man, and I don't mind telling you, Kate, I'm scared to death. What if I don't raise the little ones right?"

"The fact that you worry about that is a good sign you'll do a fine job of rearing them. And don't forget, I'm here. I've done a good job bringing you up. Also, there's Stubby. He's already crazy about the little tykes. Especially little Mercy."

"Did you see them?" Flint asked as he took a bottle of whiskey from a cabinet and splashed some into a glass.

Kate gave a soft laugh. "Stubby let me have a peek at them, warning me all the time not to wake them up."

When Flint sat down in the matching chair beside Kate, she asked, "How's things with our new neighbors? Has that pretty little Lauren taken a cotton to you?"

"Taken a cotton to me?" Flint snorted. "She's more likely to take a shot at me."

"Now why would she do that? You've been behaving like a gentleman, haven't you?"

"I think so. I've been trying to."

Kate gave him a soft look. "That doesn't come easy to you, huh, Flint? I tried, but I'm afraid I didn't have much success with that part of bringing you up."

"You did a fine job with me, Kate." Flint reached over and picked up her hand. "My own mother couldn't have done any better."

"Even though I blistered your little butt a lot of times?"

"I'm sure I had it coming." He looked at Kate with solemn eyes. "Kate, you won't ever spank little Mercy, will you?"

Kate lowered her lashes to hide the amusement in her eyes. "If the time ever comes that Mercy needs to be punished, I'll leave it up to you to give her a switching."

Flint actually flinched at the idea of punishing Mercy. "I'm sure she won't need any chastising. She's a very sweet child."

It's certain you will never punish her for anything, Kate thought, then switched the subject. "Have you seen Lauren Hart while I was gone?"

"A couple times," Flint answered, then complained, "She's the most unfriendly woman I've ever met. An aunt of her's showed up today . . . a young fellow came with her."

"Have you met them yet?"

"Yeah, I think so."

Katy gave Flint a puzzled look. Why the short answers? She knew him well, and knew that there was something he didn't like about the aunt and her companion.

"Did you like them well enough?"

"Yeah. They're all right, I guess. They're in the saloon in Jackson Hole now playing poker."

Kate yawned. She had been traveling since early morning, and her body was crying out for rest. She stood up and stretched. "I'm going to bed, son. It's good to be home. I think I'll postpone my trip to Utah for a while. Looks like I'm needed around here right now."

"Thanks, Kate. It's good to have you home. I don't mind telling you that I've been pretty nervous, thinking about taking care of the children by myself."

"I'm home now and things will be just dandy. The young'uns will bring some life into this big old house. I'll see you in the morning."

Chapter Twelve

It was eerily quiet outside when Lauren a-
wakened. She had finally fallen asleep last night
to the sound of wind whipping around the
house. She was thankful to be in this warm, dry
place instead of the drafty cabin where she'd
grown up.

She snuggled deeper into the covers to warm
her shoulders. A contented look came over her
face. She had never slept so warm in all her
memory. There were no holes in the blankets
that covered her, and her new flannel gown was
long and full, wide enough for her to tuck her
feet into its hem.

As Lauren's shoulders and nose grew warm,

she began to think of her neighbor, Flint Mahone. He was the most handsome man she had ever seen. A wry expression twisted her lips. She wasn't the only female in Jackson Hole who thought that way either. It hadn't missed her notice how the women, young and old, fawned over him. The big arrogant rooster took their adoration as though it was his due.

Well, he wouldn't get any sighs and coy looks from her. She would give all her attention to Colly King. He was handsome too, and had nice manners. She felt sure he wouldn't be caught in the street with a loose woman plastered to his side.

Lauren heard Dud stirring around in the kitchen, and sniffed the aroma of frying bacon and brewing coffee. She decided to lie in the warmth of her bed until Dud called her to breakfast.

As she lay snuggled down in the covers, she found herself wondering if and when Flint Mahone would come to help drive the wild cattle out of the brush. If he didn't come soon, snow would fall and the drive would have to wait until next spring.

She had just made up her mind that he probably wouldn't come at all when Dud called out, "Come and get your breakfast, Lauren, before I give it to Wolf."

Lauren sat up, swung her feet to the floor, and shoved her feet into a pair of new fur-lined moccasins. She shrugged into an equally new robe, the first she had ever had, and walked across the short hall to the kitchen.

"It sure smells good in here," Lauren said as Dud lifted a black cast-iron kettle from the stove and poured its hot water into a basin.

"It's wet and cold out there," he said as he hung a clean towel on a nail beside a small mirror.

"I'm happy to see it didn't snow again." Lauren looked out the window over the dry sink.

"Me too," Dud remarked as he filled two plates with bacon, fries, and scrambled eggs. "But I wouldn't be surprised if we had snow today or tomorrow. It's colder than a whore's heart out there. If Flint is gonna help me with that cattle drive, I hope he'll show up today. Cattle are dumb. You can't herd them in a blizzard."

"I wouldn't depend on him showing up ever," Lauren said as she sat down at the table. "He probably went to the saloon last night and is still there."

"I think you're wrong." Dud filled their coffee cups from the pot. "The man has to be dependable and not afraid of work or he wouldn't own that big ranch. To have something like that in your thirties takes a lot of work."

Lauren made no answer to Dud's remark, and he didn't add to it. As they ate breakfast and drank the strong, fragrant coffee, they talked of their plans for the ranch; then Lauren brought up the subject of the aunt she had never known about.

"Why wasn't I told that I had an aunt?" she asked Dud just as he raised his coffee to his lips.

Dud set the cup of coffee back down untasted. When he didn't answer right away, Lauren pressed, "Well, why wasn't I told? Was she an outlaw too?"

"Dad-gum it," Dud grumbled, "I don't really know. Besides, it's not my place to tell you." He lifted the coffee cup to his mouth again.

Lauren knew from the stubborn look on his face that Dud would say no more about it. She heaved a silent sigh. Maybe someday Aunt Lillie would tell her. At any rate, she liked her new relatives. Actually, Colly wasn't related to her, she realized, and fell to thinking about him. He was so different from Flint Mahone. He had nice manners, a nice way of talking and acting. He didn't strip her clothes off with his eyes the way that ruffian Flint did.

Lauren had just refilled her cup when Dud, taking the pot back to the stove, said enthusiastically, "I knew you were wrong about Mahone. Here he comes now. And four of his hands are with him."

As Dud shrugged into the heavy mackinaw he had bought in Jackson Hole, Lauren rose from the table and walked to the window. She stood back out of sight. She did not want the arrogant rancher to catch her peering out at him.

"I'm going to take Wolf with us, if it's all right

with you," Dud said, pulling his hat low on his forehead.

"Go ahead. But make sure those cowhands know he's a pet and not to be shot at."

"I'll make sure they know that," Dud said.

"I'm afraid we'll have to make another trip to Jackson Hole to visit the gambling parlor again," Lauren said. "Cattle will eat a lot of hay over a long winter."

Dud nodded thoughtfully. "Why don't you take whatever's left in the tin can and buy as much hay as possible?" he suggested. "That way we'll have fodder waiting for the animals when they arrive." With that advice he was out the door, and the wind slammed it behind him.

How much money did they have left in the tin can? Lauren chewed at her lower lip. She hoped there was enough to buy a load or two for the time being. She walked to a cupboard and took from the shelf the tin box she and Dud kept their cash in. Sitting back down at the table, she took out a thin sheaf of greenbacks. She counted them out and sadly shook her head. She thought there was barely enough to buy the animals' supper. She'd best get going. It was suddenly looking mighty gray outside; maybe they were in for more rain, maybe even snow.

She cleared the table, stacking the dirty dishes in the dry sink. Ten minutes later she was dressed in her warmest clothing and taking the money from the tin box. In another ten minutes she had the team hitched to the wagon.

She climbed onto the high seat and clucked to the horses.

As the wagon bounced along, a cold wind blew down from the mountains, causing a thin layer of ice on the puddles along the track. Lauren pulled her hat down to her eyebrows, pulled the collar of her heavy jacket up around her ears, and hunched down. Clouds of steam issued from her lips, as well as from the horses.

Twenty minutes later Lauren gave a loud sigh of relief. It was evident that she was nearing Jackson Hole; she could see slender clouds of smoke curling up behind the tall pines. A minute later she rounded a bend and Jackson Hole lay before her.

She drove straight to the livery. The owner could either sell her some hay or tell her where she could buy some.

When Lauren drove through the wide doors into the livery, a mostly bald-headed man with a fringe of brown hair came out of the dim interior of the long building.

A warm smile curved his lips. "How can I help you, miss?" he asked, reaching up to assist her to the straw-scattered floor.

Lauren smiled back at him as she laid her hands in his. "I need to buy half a load of hay . . . just enough to hold me over until tomorrow."

"That's about all I can spare right now," Baldy Jenkins said as he led the way down the wide aisle of the livery. "The place to go if you need a good supply is Ty Summers' place. He can let you have all you need."

"I'm happy to hear that." Lauren smiled widely. "I know his wife, Janice."

Baldy stopped in front of a stack of baled fodder. "I'll have to find my grandson to load your wagon. Why don't you go down the street to the cafe and get yourself a cup of coffee and thaw out? It will take a little while to find Pete and then load the hay."

Lauren entered the Range Cafe, and blinked as the warm air in the small room brought tears to her eyes.

"Come sit with us, dear," suggested a warm female voice from a far corner.

Lauren brushed the wetness from her eyes and recognized her aunt and Colly King. "Aunt Lillie—" she smiled, walking over to the table— "what brings you out so early?" she asked as Colly rose and pulled a chair out for her.

"Although our rooms are comfortable enough at the hotel, it's not like living in your own home. We have always lived in a house. We wanted to have an early breakfast, then start looking around for any property that is for sale."

"I take it you're only interested in a house, not a ranch," Lauren said after she had ordered a cup of coffee.

"A ranch is not for us." Lilly laughed at the idea of her and Colly running a ranch. "We're city folk. Running a saloon is what we do best."

"And don't forget a gambling hall," Colly added, a devilish smile creasing his handsome face.

Lauren started to voice her approval of a gambling hall, but something told her not to venture any opinion about it one way or the other. She guessed she kept her silence because she didn't want her aunt to know that she gambled sometimes, out of necessity. The very lady-like woman might frown on a female playing poker.

"So why are you in town so early?" Lilly asked.

"Dud is going to spend the day driving our cattle out of the brush. He says that we're in for a blizzard before the week is out, and we don't have a blade of hay in the barn. So I made a trip to the livery to buy some."

"How many head do you have?" Lillie asked.

"Our neighbor Flint Mahone thinks there's two or three hundred."

"Three hundred?" Colly asked in some surprise. "That should bring you a good amount of money when you drive them to market."

"Three hundred is a small number, compared to the two thousand that Flint Mahone plans on driving into Kansas come spring."

Colly gave Lillie a wry smile. "Ma," he said, "maybe we should go into the cattle business after all."

Lillie smiled and shook her head. "Ranching

175

is hard work. Believe me, it's not for either one of us."

Colly nodded and answered good-naturedly, "I expect you're right. I just got carried away for a while, thinking of all that money Mahone is going to be making a few months from now."

Lauren heard the envy in the handsome man's voice and before she knew it, she was defending Flint. "I suppose it's true he makes a lot of money, but he works like a dog for it. According to his housekeeper, he's up before dawn and seldom gets home until well after sundown."

"He's quite a man, isn't he?" There was a flicker of irritation in Colly's eyes.

"I'm not saying that," Lauren quickly amended. "I don't know what kind of man he is. I only said that he's a hard worker and deserves the money he makes."

"You're right, dear," Lillie said. "If he puts that much time into running his ranch, he deserves the money he makes."

Colly didn't like the way the conversation was going. "Lauren," he said, "I've been wondering. If I hired a buggy, would you go riding with me tomorrow? You could show me your ranch, some of the countryside."

"I don't know anything about the countryside. Dud and I only arrived here three days ago ourselves. I only know a little about the river road."

"We'll just have to explore the area together then. What about it?"

Lauren hesitated a moment, then answered, "I suppose we could. That is if it doesn't snow. I'm told that they have terrible blizzards around here, and it looks to me like dark clouds are building up in the north."

Lauren finished her coffee and reached for the jacket she had draped across the back of the chair. "I think I'd better get started for home just in case a blizzard is on the way right now."

Colly jumped to his feet to help her on with the jacket. "I'll see you tomorrow around one o'clock," he said softly.

"When will I see you again, aunt Lillie?" Lauren asked as she pulled on a pair of fur-lined gloves, the first she'd ever owned.

"Just as soon as Colly and I have found a house, he'll come out to your ranch and bring you into town. It's too bad that crusty old Dud makes it impossible for us to live together. At any rate, he can't keep us from seeing each other as often as we want to."

When Colly would have gone with Lauren to the livery, she smiled and shook her head. "It's only across the street, Colly. Stay here and have a cup of coffee with Aunt Lillie."

As Lauren walked across the muddy street she pulled the jacket collar up around her throat. The wind was picking up and there was the feel of snow in the air. She hoped that Baldy

Jenkins had located his son and now had the wagon loaded.

Lauren smiled her relief when she entered the livery and saw her wagon loaded and waiting for her. Baldy came from the back of the long building. "I've been hoping that you'd show up pretty soon," he said. "We're in for some bad weather. I think you'll beat it if you leave right away."

"I'm leaving right now." Lauren pulled the thin sheaf of money from her hip pocket. Handing it to the friendly man, she climbed into the wagon and yelled, "Gidda-yup."

As the wagon was pulled along at a fast clip, Lauren kept her eyes on the horizon. She could see great black thunderheads piling up. There was going to be an electrical storm. She had to get home fast, and reluctantly she laid the whip on the horses' rumps. When she pulled into the barnyard, the trees around the buildings were bowing before the heavy blasts of wind. The first crackling lightning and booming thunder sent bolts of fear through her, but she managed to drive the wagon into the barn and unharness and stable the horses.

As she ran toward the house, letting loose little squeals every time lighting zigzagged across the sky, the first slash of rain came. Almost hysterical, she jumped up on the porch and banged open the kitchen door.

*   *   *

For hours they had chased the wild ones through brush, across ridges and windfalls. The cattle, their heads hanging low, bawled for water. As they continued to drive the animals through stands of timber and tangles of brush, the cowhands were beginning to look haggard and worn. Flint had noticed a stirring of wind among the trees, and a frown had creased his forehead. Looking westward over his shoulder, he'd seen that the mountain peaks were shrouded with clouds, and knew they were in for some bad weather. Snow, or rain, was on its way.

When the thundering and lightning began, the cattle were spooked. They were poised to stampede. A slicker bulged at the cantle behind him, and he pulled it free and shrugged into it as he rode up alongside Dud.

"Dud, all hell is gonna break loose any minute," he yelled over the roar of the wind. "We're a couple miles from your range. We've got to make the cattle run, keep their minds off the lightning."

Dud nodded, and they both let loose an Indian yell and touched spurs to their horses. The longhorns increased their pace, bawling their distress.

The cowhands raced their mounts alongside the herd, yelling and popping their long whips. It wasn't long before they could make out the dim shapes of the ranch buildings.

Almost at the same time the first drops of rain

fell. Flint stood up in the saddle and yelled to his men, "Drive the animals into that gully down by the river. They can find a little shelter there."

"Come on to the house, Flint," Dud invited. "Have a drink, warm your innards."

Flint was chilled to the bone, but he didn't think he could face another one of Lauren Hart's cold looks.

"Another time, Dud," Flint called. "I'd better get on home. The young'uns may be afraid of all the racket the storm is causing."

"A lot of thanks for your help," Dud called after Flint's fast-disappearing stallion.

Lauren saw Dud hurrying from the barn and glanced around the kitchen, then walked into the sitting room. A big fire was blazing in the fireplace and a bottle of whiskey and glasses were sitting on a table next to a chair. Everything was ready for Dud and Flint. They could have a glass of whiskey, then some coffee if they wanted it.

She went back into the kitchen just as Dud opened the door, and was almost knocked down by Wolf in his hurry to get in and lie down before the fire.

"Did you get the hay?" Dud asked as he held his hands over the cookstove, which was radiating heat through the kitchen.

"I could only get half a load from Baldy Jenkins, the owner of the livery. That's all he had on hand. He said to go to the Summers ranch, that Ty Summers would sell me all I want."

Dud poured himself a cup of coffee and sat down at the table. "I don't suppose we've got much money left, have we?" he asked as Lauren set a plate of roast beef and potatoes in front of him.

"You suppose right." Lauren placed her own supper plate on the table. "There's about twenty dollars in our little cache."

"Enough to get you into a game," Dud said as he cut into his roast beef. "When will you go? You can't count on the weather. This rain that's pounding us could turn into snow overnight."

"You're right. I guess we'd better go tomorrow."

Chapter Thirteen

Flint came awake with a little bare arm thrown across his waist. The room was cold and though Mercy shivered, she didn't release her hold on him. The child must have crawled into his bed sometime during the night. He carefully pulled the covers up around her small shoulders, and smiled when she scooted a little closer to him.

Don't get too comfortable, little one, he thought. Your Uncle Flint has to get up and see what the weather is like outside.

So thinking, he carefully removed Mercy's arm and swung his feet over the edge of the bed. When he had taken clean denims and a flannel shirt from the wardrobe and pulled them on over his long-legged, one-piece underwear, he made sure Mercy was well covered, then picked up his socks and boots and walked down the hall to the kitchen.

Kate looked up from the frying pan on the big cookstove. "How did you manage to get away from the little one?" she asked grinning. "When I looked in on the two of you before, she was clinging to you like a little monkey."

Flint smiled too as he worked the handle on the small pump fastened to the sink. "It wasn't easy," he said as the washbasin filled with water. "I had to move more carefully than I have done slipping away from Indians."

Kate placed a plate of bacon and eggs on the table, and as Flint took his seat at the head of the table, she placed her own plate across from him. "Them young'uns have certainly taken to you, Flint." She took a hot biscuit from a platter and as she broke it in half and spread butter on it, asked, "Do you think you can live up to their good opinion of you?"

Flint washed a mouthful of food down with a swallow of coffee. "I don't know if I can or not, Kate, but I'm sure as hell going to try. I'll probably make a lot of mistakes along the way."

"Ha!" Kate snorted. "What parent hasn't? The main thing for you to remember is that you'll always be there for them. Let them know that they can depend on you. That's the most important thing in raising kids. I did that with you and Jake and you two turned out fine."

Flint looked at Kate with dry amusement. "Katie, my love, you think that out of love. I doubt if there's a handful of people in Jackson Hole who think I've turned out fine."

"If that's true, the rest of the people don't know how good you are inside."

"All right, Kate, I won't argue with you. I'm a saint," he added as he stood up to fetch the coffeepot from the stove.

As he refilled his and Kate's cups, she asked, "What are you going to do today?"

"I'm thinking we should drive the rest of Dud's cattle back to his range. We didn't get them all yesterday. Some of those old mossy-horns have lived back in the brush for years. They're as wild as can be."

Kate looked at Flint over the rim of her coffee cup. "Have you looked outside this morning, Flint?"

"No, I haven't. Why?"

"Just go take a look. I think you'll change your plans then."

Flint wiped a swath of moisture away from the kitchen window and peered outside. A muttered exclamation fluttered through his lips. Sometime last night the rain had turned to snow. Although it wasn't snowing, there was half a foot of snow blanketing the ranch.

"It's worse in Jackson Hole," Kate said. "That old Indian stopped by for a cup of coffee. He said there's a foot of snow in Jackson Hole. He said a crew of townspeople are busy clearing off the boardwalks and street.

"So what are you going to do today?"

"First I'll get the men up, have Stubby make them a good hearty meal. After that we'll get shovels and start clearing the snow away. Then I'll try to get to Jackson Hole and give them a hand with clearing away the snow."

Kate spooned some sugar into her coffee. "I guess Lauren and that crabby old Dud will be all right."

"They'll be fine," Flint said shortly. "Those two could lick the Devil if need be."

Kate hid her grin by lifting the coffee cup to her lips. If she was correct in her thinking, Flint wasn't making any headway with the little beauty. His pride must be hurting pretty bad. She set her cup down with a satisfied click. It was time that young man got his comeuppance. Of course she hoped that in the long run he would get the girl. It was high time he got married and settled down.

As Lauren guided her stallion on a set of tracks made by a previous rider, all she could hear was the muffled sound of her horse's hooves and the creak of saddle leather. She was getting a later start than she had planned for her trip to Jackson Hole. But she had to do what she must do and get home in time to feed the cattle. She had to win some money at the poker table, then ride out to the Summers ranch and buy the needed hay.

She could do all that if the weather held. A glance at the sky showed it was still clear, with only a few white clouds in the north. She would be fine, she decided, and leaning forward, gave the stallion a pat on his proudly arched neck. She'd had such a warm feeling this morning when she helped Dud scatter hay on the snow for the cattle to eat. As they munched down the dry grass, she'd smiled. It was because of her they'd had something to eat.

"And if they are going to have something to eat this evening, I'd better get my butt down to Jackson Hole and win some money," she muttered to herself.

As Flint rode along, the stallion snorted from the cold. "Just hang in there, Shadow," he said quietly to the horse. "We'll be in town pretty soon and you can be in a warm stable at the livery."

He was nearing Jackson Hole when up ahead he saw a magnificent sorrel horse and rider. The horse belonged to Lauren Hart. He peered against the weak sun and recognized her as the rider. What was she doing out on a freezing day like this? he wondered.

He kept Shadow to a shuffling walk, slow enough so that he could keep Lauren in sight, see where she was going. His face darkened when she steered her stallion to the hitching rack in front of the Trail's End saloon. When she swung out of the saddle, he saw that she was disguised as a male. His face took on a grim look. Was she going into the saloon to play poker? Were she and Dud so hard up she had to play cards in order to feed the cattle?

It would have been better, he thought, if he hadn't driven the longhorns down to their ranch. But she and the old man were so happy when they learned about the cattle.

Flint turned Shadow's head to follow Lauren. She was disappearing into the saloon as he arrived at the hitching rack. There were only three other horses besides Lauren's tied up. His lips twisted in a half smile. There weren't too many hearty souls who would venture out in the hellish cold today.

He stopped first at the bar and ordered a glass of whiskey. "It's kinda slow today, huh, Hank," he said to the tall, thin, balding bartender.

"It sure is. I ain't gonna make much money today. It will pick up a tad this evening when the businessmen come in."

"What about the gambling hall? Is there any action in there?"

"There wasn't a great deal until the kid came in. You remember him, he cleaned out everybody. The men will be wanting to get their money back. It should be quite interestin' to watch. That kid was the best I ever saw."

"Do you think he cheats?"

"Nary a bit. I watched that kid close. He's got

a sharp memory. He remembers the cards that have been dealt. He's just card savvy. Are you gonna watch the game?"

"Not right away. Later maybe. In the meantime I'll have another drink."

Flint took his fresh drink and moved down to the end of the bar where he could see the poker players. Lauren sat with her back to him and he was disappointed about that. However, it wasn't very long before he knew she was winning most pots from the way she'd bend at the waist and rake the money toward her. And he could tell by the dark looks that the men were shooting at her, they were getting a little perturbed at her taking most of the pots.

Flint took a step into the gambling room when four men, rowdy and loud, walked into the saloon. It was Jonas Kile and his three sons. All four looked pretty much alike. They had bearded, straggly hair and clothes that had never known the feel of soap and water. Their faces were sullenly malicious as they bypassed the bar and stomped into the gambling room, going straight to the table where poker was being played.

Flint grew tense. There was going to be trouble and Lauren would be right in the middle of it. He reached down and loosened the colt in the holster tied to his leg.

"We're gonna join you men, if you don't mind," Jonas said in a loud, gravelly voice.

Without waiting to be invited, he and his sons pulled out chairs and sat down.

The four players, including Lauren, frowned but didn't voice their resentment of the four intruders. As the cards were being dealt, Jonas looked at Lauren and sneered, "Since when has green kids been allowed to play poker with grown men?"

As his sons snickered, one of the players said, "Don't let his youth fool you. He's as good a player as any man sitting here."

"Hah!" Jonas snorted. "We'll soon see about that. There ain't no way a kid between grass and hay is gonna beat me in cards."

"Don't say you weren't warned," the dealer said as he finished dealing the cards.

As those at the table expected and hoped, the Kile men started losing right off. None of the four were very good at the game, and within half an hour two of the sons were broke and had dropped out of the game. The remaining Kiles were sour, evil-looking men.

As the game continued, Flint became aware of a man and woman sitting at a table in a far corner of the room. He was surprised to recognize Lillie King and her stepson, Colly. Why were they watching Lauren so closely? he wondered.

Flint jerked his attention back to the poker game when suddenly Jonas was on his feet, yelling and swearing. "You little bastard, I knew you was cheating."

"No! I've never cheated at cards in my life," Lauren denied sharply. "You don't have the slightest notion of how to play, nor do your sons."

"You little piss-pot," Jonas made a jab at his gun. Before he could clear leather he found four guns trained on him.

"Look, Kile," one of the men said, "I've played with the kid before and I know for a fact that he doesn't cheat. And I agree with him, you don't know spit about playing poker. Now get the hell out of here!"

Flint holstered his Colt as Kile was sent spinning toward the door. He grabbed for it again when the oldest son, Herbert, short and fat like his father, drew his gun. Flint took one long step and was beside him. He drove his heel hard into the man's instep, then stepped back and kicked him in the groin.

Herbert let out a high-pitched scream and grabbed his crotch. "You've broken my foot," he complained plaintively.

"You're lucky I didn't break your damn back. Now take the rest of the Kiles and get the hell out of here."

Herbert, bent over, started for the door, the rest of his kin following him, the father bringing up the rear. Then, just as everyone was breathing a sigh of relief, Jonas, as he walked past Lauren, grabbed her and used her to shield his body as he walked backwards to the door.

"The first one that follows me gets a bullet between the eyes," he ground out.

Every man there knew that the dim-witted bully would do as he threatened. They stood helplessly as Jonas backed toward the door. Flint was praying that the Kiles wouldn't discover Lauren was a girl before they turned her loose, but suddenly Jonas cackled, "Hey, boys, this ain't no young fellow we have here. It's a girl. I got me a handful of tits."

"Ain't we gonna have fun tonight," Froggie practically drooled.

"I go first with her," Herbert declared. "I'm the oldest."

"You'll go first after I've had my fill of her," Jonas growled, and backed outside. He paused long enough to warn, "If you try to follow us, we'll do her some harm. Like taking a whip to her."

While the men were arguing what best to do about Lauren's kidnapping, Flint hurried into the barroom and slipped outside through the kitchen door. As he ran to the front of the building, hugging the wall, he gripped in his fist Lauren's winnings, which he had swept off the table as he left the gambling hall.

He rounded the corner just in time to see Jonas throwing Lauren onto her sorrel and climbing up behind her. One of his sons grabbed the reins of his father's horse. They had disappeared out of sight down the river road before Flint untied his stallion and sprang into the saddle.

Flint soon came within sight of the running horses, but he held Shadow back so the men wouldn't know they were being followed. All he could do was trail along behind them, waiting to see where they would hole up.

Flint figured he had been following them over two hours. A wind had picked up, and it looked like it would snow again any time. It was getting late, with shadows lurking beneath the trees. He worried that Lauren would catch pneumonia. How tired she must be, how frightened of what lay ahead for her. He felt sure she was still a virgin and his blood ran cold at what the three men would do to her.

Suddenly the horses' tracks turned off the river road and began to wind up the mountain. Why, he wondered. Their run-down place was in the foothills, in the opposite direction.

When Jonas brought his horse to a halt in a copse of pines and slid off its back, Flint realized what the old goat had in mind. He was smart enough to know that he couldn't keep Lauren overnight, but he was dumb enough to think that he could use her before turning her loose.

Flint rode in as close as he dared without being seen. He cringed when he saw Jonas jerk Lauren out of the saddle and fondle her breasts. He ground his teeth in helpless anger when Kile flung her down in the shelter of a tree and began to tie her hands and feet together. He could barely contain himself when Jonas tore open her jacket and then her shirt.

"Hey, boys," he called, "ain't them the purtiest things you ever saw? Soft and white." Spittle dribbled from the corners of his mouth as his callused and dirty palm covered one of her breasts and squeezed.

When Lauren let out a cry of pain all four men tittered. "Let me make her squeal," Herbert pleaded, kneeling down beside Lauren.

"None of that until we make camp and fix something to eat. Then we'll have lots of fun before we turn her loose."

"Paw," Froggie whined, "let me mate with her first. I ain't never had me a virgin."

"The hell you ain't. What about them young Injun girls I bring to the ranch every once in a while? They ain't more than twelve years old. Ain't no buck covered them yet."

"Yeah, but you and the boys used them a lot before I ever got my turn. They was always wore out. They didn't hardly know what was happenin' to them."

"That's how it is with the youngest in the family, Froggie," Jonas said carelessly as he walked over to the fire the two older brothers had built. "If you want a virgin, you gotta go out and find one yourself."

Flint hunkered down at the feet of his stallion, figuring how best to slip in and cut the ties that bound Lauren, then get her out of there.

The coffee smelled good as Herbert filled four tin cups he had dug from a grub bag. As they sat around the fire drinking the dark brew, Flint decided now was as good a time as any to go after Lauren. He stood up and checked the cylinders in his Colt. All were loaded. He glanced upward. It was clouding up, great banks of solid gray, more snow was on its way. He started out, creeping warily from tree to tree.

When he came to the tree that Lauren was bound to, Jonas and his sons had finished eating and were now passing a bottle of whiskey around. He could tell by their slurred words that they were well on their way to becoming drunk. It was time he freed Lauren and got her out of there.

With his hand on his bowie handle, Flint moved as silently as an Indian until he stood behind Lauren. Now if he could just alert her without making her cry out, it should be quite simple to slice through the leather thongs and free her. The men were gathered around the fire, the flames blinding them to any movement outside its circle of light.

He squatted down beside Lauren, making a shushing noise so Lauren would make no sound as she jerked her head around to gaze at him.

Tears of thanksgiving welled up in her eyes. He gave her a warm smile as he cut her bonds. When he pulled her to her feet, she tottered a moment, then caught her balance. She silently pointed to her sorrel stallion, which was tied to a bare-leafed aspen.

Flint put his lips to her ear and whispered, "Stay here while I go get him."

Luckily, the stallion was very gentle and though Flint was a stranger to him, the horse followed him quietly.

Flint found Lauren in the shadow of the tree where he had left her. He boosted her into the saddle, then led the stallion toward the spot where he'd tethered Shadow.

No sooner were they both mounted than the clouds let loose a fresh onslaught of snow and freezing rain. It slashed at all bared flesh, icy cold and stinging. Flint and Lauren pulled their hats down to their eyebrows for they were almost blinded by nature's blast.

Flint had no idea where they were, was not even sure of the direction home. He couldn't see two feet in front of him. He cautioned Lauren to keep him in sight. Then he gave Shadow his head and prayed for the best.

He shaded his eyes with a hand and peered through the curtain of white. He could dimly make out a wall of pines. Once Shadow almost walked into a small herd of deer that had taken shelter in a copse.

Another five minutes passed, and Flint began losing hope of ever seeing his ranch and little relatives again. Then Shadow walked into the ruins of a log cabin.

"Lauren," Flint called over the whistling wind

that almost sucked the breath out of his lungs, "stay on your horse while I inspect this building. It's not whole, but it may offer us some protection. I want to make sure there are no wolves or cougars inside."

Flint found that there wasn't much left of the building; only one side of the cabin was standing. Luckily, it was the portion that held a good-sized fireplace.

After he had hurriedly inspected it for animals and found none, he came to the conclusion that the log structure had been struck by lightning and had partially burned.

Flint noticed as he groped his way outside that there was a good supply of wood stacked near the hearth. As soon as he got Lauren inside he would build a roaring fire. She must be chilled to the bone.

Holding Lauren by the arm and gripping the reins of both horses, Flint fumbled his way into the ruin. He could vaguely make out the opening of the fireplace, and he led Lauren to it.

"I'll build a fire as soon as I tie the horses in a far corner." Lauren barely nodded her understanding.

Flint was thankful that they were out of the worst of the weather, but enough sleet and wind still managed to swirl around, making their teeth chatter. As he unsaddled the horses, he wished he had blankets to throw over them.

The animals seemed content enough to be in

this small sheltered area, Flint made his way back to Lauren and the fireplace.

By feel alone he cleared away a space in the firepit, then felt for some of the wood he had seen earlier. His fumbling fingers encountered instead a woven basket. Inside it he found small pieces of kindling. He piled the sticks and pine needles in the spot where he had cleared away the ashes, then added short pieces of wood on top. The wood was tinder-dry and he had no doubt that it would catch fire quickly.

His fingers were so stiff from the cold that he had to make three attempts at striking a match. But once he finally got a flame to the kindling, the wood caught immediately and flames roared up the chimney.

"Sit as close as you can to the fire, Lauren," he said, then laughingly added, "but don't catch on fire." She laughed also, but it was a weak sound.

Flint walked over to Shadow and took from the cantle a tarpaulin. By now the flames from the fire were lighting up the small area enough for him to see what he was doing.

The tarp was a good six feet by six feet square. He took his bowie from his back waistband and cut three holes in the top of one side, then cut a hole in each end on the bottom. Next he took from the saddle horn some strips of rawhide, such as every cowboy carried, and threaded the leather thongs in the three top holes. He fastened one to the corner of the fireplace, then the next one to one of the remaining rafters, and the last to a pine that had been badly scorched by the fire.

When he had tied the two bottom ends, one to the fireplace and the other to the tree, the wind was considerably less within the small shelter.

"I expect you're hungry." Flint looked at Lauren as he held his hands over the flames.

"Yes, I am, but I try not to think about it."

"I have some pemmican if you feel like gnawing on a piece."

"I like pemmican," Lauren said, then with twinkling eyes added, "That is, if it's not too old."

Amusement deepened the creases in the corners of Flint's eyes. "I promise it's no older than five years."

Lauren chuckled at his levity, and they sat in companionable silence chewing on the mixture of berries and suet. The crackling of the fire in the frigid night was a thing of pleasure to them. With the edge of their hunger blunted and the heat from the fire seeping into their flesh, they relaxed and fell into sparodic conversation.

"How are you doing with your little relatives?" Lauren asked.

"We're getting along very well, I think. They like me and worry when I stay away too long. I've been thinking about them, hoping they won't fret too much when I don't show up tonight."

"I've been thinking about Dud," Lauren said, a worried frown marring the smoothness of her forehead. "I know he must be sick with worry and frustration. He can't even send Wolf out to find me. The sleet and snow would kill all my scent. I wonder how long this freezing stuff will continue to fall."

"I don't think it will last too long. It's still too early for real winter weather.

"If you don't mind my asking, where do you and Dud hail from?" Flint said.

Lauren was so slow to answer his question that Flint gave her a quizzical look, wondering if she hadn't heard him.

Finally she answered, "We come from the badlands of the Dakotas." Her words were so short and crisp, Flint knew it would be useless to question her further. She did not want to talk about her past.

He brought up the subject of horses instead. "Dud told me that his main interest is in raising horses."

"Yes, that has always been his dream. He wants to raise purebloods. Me, I love the little burros around here. They are so small and cute."

"They're ornery little critters," Flint said, crossing his feet on the hearth. "They don't respond to affection. Most of them will kick a man every chance they get."

"I think if a person got one young enough he would be as gentle as a pet dog."

"Well, if you try it, I wish you luck." Flint chuckled. "I think you'd have more luck trying to tame a buffalo. But I will say this for burros. They are patient animals and are usually easy to catch. They never stumble or fall."

It was quiet for a while, only the wind and sleet breaking the silence. Then Lauren said, worry in her voice, "I hope our poor cattle don't get too hungry. I was supposed to ride to the Summers ranch and buy some hay."

"They'll be all right. Wild like they are, they have survived bad winters without any help from man. When we get out of here, I'll ride to Ty's place and have him deliver you some hay."

"We'll appreciate that." Lauren gave him a warm smile.

"It's nothing," Flint said and rose to put more wood on the fire. When he sat back down, he was closer by six inches to Lauren. In fact, their shoulders were almost touching.

A blast of wind swept down the old chimney, stirring the fire, blowing the flames. "It doesn't seem to be letting up any," Flint observed. "We might as well try to get some sleep and hope tomorrow morning we can find our way home."

Lauren looked down at the narrow strip of floor in front of the hearth, then up at Flint. "I don't see how we can get any rest in such cramped quarters. Besides, we'd have to lie in the dirt, and we don't have any blankets."

"I know that all you say is true, but I have a

bedroll that will fit nicely in this narrow strip of floor."

"And who will use your bedroll?" Lauren gave him a suspicious look.

"I thought that we could share it. We'd keep warmer that way."

"You thought that, did you?" Lauren gave him a look that made him glance away, a sheepish smile on his face. "I hope you don't think I would try to take advantage of you," he said stiffly after a while.

"No, I don't think that for a minute. But you might as well know that if you did have that in mind, you'd have a big fight on your hands. I know just where to hit and kick that would do real damage to a man."

"You do, do you?" Flint grinned at her. "Who taught you that?"

"Dud, of course."

"I should have known that," Flint grunted, and rose to get the bedroll. When he unrolled it in front of the hearth he said, "I'll sleep next to the fire because I'll have to feed it wood all night. If I had to climb over you every time, you might become frightened and do harm to my manhood."

"I might very well do that," Lauren agreed, and stretched out on her side of the blankets.

She didn't think that she would sleep at all, but it wasn't very long before she was being lulled to sleep by the brittle crackle of sleet hitting the partial roof. She was unaware that Flint sat on the hearth gazing longingly at the beauty of her face in the firelight.

Flint's sleep was fitful when he finally stretched out in front of the fire. He knew he had to keep the fire going; but far more disturbing to his rest was the nearness of Lauren's body next to his own, which kept him in a state of sexual arousal the likes of which he had never experienced before. He told himself that he must do something to keep this woman off his mind.

He didn't know when he had fallen asleep, but suddenly he was awakening to gray morning light. The fire had burned down to red coals. He sat up and reached for some wood. While he was stacking it onto the coals he heard the gentle patter of rain.

"Pray God it's not a cold rain," he whispered as he lifted a corner of the tarpaulin and stepped outside.

His prayer was answered. It was a slow, steady rain, not sleet or snow. The snow was melting from the ground and trees. He rushed back inside the makeshift room.

"Good news, Lauren," he said, gently shaking her shoulder.

She raised herself up on an elbow and looked at him out of sleepy eyes. "How can you call it good news when it's still raining?"

"That's the good news. It's raining and not sleeting. We can see our way to get out of here now."

"Let's go!" She scrambled out of the bedroll, groaning a little from sore muscles.

While Flint took down the tarpaulin, Lauren rolled up their blankets and tied them on the cantle of Flint's stallion.

When they had mounted and Flint took a look around, he gave a satisfied laugh. "I'm not real familiar with this area," he said, "but I know where we are. We should be home in an hour or so. Or at least you should. I'll be breaking off to see Ty Summers about some hay for your cattle."

"I've got to tell you something about that, Flint," Lauren began hesitantly. "I don't have the money for the hay right now. I'll have it in a couple days."

Yes, Flint thought to himself, after you've visited the gambling hall again. He unbuttoned his jacket and reached into his vest pocket. "This is yours," he said, and handed her the greenbacks he had swept from the table the previous night.

Lauren looked at him, her eyes wide with surprise. "How do you know this is mine?" she stammered.

"Because I saw you win it."

"But how did you know that . . ."

"I just knew." Flint gave her a devilish smile.

"So now my secret is out," Lauren said with a sigh.

"I won't give you away, but you're taking a big chance every time you go there. You should have learned that last night."

"I know that, but we had to do something. Dud is too old to start herding cattle again." She smile wryly. "Other than gambling, I haven't the slightest idea how to earn a living."

When she saw a twinkle appear in Flint's eyes, she snapped, "You can forget that. I wouldn't know how to please a man even if I wanted to."

"I'm sure any man would have the patience to teach you." Flint gave her a lazy look.

Lauren ignored his remark and said, "Let's get going. I want to get home as soon as possible. Dud will be out of his mind with worry by now."

Chapter Fourteen

A faint patter of rain awakened Dud. He sat up in bed. It was about an hour past dawn, he judged.

Dud rolled out of bed, flinching when his bare feet hit the cold floor. He hurried into the sitting room and added wood to the fire, which had almost gone out. When it blazed, giving out welcome heat, he went to the kitchen and built a fire in the big stove. He pulled an almost full pot of coffee to the front of the stove to heat. He had brewed the coffee last night as he paced the floor worrying about Lauren.

As he got dressed and pulled on socks and boots, he thought back over the night.

He hadn't gone with Lauren to the gambling hall. There were many things to do around the ranch, the most important being repairs to the corral. There were so many rails missing in the pen, the horses would have no problem getting out, nor would wolves or wildcats have a problem getting in.

He hadn't worried about Lauren going alone in the daylight. There would be people around; no one would do her harm. He had been kept so busy making the corral tight and safe, he hadn't been aware that the day was practically gone and Lauren hadn't returned.

When he'd realized how late it was, Dud had run to the house, grabbing up a piece of cold sourdough and washing it down with swigs of cold, strong coffee. Fifteen minutes later he was racing over the snowy ground, riding toward Jackson Hole.

It was bitterly cold when he got there, and worse yet, Lauren wasn't in the gambling hall. When he'd asked the bartender, Hank Jones had said that the young man had been there.

Dud's heart had felt like it had dropped to his feet when the bartender told him how a man called Jonas Kile had accused Lauren of cheating and one of his sons had pulled a gun on her. Flint Mahone had knocked the gun out of his hand, and it had looked for a while as if Kile and his sons would leave the gambling hall.

"But they didn't," Hank said. "Old man Kile grabbed your young friend and held him in front of him as he walked backwards toward the door. Flint slipped out the back door then, and I expect he's still following them."

"So will I," Dud grated, and turned to walk toward the door.

"Hold on, old feller," Hank said, stopping him. "It's going to be dark soon and they've got a big head start on you.

"Leave it up to Flint to catch them. He'll find the kid and bring him home safely. You'll see."

Never having felt so helpless in his life, Dud acknowledged that Hank was right. He didn't know the area and would probably get lost instead of helping Lauren. So, he said good night to Hank and rode home.

Now, as Dud waited for the coffee to heat, the rain was falling steadily outside. He filled a cup with the strong brew, went outside, and stood on the porch to drink it. As he squinted his eyes at the rain, he realized that it was no longer sleeting and that the snow was melting.

He finished his coffee in one long swig and returned inside. He would try to find Lauren now that it was light.

He was in the process of saddling his horse when the sound of hoofbeats made him glance out the open barn door.

"Well, I'll be jiggered," he exclaimed, a wide smile breaking over his wrinkled face. "Lauren!" he called, hurrying out to take her stallion when she drew rein. "Where have you been, girl? Did Flint help you get away from them rotten bastards?"

"Yes, he did, Dud. I hate to admit it, but he saved me from something worse than a beating. Those miserable Kiles discovered that I was female. I don't have to tell you what they had planned for me. Flint slipped into their camp and freed me from the tree they had tied me to. He managed to free the sorrel too, and once I had mounted, we carefully rode away from the Kiles. It was by accident we found the ruins of an old cabin. Only one wall and the fireplace were standing. The rest of the building had been burned out.

"We stopped there because we couldn't see where we were going in the dark and sleet."

Dud was quiet as he unsaddled the stallion. When Lauren began to wipe the sorrel down with a couple burlap bags she found hanging on a nail, he asked gruffly, "Did Mahone behave himself with you?"

"He was a perfect gentleman, Dud," Lauren answered as she hung the sacks back on the wall.

"That's good." Dud's face beamed. "I kind of like him. I'd hate to have to shoot him."

Lauren hid her amusement by leaving the barn and walking toward the ranch house. There she went straight to her room and changed into warm, dry clothing. She carried her wet boots into the sitting room and placed them on the hearth to dry out.

As she pulled on a pair of heavy woolen socks, she smelled the aroma of frying salt pork, and swallowed the saliva that gathered in her mouth. She was starving. She had only had pemmican for supper the night before.

There wasn't much said as they consumed the meat and sourdough. Then, when Dud had replenished their coffee cups, he said, "I don't suppose you had time to make much money at the poker table yesterday, what with that Kile bunch comin' in and makin' off with you."

Lauren gave an amused chuckle. "I had luck like you couldn't believe before that bunch came busting into the room. I had in front of me more than the amount we needed to buy hay. Then the first thing I knew Old Man Kile was accusing me of cheating."

"Ah, that's a shame." Dud looked sick. "They got your money then?"

Lauren shook her head. "They didn't get one thin dime. Flint had enough presence of mind to grab up my winnings as he ran out the back door. He has it now. He's on his way to the Summers place to buy our hay."

Dud's smile was so wide, Lauren feared his face would split. "You don't know what a relief that is, girl. The cattle started bawling for food an hour ago. It near broke my heart to know that they was hungry."

"Well, they'll have enough to eat this winter," Lauren said, "and you and I will have a little spending money to last us a while. You won't

have to worry about running out of tobacco."
She grinned at Dud, knowing that was a big
worry of his. He would rather go without food
than not have his cigarettes.

Dud had pulled the makings out of his vest
pocket, and was tapping tobbaco into a thin
white square of paper. When he had moistened
one side with his tongue and lapped the two
pieces together, he said as he lifted a flaming
twig from the fireplace, "When I came lookin'
for you last night, I saw your aunt and her fancy
stepson sitting in a dark corner in the gambling
hall. I thought it strange he hadn't gone with
Flint to ride them Kiles down."

"So do I." Lauren set her cup down. "I wasn't
aware that they were there. Maybe they came
later."

Dud shook his head. "I asked the bartender
how long they had been there. He said they had
been there all afternoon. He said they just sat
at that table watching everyone who came in."

"They probably didn't recognize me."

"I somehow doubt that," Dud griped. "I know
Lillie. She don't miss nothing. I'm tellin' you
again, girl, don't trust her."

The subject of Lillie was dropped when the
creaking and groaning of wagon wheels was
heard approaching the cabin. Lauren and Dud
pushed away from the table and hurried outside.

Two teams of sweating horses, each pair pulling a load of hay, were approaching the barn.

Flint drove one pair and Ty Summers handled the reins of the other. The rancher waved his hand at Lauren and called, "Them cattle will sure appreciate the sight of this dry grass."

"They sure will," Lauren called back, and hurried inside to get dressed.

She pulled on an oversized black slicker that had once belonged to her father, and waded through the slush and mud, the mire making sucking sounds under her boots.

The wagons had been drawn into the huge barn. Flint had almost finished pitching his load up into the loft, and was about to back the team up, ready for departure.

"Won't you and Ty come to the house and have some coffee before you leave?" She smiled up at him.

"Thank you, Lauren, but I've got to get home. The kids will be wondering what has happened to me."

Lauren managed to keep her disappointment from showing, but it was churning inside her. Her voice was calm when she said, "Thank you for all you've done for me and Dud."

She wheeled and hurried toward the cabin then. She would not let him see how his refusal had affected her.

Flint watched her go, tempted to call out that maybe he would take the time for one cup. Then the images of three little worried faces appeared in front of him and he drove the team toward the Summers ranch. As the team splashed through the mud and slush and the rain softly peppered his slicker, Flint was lighthearted. Lauren was softening toward him. When he delivered Ty's team he would go home, eat, spend some time with his little charges, and then go after the Kiles.

Flint was humbled by the way the children greeted him. Kate watched the way the boys clung to his long legs and the way little Mercy almost choked him, hugging him so tight around the neck.

"Flint," she said soberly, "you're obliged to stay alive for those children's sake. It would be hard on them if they ever lost you."

When Flint finally got to the table, dragging the boys clinging to his legs, he looked up at his housekeeper and said with a sigh, "That's a big burden you're laying on me. You know that in these Western lands death can come suddenly and without warning. All I can promise you is that I'll be more careful from now on. However, I'll not spend my time in the house like a scared old maid."

He looked at the children, who were spooning stew into their mouths. "I want you kids to listen to me now. I'm serious about what I'm saying. There will be many times when I'll get home late, or might not come home at all. But when that happens it's because it can't be helped. But I *will* come home, and I don't want you kids worrying about me, or thinking that I have deserted you.

"Do you understand that?"

The boys nodded solemnly. "Yes, Uncle Flint," they said in unison. Mercy said that she would cry, but she would do as he said.

Flint leaned over and kissed the top of her head. "You're my brave little girl." Inside he prayed that one of the Kiles didn't kill him when he went after them.

The fine rain that had fallen steadily all day hadn't let up much as Flint started his mustang up the mountain that afternoon. He gave thanks that the horse was mountain-born and mountain-bred. He had been captured wild and was still wild at heart.

Flint almost rode past the group of buildings in the foggy mist. He reined the horse in and gazed at the old weather-beaten buildings, aged by wind and sun, with warped doors and shutters. Neglect had contributed a big portion of the buildings' decay.

Through the uncurtained window, he made out Old Man Kile and his oldest son Herbert. He rode the horse around to the back of the cabin. Dismounting, he hunkered down in the bushes that grew there and listened.

He could hear the mumbling of male voices, but couldn't make out what they were saying. As he debated what he should do, a sharp female cry came from inside.

"Those bastards," he ground out. "They've got a woman in there." When another cry of pain rang out, followed by a coarse burst of laughter from the men, Flint was half blinded by the rage he felt. The female was being sexually abused and the Kile men were enjoying it.

Hardly aware of his actions, Flint ran around to the front of the cabin, threw open the door, and lunged into the room. Red-rimmed, blood-shot eyes stared at him. He glanced briefly at the squalor and sordidness of the room, then saw a young Indian girl, no older than twelve, lying on a narrow cot. Froggie was bending over her.

Flint swung his gaze around the room, making note of where each Kile stood. Herbert, the oldest, was at the stove frying something in a battered skillet. John Henry, the second son, sat at the table. That was good. All three were in a position where he could keep his eyes on them. Froggie was noted for being slow and a coward. Flint didn't worry about him. He had to keep an eye on the old wolf, who was glaring at him, an ugly expression in his eyes.

Keeping his eyes on Jonas, Flint ordered, "Froggie, get yourself over here where I can see you."

"I ain't gonna do it," Froggy blustered, then whined, "I ain't finished with her yet."

Flint walked over to the cot, a cold smile on his handsome face. With a lightning move he hit Froggie between the legs with the butt of his rifle. Froggy screamed his pain as he went sprawling in the dirty blankets.

"You're finished with her now, aren't you?" he asked sardonically.

"What's the matter with you, man!" old Kile bellowed, rushing toward Flint. "You've ruined him."

"Stand back, old man, or I'll ruin you too," Flint threatened as Jonas snatched a seven-inch blade from his waist and rushed at him, followed by his sons.

Flint got off several shots, wounding Herbert and John Henry, before he had to stop to reload.

He crouched, wondering how he could defend himself against the vicious-looking blade Jonas still held. From the corner of his eye he saw the Indian girl spring off the bed and rush to the stove. And though he felt sure that the handle on the skillet had to be hot, she snatched it up and brought it down on Jonas's head. He screamed as hot grease spilled over his head and ran down his filthy underwear. While he was hopping around, half blinded, Flint called to the girl, "See if you can find some rope or cloth you can tear into strips. Then tie them up. They're going to take a short journey."

"Behind you!" the girl yelled.

Flint spun around and saw fat Froggie advancing on him, a long knife in his hand. When the youngest Kile got close enough, Flint stamped hard on the man's instep. When he bent over in pain Flint drew back his fist and hit him hard in the stomach.

The girl had, in the meantime, securely tied the father and two wounded sons.

"Good girl." Flint gave her a warm smile. "Are you all right?" He knew that she had been terrified, but all he could see on her face was the joy of having been rescued from the Kiles.

"I have never felt better in my life," she said, and proceeded to tie Froggie's hands together. She looked at Flint and asked, "What are you going to do with them?"

"How far is it to your village?"

"About three miles."

"Do your people know that Jonas has kept you here in his cabin?"

She shook her head. "They don't know where I am. The old man grabbed me when I was in the woods digging roots."

"Will they be happy to see you?"

"Oh, yes, they will be very happy."

"Good. Now, while these brave men take off their boots, you dress yourself real warm. Put on their jackets. I'm sure they won't mind, will you, fellows?"

"The hell we won't," Jonas railed, rubbing his burning eyes. "Just what are you cookin' up to do with us?"

"Well, first off, we're going to take this child home and you're going to explain to her parents how sorry you are for taking their daughter and using her worse than you would a whore."

The faces of all four men turned gray with fear. "My God, man, you can't do that."

Flint grinned lazily, a taunting grin. "You want to bet?" he said, and nudging Jonas in the back with his Colt, prodded him toward the door.

"You know they will kill us," John Henry protested nervously.

"Most likely." Flint gave him a push that sent him out onto the porch. He waved his gun at the other three, motioning them to join their relatives.

"What about our boots?" Froggie whined. "Our feet will be cut to pieces."

"I wouldn't worry about my feet if I were you. You'd be better off to give your neck some thought. And stay away from them horses," he warned when the men headed toward the barn, which looked ready to fall down at the next stiff breeze.

"Come on now, Mahone." Jonas was talking fast and nervous, afraid. "It's bad enough that we don't have boots or jackets." His teeth chattered. "It's inhuman to make us walk barefoot in the woods, in the rain."

"You still won't suffer the way that poor girl did at your hands. Your sins are beyond redemption. Now step along. It's time for you to pay the piper."

The girl, who Flint learned was named Little Dove, mounted one of the Kiles' horses, and Flint led the captives up the mountain. There was no conversation between father and sons. What was awaiting them at the end of their journey was heavy on their minds. There were, however, muttered curses as one or another of them placed his bare foot on a sharp stone or a piece of dead tree branch.

It was still raining, but Flint and Little Dove were quite dry under their black slickers.

The day was melting into twilight when they scented wood smoke and cooking meat. They were nearing the Indian village. When several dogs set up a raucous barking, they knew they had arrived at Little Dove's village.

"Cut us loose, Mahone," Jonas begged. "I promise we'll leave the area and never come back."

Flint gave a scornful grunt. "Anyone who would believe that would believe that the Sweetwater could flow up the mountains. Get going." He gave the rope that fastened then together a jerk and kept the men at a fast trot.

They entered a clearing in a pine grove, and Little Dove called out in her native tongue. Tent flaps were flung open and a spate of welcoming cries penetrated the rain and fog. When around twenty people surrounded the cowering Kiles, Flint handed the rope that bound them together to an older man who appeared to be the chief.

"Little Dove will explain everything," he said, and turning the mustang around, he headed back down the mountain.

He hadn't gone far when the first scream echoed through the mountains.

Chapter Fifteen

Lauren cantered along the river trail, the stallion's hoofs making little noise on the soft damp earth.

The snow that had covered everything had disappeared three days ago, leaving behind slippery mud.

She wouldn't be out today if she didn't need a few items from the grocery store. Number one, according to Dud, she must purchase some smoking tobacco. He had run out last night, and he was a bear if he didn't have any weed to stink up the cabin.

But more important as far as Lauren was concerned, she had to buy the items she needed to bake cookies. She was having company to-morrow. Kate Allen and Janice Summers had sent word they would be coming around two o'clock in the afternoon.

A nervous frown creased her forehead. She knew so little about cooking, and absolutely nothing about baking. There was no use asking Dud to help her. Although he had a sweet tooth, he knew nothing about how to make something that would satisfy his craving.

As Lauren neared Jackson Hole, an idea struck her. She would go to the little cafe in town and ask if the owner would sell her a pound of cookies to take home with her.

Her mood had lightened considerably as she entered the main street of town which was a quagmire of mud. She rode straight to the cafe and dismounted. She looped the reins over the hitching post and entered the small eatery, where the floor was almost as muddy as the boardwalk outside.

As Lauren stood, undecided whom to approach about buying the cookies, a warm female voice spoke from a corner table. "Come sit with us, Lauren."

Lauren peered across the room. "Aunt Lillie," she exclaimed, and walked toward her aunt and Colly. "I didn't expect to see you two." She smiled as she sat down in the chair Colly King pulled out for her.

"I'm used to having a late breakfast and can't

seem to break the habit," Lillie said. "Have you eaten this morning, dear?"

Lauren remembered the cup of coffee and the slice of stale bread she had consumed a couple hours ago. She nodded, then said, "That was some time ago."

Lillie hid her amusement by lifting the coffee to her lips. Her niece was hungry. She placed the cup back in its saucer. "May be you can find room for a bite or two more. The bacon and eggs are quite good," she added, and told Colly to call the waitress over.

"What are you doing in town so early, Lauren?" Lillie asked once the food had arrived.

Lauren looked embarrassed. "I came in to buy the ingredients for making cookies. I met this young mother and the housekeeper of Flint Mahone. When I invited them to come calling, I didn't stop to think I should offer them something to go with the coffee."

Lauren looked at Lillie and said plaintively, "I don't know spit about baking anything." She folded her hands as though in silent prayer. "Do you maybe know how to make cookies?"

Lillie's peal of laughter rang through the small cafe. "Honey, you're looking at the best bakery cook this side of the Rockies. I can bake you most any kind of sweets you'd want."

"Oh, thank you, Aunt Lillie." Lauren squeezed her aunt's hand. "Do you think you could find the time to teach me a little about cooking?"

"I'd love to, child. When would you like for me to come out to your place?"

"Is today too soon?" Lauren asked hopefully.

"Go get what you need and we'll leave right away."

"Would you go with me?" Lauren asked timidly. "I really don't know what to buy."

"Of course, honey. Just as soon as I finish my coffee."

"You're welcome to come to the ranch too, Colly," Lauren said, having noted that the handsome stepson looked a little disgruntled.

When Colly only shrugged indifferently, Lillie said with some amusement, "Don't mind Colly's dark mood this morning, Lauren. He's put out at me because I have decided that I'm too old to open up another gambling hall. I'm going to open a ladies' dress shop."

"That's wonderful, Aunt Lillie," Lauren exclaimed, then looked at Colly's sour face. "Maybe you could open your own gambling hall, or even a saloon."

"I was going to suggest that to him," Lillie said, "but he's been so grumpy I decided to let him stew a while."

"Do you mean that, Ma?" Colly's face became animated and his eyes sparkled.

"Of course I mean it. For the life of me I can't see you in a ladies' shop, handling silk undergarments and stockings and garters." When a devilish twinkle appeared in Colly's brown eyes, Lillie snapped, "On second thought, you probably know more about such than I do."

Lillie stood up, gathering her wrist purse and gloves. "Come, Lauren, let's get your shopping done so we can get started making cookies."

When Lauren and Lillie entered the mercantile, Florence Richards was dusting a shelf of airtights. She barely nodded her head at Lauren and ignored Lillie completely. When Mrs. Richards continued to flip a rag over the tin cans, Lillie spoke in her most arrogant voice.

"My good woman, if your shelves of merchandise are more important than your customers, we shall go elsewhere."

"And maybe we'll run into your husband on the way," Lauren said, remembering how this woman had treated her earlier.

Florence shoved the cloth beneath the counter and asked ungraciously, "Well, what is it you want?"

Lauren and Lillie looked at each other with raised eyebrows. Then Lillie lifted her chin and there was a glint in her eyes as she said, "Come, Niece. We don't need this cow's insults. We'll go to the other store. I'm sure they'll appreciate our business."

Just before she slammed the door behind her Lillie said, "When I open my shop, I'm going to tell all my customers to bypass this store."

Florence stared after them, her mouth working like that of a puppet, but no sound came through her lips.

"Colly," Lillie said as she and Lauren started

to cross the street, "bring the surrey around in a half hour."

"Yes, Your Ladyship." Colly tipped his hat with a mischievous grin. "It shall be as you wish."

"Go on, you scamp," Lillie ordered, a twinkle in her eyes.

Colly walked them across the street, then went whistling down the boardwalk, making his way to the livery.

The store Lauren and Lillie entered was smaller than the one across the street, but the merchandise was dust-free and stacked neatly on the shelves. The floor was swept clean, including the corners.

Robert and Esther Thomason, owners of the store, greeted them with warm smiles. "Welcome to our establishment, ladies. I'm Robert and this is my wife Esther."

Lillie extended her hand. "I'm Lillie King and this young lady with me is my niece, Lauren Hart."

When everyone had shaken hands, Robert said, "Could you be the Miss Hart who now owns the old Hayes ranch?"

Lauren nodded. "Yes, I am."

"I met a friend of yours this morning. Said his name is Dud Carter."

Lauren's smile was warm as she said, "Dud is my oldest and dearest friend. I've known him as far back as I can remember. He's a fine man."

Lillie didn't add anything to Lauren's glowing

description of Dud, but the snort she gave spoke volumes. Lauren frowned at her, then gave her attention to the Thomasons.

"Aunt Lillie and I want quite a few things." She looked at Lillie, hoping she would take over. The only things Lauren had ever shopped for were beans and coffee and sugar and salt pork.

Lauren became more and more nervous as the ingredients continued to build on the counter. She was almost positive that she didn't have enough money to pay for the items, and Aunt Lillie hadn't finished yet.

When Lillie finally finished and Robert was totaling up the bill, Lauren became nauseous. When Mr. Thomason handed her the bill, she was on the point of rushing outside and losing her breakfast.

Lillie took the slip of paper from her shaking fingers, and said very nonchalantly, "Lauren would like to open an account with you. She will pay you monthly . . . if that's all right with you."

"Certainly." Robert beamed. "We'd be pleased to carry Miss Hart."

"How did you know Mr. Thomason would carry me on his books?" Lauren asked when all their purchases had been carried outside and stowed in the topless surrey Colly had driven up in front of the store.

"Because you're a ranch owner, honey. Store owners know that eventually they'll get their money . . . usually at the end of a cattle drive."

"I guess I've got a lot to learn about regular living," Lauren said as Colly helped her into the surrey.

"Don't worry about what you don't know, Lauren," Colly said softly as he placed his hands on her small waist and lifted her into the vehicle. "Stay just the way you are."

Lauren gave him a puzzled look when his hands remained on her waist longer than necessary. And she didn't like that soft look in his eyes.

When she gave a nervous twitch of her shoulders, Lillie said sharply, "We'd like to get to the ranch before dark, Colly."

"Of course," her stepson said, and hopped into the surrey, sitting so close to Lauren, their thighs rubbed against each other every time they hit a rut in the road.

Lauren gave a silent sigh of relief when they pulled up in front of her home. She hurried off the seat and had her arms full of supplies before Colly finished helping Lillie to the ground.

Colly frowned at her action. He couldn't believe that he had been rebuffed in such a subtle way. No woman had ever done that to him before.

"Come on, Colly." Lillie poked him in the ribs. "Let's get these supplies inside so Lauren and I can get started on her cookies." When he would have followed his stepmother inside, she ordered, "You might as well go back to town and wait a while. Come back in two or three hours."

"I'm getting tired of making this same trip," Colly grumbled, but he walked back down the steps and climbed into the surrey. He brought the short whip down sharply on the horse's rump, making it lunge forward so that he had to fight to keep the animal in control.

Lillie grinned as she opened the kitchen door and went inside. She must have a serious talk with that young man. It would be nice if Lauren did take a liking to Colly, but it didn't look as if she would . . . not in a romantic way, that is.

As Lauren and Lillie creamed together butter and sugar, beat eggs, sifted flour, then stirred in a handful of raisins, Dud and Flint were busy chasing wild cattle out of brush, gullies, and stands of timber.

The sky was turning pink behind the mountain when Flint drew rein and pushed back his hat from a sweating brow. "I think we've got all we're going to find. We can make a sweep through here come spring and get any we may have missed," he said to Dud.

"Man, I tell you I'd forgotten what it was like chasing wild cattle. I know for sure now I'm gonna raise horses. They couldn't be as bad as them damn longhorn steers. There was a couple old devils that kept charging my horse. There was one I thought I'd have to shoot."

Flint took the makings from his vest pocket and started building a cigarette. "I think you have the right idea about raising horses. Horses can manage to survive where cattle would die. Horses uncover food by pawing the snow off the dead brown grass. Cattle are too dumb to do that."

A pleased smile lit Dud's eyes. He hadn't known that wild horses could more or less look after themselves. He only wanted to raise them because he liked them.

"Well, let's get these devils home." Flint tossed the cigarette butt into the trampled mud stirred up by the cattle. The glowing end quickly burned out.

They crested the top of a long hill and below them, about a mile distant, was what was known now as the Hart ranch. With whooping and yelling they drove the herd of almost a hundred head downward. They bunched the cattle on a nearby flat.

"This is a fine place for them to winter over," Flint said. "It's not too far to haul hay to them, and when spring comes there will be plenty of buffalo grass for them to eat."

"Where will I keep the horses I intend to catch? Can they stay with the cattle?"

"You've got to locate a dead-end canyon. Once you drive the horses inside it, you'll need a barrier of some kind that you can draw across the open end. Maybe brush or a good strong gate. You've got to make sure there's grass and water for them.

"Have you ever broken a horse to saddle?" Flint asked.

"I did a lot in my youth. I don't beat a horse into submission. I first teach him to trust me. After that it's easy enough to turn him into a fine riding animal."

"I can understand that," Flint said, then added with a grin, "I always found that tactic worked with women too."

"Most times it works that way," Dud agreed with a chuckle. "But there's some women you can't fool with honeyed words. They can see right through them. If you're in mind to use that approach on Lauren, you might as well forget about it. She's probably got you pegged already."

"Hey, I'm not so bad," Flint protested. "I admit I do a little carousing around once in a while."

"Oh, yeah? That's not the way gossip has it. It's said that you're a womanizer. That you've laid with most of the young single women in the area, and all of the whores. Is that true?"

Flint's face went brick red. "Only partially," he said, trying to make light of his reputation. "Some of the single girls are so downright ugly I wouldn't poke them in a fit."

"Hey," Dud laughed. "You don't have to explain anything to me. I'm not claimin' to be a saint. Come on, let's get up to the house and warm up with a glass of whiskey."

"I don't know," Flint said doubtfully, torn between his desire to see Lauren again and his dread that he would find scorn in her eyes.

Before he could answer one way or the other, Dud touched spurs to his stallion, making him gallop toward the ranch house.

Both men frowned when they drew rein in front of the house and saw Colly King stepping down from the rented surrey. "What's he doing here?" Flint asked as they drew near Lillie's stepson.

"Hell," Dud growled, "I'll bet money Lauren's Aunt Lillie is inside the house. I wish I'd gone home with you." Dud's face looked like a storm cloud as he dismounted and looped the reins around the hitching post close to the porch.

"Hello, Dud." Colly nodded to the older man as they met at the porch steps. "You look like you've put in a good day's work."

"You could say that," Dud answered. "My neighbor here"—he nodded toward Flint—"has been helping me chase wild cattle out of the brush all day."

"Glad to see you again," Colly said pleasantly, reaching his hand out to Flint.

Lauren became all flustered when she saw the three men step up on the porch. She looked down at the apron that covered her pants. It was covered with spilled flour and milk. She, who had never before cared what she looked like, now wished she could fall through the floor. It didn't occur to her that her face was liberally streaked with flour and that strands of hair had escaped the blue ribbon that held the curls in place and now straggled down her cheeks.

But the two young men who gazed at her thought she was the most beautiful woman they had ever seen. Each one vowed on the spot that she would be his before the end of the year.

"When did you learn how to bake cookies?" Dud asked as Lauren placed a sheet of cookies on the table.

When Lauren looked up to explain she hadn't made them, Dud spotted Lillie coming from the larder. "Humph," he growled. "If you had a hand in baking them, they won't be fit to eat."

"Now, Dud," Lillie scolded, "you used to say I was the best cook in our area."

"That was when I was young and had no sense," Dud snapped back as he squatted down and opened the door to a cupboard situated beneath the sink. "Come on into the family room, Flint," he said, straightening up with a bottle of whiskey in his hand. "We'll have that drink we was talking about."

The last thing Flint wanted was to let the handsome Colly have Lauren all to himself. Avoiding eye contact with Dud, he said, "I think I'll have some of those cookies first . . . that is, if I'm offered."

"Of course you're offered." Lillie smiled at him and slid a sheet of cooled cookies onto a platter. "There will still be plenty left for Lauren's company. Help yourself while I pour us all some coffee."

Dud stomped off into the sitting room with Lillie calling after him, "Are you sure you don't want any cookies and coffee?"

There was laughter in her voice, and Dud muttered, "Go to hell."

"What's that you say, Dud dear? I didn't quite get it all."

Lillie and the two men laughed at her sly quip, but Lauren remained silent. Dud was her longtime dear friend and she wouldn't laugh at his expense. However, she thought, he must get over this hard feeling he had for Lillie. She liked her aunt a lot and wanted her to be part of her life from now on. That couldn't happen if Dud and Lillie were always snapping and snarling at each other.

Everyone sat down at the table and when Lauren had filled three cups with coffee, the only empty chair left was at the head of the table. She grew nervous noting that Flint and Colly would be sitting on either side of her. Colly, as usual, wore a black suit with a white shirt and a black string tie. Flint had washed his face and hands at the small pump in the sink and slicked back his hair. It was still unruly, though, and an errant curl hung down his forehead, giving him a roughish look.

Flint didn't have much to say, but Colly made up for his silence. The more Lauren laughed at his glib sallies, the darker Flint's brow grew. He knew he didn't compare well with Colly King when it came time to amuse a lady. Flint was so sure of himself around whores and loose women, but he was finding now that around decent young women, he was quiet and darn near tongue-tied.

He drained his coffee and pushed his chair away from the table. "Thank you, ladies, for the coffee and cookies. The cookies were delicious, Miss Lillie."

"Are you leaving, Flint?" Dud stood in the kitchen doorway.

"The kids will be anxious to see me and I want to check if the hands have put out hay for the stock. We may have snow by tomorrow morning."

Flint picked his hat off the floor where he had placed it beside his chair. "Ladies." He smiled at Lillie and Lauren, and settling the Stetson on his head, walked to the kitchen door.

Dud followed him outside. "I want to thank you for all the work you put in for me today," he said, standing on the edge of the porch. "And I'm sorry you didn't get the whiskey I promised you."

"That's all right. I've got plenty at home."

"I've been mad at Lillie for a long time. Do you think I'm wrong to try to keep her away from Lauren?"

"I don't know. She seems like a nice woman to me. Now don't get mad at what I'm going to say, for I don't mean no insult. But it strikes me that Lauren could learn from Lillie how to be more ladylike."

Dud looked out into the gathering darkness a minute, then said, "You may be right, but it just hurts too much to have her around."

Chapter Sixteen

When Flint awakened the sun was still behind the mountain, but dawn would soon be arriving. Last night he had decided that today he would go deer hunting. It could start snowing any day now, and the deer would head for higher country for the protection of the pines and boulders and crags. The fierce blizzards would not reach them up there the way they would down on the flat plains.

He raised himself up on an elbow and looked down at the short-legged cotlike bed where Mercy lay sleeping. It had been his old bed when he was around her age. Kate had dragged it down from the attic.

Mercy had fallen into the habit of creeping into his bed every night, and Flint knew that situation could not continue. He had sat her on his lap and reasoned in soft tones that she was a grown-up young lady now and must have her own bed. "And it will be right here next to mine," he coaxed.

He'd had to make all kinds of concessions, though, before she agreed to the new bed arrangements. The lamp had to be left lit all night, he had to hold her hand until she fell asleep, and he had to tell her a story every night. He had wondered at the time if he could remember any of the stories Kate used to tell him.

He grinned to himself, recalling how night before last he'd had Kate refresh his memory of the old childhood stories.

Flint sat up and flinched when he swung his feet to the floor. The Mexican tiled floor was like ice. He grabbed clean clothes out of the wardrobe, snatched up his boots, and hurried down the hall to the kitchen.

This was his favorite room of the house, especially in cold weather. The big black cast-iron stove was always burning, sending a comfortable warmth into the room. And there was always the aroma of something cooking, either a roast, or fresh bread, or a cake or pie.

There was no doubt about it, he thought, tugging his denims on. The kitchen was the heart of a house.

"How come you're up so early?" Kate asked,

taking a pan of biscuits out of the oven.

"I'm going to go get us a deer. They come out early in the morning to graze. A small herd has been coming to that meadow back of the creek all summer."

"I'm having company today," Kate said as she broke three eggs into a frying pan of bacon grease.

"Do you mean to tell me that you're finally going to let a man court you? Who is the lucky fellow?"

"You know it's no fellow." Kate gave him a slap on the back of the head. "Lauren Hart is coming over this afternoon. Janice Summers and I visited her the other day. Now I'm going to show her how to bake bread."

Flint's only answer to that statement was a grunt. Kate hid her amusement as she poured their coffee. She knew Flint, knew he had quite a crush on the beautiful Lauren and that she wouldn't give him the time of day. He wouldn't admit it, but that bothered him no end. He was used to getting any female he wanted. It would do him good to be set back on his heels for once.

Flint drained the last of his coffee and stood up from the table. As he took his heavy mackinaw from one of the pegs on the wall next to the door, he said, "I'll be home for lunch."

When he set his hat on top of his head and stepped outside, Kate thought, her eyes twinkling, "I imagined that you would. Not that Miss Lauren Hart has anything to do with it."

When Flint left the house and headed toward the barn, it was a cold, bright day. Ice flashed on the trees, sending rainbows slipping among the branches. He entered the horse barn and stepped inside the stall of his favorite mustang. A sturdy little bangtail was what you needed when you were going to travel rough country. They were surefooted and had the stamina to last all day.

The stable hand had already pitched hay to the horses, so all Flint had to do was throw a saddle on the little horse. He led him out of the barn, mounted him, then headed for the meadow where the deer liked to graze.

When Flint came upon a faint trail, he followed it for some distance. He figured he was about three miles from the ranch when he spotted three deer—a stag with an antler spread of about six feet, a doe, and a yearling. He guided the mustang into a stand of pines and pulled his Winchester from its sheath.

He had the stock at his shoulder, his finger curled around the trigger, when suddenly the big buck dropped to the ground. Its legs flailed once, and then it lay still.

"What the hell?" Flint grated, looking around for the puff of smoke that would tell him where the shot had come from. But he hadn't heard a shot.

That mystery was cleared up when a figure darted from the trees, a bow and arrow in his hand. Flint smiled wryly. An old brave had beaten him to it.

He nudged his mustang and rode toward the Indian. The old fellow looked up at his approach, a threatening look in his faded eyes.

"Go find your own deer, white man," he said. "This one is mine. Hungry women and children are waiting for it."

"I am not a man who would take food from women and children," Flint said gravely, but he wanted to laugh at the idea of this old man wanting to fight him for the deer. "I can find another, but I don't see your pony. Do you plan to carry this big buck to your village?"

The old fellow lifted his chin proudly, and thumping his chest said, "Black Bear can do it."

"I'm sure you could, Black Bear, but we both know my horse could do it much easier. Let's tie the animal on my mustang's back and take it to your village."

"Your words make sense," Black Bear said after pretending to think over Flint's offer.

Flint took a pegging rope from the saddle horn and strapped the big buck onto the wiry little mustang. He looked at the frail old man and asked. "How far to your village?"

"One mile maybe, as the crow flies."

"Climb up on the horse and hold the deer so it won't fall off."

Flint saw in the old brave's eyes that he wanted to refuse, but it was also plain that he was ready to drop from exhaustion. His spent condition made him silently climb up on the mustang's back and pick up the reins.

When they came to a clearing and children and barking dogs ran to meet them, Flint knew they had arrived at the village. As the old man bragged about killing the deer, pointing out how his arrow had gone straight to the animal's heart, Flint hurriedly untied the deer and pulled it to the ground. He wanted to continue hunting for his own deer. There had been a drop in the temperature. He could smell snow in the air. No one noticed when he rode away.

Flint followed another trail, this one more heavily traveled than the one he had walked previously. He found that the farther he followed the narrow trail, the more rugged the country became. He was not unfamiliar with the area, but he didn't know it all that well either.

It was around noon when an icy cold wall came down from the mountain. An owl hooted a mournful, lonely sound back in the trees announcing that snow was on its way.

Within minutes he was in a thick white blanket of snow. Luckily there was no wind. There would be no drifts to fight. He had just admitted to himself that he was turned around, hopelessly lost, when the little mustang found his way into a deep gully. Flint swung to the ground and inspected the area.

The ravine was deep, its sides at least three feet higher than he was tall. Its banks were rocky and lined with thick brush. Following a bend in the deep depression, he spotted a high pile of driftwood carried there by sudden floods. The gnarled, crooked limbs were bone-dry. There would be no problem getting them to burn. He gathered up an armful and returned to where he had tied the mustang to a stunted pine. Tossing the wood down, he stripped the saddle off the little horse and removed his gear.

The first thing Flint did was to see to the comfort of his horse. He had an extra blanket rolled up and tied behind the cantle. It took but a minute to loosen the ties and spread the gray wool over the mustang's back.

His next action was to rig a large tarpaulin between two trees to hold back some of the wind and to keep the snow off him.

That done, he built a fire in the lee of a pile of boulders that had been washed down by raging waters and left in a high, wide jumble. When the leaping flames threw shadows on the opposite bank, Flint rummaged in his grub sack until he found his battered coffeepot and a small bag of coffee that Kate had ground in her coffee mill.

As the coffee began to brew, sending out its delicious aroma, Flint sat in front of the fire and began to build a smoke. Well, he would miss Lauren's visit, but there was no help for it. He had been in tighter places than this. He would weather the storm just fine.

Leaning back against a boulder, he took one

drag on his smoke, then let loose a string of oaths. A bullet had just smacked against a rock near him. He jumped to his feet, the Colt in his hand, and moved stealthily down the ravine. He couldn't see anything. He remembered his father saying, "When a man stares too long into flames, he's momentarily blinded."

Who was trying to kill him? he asked himself. He knew there were a few people who didn't much like him, but he didn't think any of them would try to dry-gulch him.

Not knowing what else to do, Flint made his way cautiously back to the fire and hunkered down behind two stunted pines growing close together. He listened. If the man was still around, he would hear him walking in the gravel of the gully bed.

After waiting for what he judged to be ten minutes, and hearing nothing out of the ordinary, Flint started to gather his feet beneath him to rise. Two shots rang out then. One bullet whacked sharply against the boulder he had taken shelter behind, and the other one struck him.

Through a roaring blackness he felt himself falling forward.

The weather was crisp and chill when Lauren led her sorrel stallion out of the barn and climbed into the saddle. Her teeth had chattered in the cold air. Weather like this in the Dakotas always meant there would be snow in a very short time. To be on the safe side she decided not to stay too long with Kate.

As the stallion cantered along the river road, Lauren hoped that Flint wouldn't be at the ranch. The way she caught him looking at her sometimes made her nervous. She got the feeling his eyes were stripping away her clothes, that his mouth was on her breasts, making the areolas swell, then pucker. It made her breath catch. Her breasts felt the way they had when she'd been in the cabin where she and Flint took shelter when they were caught in a rainstorm. Every time she looked at Flint, or thought about him, her nipples grew as hard as little stones. Just like they were now.

Lauren wondered why Colly King didn't affect her that way. He paid her a lot of attention. He was as handsome as Flint, maybe even more so. But there was a toughness about Flint that appealed to her. And beneath that rough exterior a true gentleman resided. He might make love to her until she was downright silly, but he would never force himself on her.

"As if he'd have to," she murmured as the Mahone ranch house came into view. She swung out of the saddle and gave the stallion to a stable hand who came forward.

"Lauren," Kate called, coming out onto the porch to greet her. "I wasn't sure you'd come, the weather looks so nasty."

"I did debate about it, not being able to read the weather signs in Wyoming."

243

"I guess they're about the same as in the Dakotas. But don't worry about it. I'll keep an eye on the mountain. The storm seems to be coming from that direction. I'll know when to send you home. Come on in and we'll get started on your bread."

The two women were soon involved in sifting flour into a large bowl and adding yeast and water. "Now," Kate said, "we scrub our hands real good, then start mixing everything up with our fingers. I have to feel things if I'm to know everything is all right."

Lauren gave Kate a crooked little grin. "Don't you feel a bit uncomfortable when you're making gravy?"

"Very funny." She gave Lauren's curls a tug.

"Well, you said . . ."

"I know what I said, and you know what I meant. I meant mixing pie dough, dredging stew meat in flour before browning it."

They continued to talk about making stew as they each took a large ball of dough and started kneading it. "Some people prefer deer, but I lean toward beef. Deer has a gamy taste I don't like. Course, if you soak it in weak vinegar water overnight, a lot of that wild taste disappears. And you have to add a lot of spices to it. And lots of pepper."

Lauren hoped she could remember all that as she watched Kate shape her ball of dough into a long loaf. She followed Kate's movements the best she could, and was successful in laying her loaf into a greased loaf pan.

"Now," Kate said, "we cover the loaves with a clean towel and let the dough rise to twice its size. In the meantime we'll have some coffee and the cookies I made yesterday." Amusement flickered in her brown eyes. "I've kept the cookies hidden from Flint and the young'uns."

"Where are the children?" Lauren asked as she washed the dough off her hands.

"Flint's longtime friend Asher Davis took them to town in the buckboard to keep them from under our feet while we make bread."

"I can't believe Flint let those children go off with that wild man," Lauren exclaimed, disbelief in her voice.

"I know Asher could use a little taming," Kate agreed as she washed her hands, "but he's the most decent man I've ever known. He loves those youngsters and would give his life for them if need be."

"Maybe I have misjudged him," Lauren said weakly.

"That's all right, honey. Most people do."

"Does he have lady friends?" Lauren asked, though she didn't really care whether Asher Davis had lady friends or not.

Lauren was sorry she had asked when Kate gave a snort of laughter and said, "Lady friends? I'd say he has many, but none of them are ladies, if you get what I mean."

Lauren knew all too well what Kate meant.

Whores and loose women. And as she had suspected, Flint socialized with the same type of woman. Hadn't she had proof of that when she saw him at the fur post with a whore's hand down his pants.

Kate saw the look of dismay that came into Lauren's eyes, and wished that she could recall her words. The girl was probably thinking that Flint was the same way. And since it was true, she couldn't really defend him.

She jumped up and said nervously, "I guess it's about time we put the dough in the oven."

Lauren was amazed that the dough had doubled in size. She mentioned this to Kate, who was sliding the pans into the oven. Kate opened her mouth to answer her, then gave a jolt of surprise when a gust of wind slammed into the kitchen window shutter.

"Lauren, honey, the weather has changed. The snow must have started earlier, and I was so busy gabbing I never noticed." She snatched Lauren's coat and scarf off a wall peg, and bundled her into them. Hurrying her to the door, Kate explained, "Someone at the barn will have your horse ready for you. Ride fast, girl. Get home before it gets any deeper."

Lauren's head spun as she left the house. But the urgency in Kate's voice told her to run, not walk, to the barn.

As Kate had promised, a stable boy, having noted the change in the weather, had her stallion saddled and waiting for her. He unceremoniously grabbed her by the waist and tossed her into the saddle. As soon as she gathered up the reins he gave the sorrel a sharp slap on the rump. The startled stallion lunged away into the storm. Lauren tried to control the animal, to guide it. But the stallion was too spooked and strained at the reins, seeking a different way.

Her arms and shoulders aching from trying to hold the stallion back, Lauren remembered Dud saying that in a storm of any kind it was best to let a mount choose its own way.

She no sooner loosened the reins than the stallion turned off the river road and galloped madly down a dim trail through the forest.

Gradually the stallion slowed down, worn out from his mad galloping run. Lauren drew the reins in. As she sat, catching her breath, she lifted her gaze up to the looming mountains, all black and mysterious.

It was miserably cold and Lauren hugged her arms around her shoulders. The stallion stamped his feet against the cold, and Lauren nudged him in the flank to move out. He would be a little warmer moving about.

The snow was falling so thick now she could hardly see two feet ahead of her. She pulled her white woolen scarf up around her face until only her eyes were left unprotected. She released the reins, letting them lie on the stallion's neck.

"It's up to you whether we live or die." She patted the weary animal's neck.

Lauren had given in to Nature's wrath. She wished she could see Dud, to tell him good-bye. She didn't know how long the stallion had wondered aimlessly when she suddenly felt him bracing his feet, then sliding down an embankment on his haunches. She grabbed up the reins when the stallion regained his feet, and was holding on for dear life as the animal took off down a deep gully. Lauren gasped her surprise when they rounded a curve in the ravine and she saw a campfire that had burned down to glowing embers.

Her surprise made her gasp when she saw the prone figure lying nearby. She immediately recognized Flint, and the blood running from his hairline told her he had been injured.

She slid out of the saddle, and leaving the stallion ground-hitched, she hurried to kneel beside him. "Flint—" She gently shook his shoulder. "Are you in pain? Do you hear me?"

Now that she was nearer, she could see a bullet wound in his head. Lauren laid three fingers on his inner wrist, feeling for a pulse. She didn't feel anything. She realized then that the blood that was pumping so wildly in her own veins was keeping her from feeling anything else.

She told herself to calm down, to take some deep breaths. When she lifted his limp wrist again she felt a strong, steady pulse.

Now, what could she do for him? She raked her gaze over the small makeshift camp. A campfire had been lit sometime ago, and there was a tentlike structure nearby. She imagined all this had been done before Flint was shot.

Lauren untied the neckerchief around her throat as she walked to the stallion to retrieve her canteen. Thank God she had poured fresh water into it before starting out this morning.

She returned to Flint, who was rambling on about something she could not make out. She tore a strip of cloth from the kerchief and poured water on it from the canteen.

As she wiped at the blood, she discovered that the wound wasn't at his hairline as she had first believed. The gash traveled a couple inches behind his right ear. She kept dabbing at it with the piece of wet kerchief until finally the blood slowed.

With a relieved sigh Lauren tore a two-inch strip from the neckerchief and folded it into a narrow, thick pad. She then tore two more strips of the white material and fastened the bandage in place by tying the strips around his head.

She was ready to stand up and see to her stallion when Flint suddenly spoke. "Keep an eye on my horse, will you? He's a mustang from wild stock. He's been taught by his mama to listen for varmints that might attack him. If his ears prick up and he snorts, look around real good. It means there's something out there that shouldn't be."

"Are you in much pain?" Lauren asked as she squatted down beside him.

"My head hurts a lot, Kate," Flint whined like a little boy of four or five. "Can't you put some of your salve on my hurt? The kind you make up for me and Jake when we fall down and scrape our knees or elbows."

Lauren shook her head. He was delirious. He thought she was Kate, his housekeeper.

He was hurting, she knew. His face was gray with pain. She laid her hand on his forehead, and kept it there when he said quite clearly, "Go by the river, Kate. It's a winding stream and long, but smooth. And there will be trees and grass along its banks. Asher and I have traveled the ole Snake a lot of times."

He is definitely out of his mind, Lauren thought, removing her hand. His brow was cool. She started to stand up when Flint began mumbling again. "Have you seen the new owner of the old Hayes place, Kate? She's really beautiful and really bitchy. I'd give six of my purebred horses for a chance to mate with her. Asher thinks she's still a virgin. Do you suppose she is?"

Flint switched back to his little-boy complaining then. "Kate, I'm so cold. Jake keeps taking all the covers."

Lauren looked frantically around the rocky gully. What could she do? She quickly added more wood to the fire, then took the saddle from her stallion. Leaving the saddle blanket on its back, she freed the bedroll that had been fastened to the cantle. She spread her bedroll on top of Flint's, which had been spread out close beside the fire. She dragged the saddles up to the blankets and placed them like pillows at the head of the bed.

That should do it, she thought. But now how was she to get Flint onto the makeshift bed? He seemed to have drifted off to sleep.

"Flint," she said softly as she gently shook his shoulder, "can you stand up and walk to the nice warm bed I've made for you?"

"Of course I can, Kate," He looked at her, a nearly blank expression in his eyes.

Like a child, he lifted his arms to her, and Lauren grasped him under the armpits and with many grunts heaved him to his feet. She was almost brought to her knees by the time she got him where she wanted him between the blankets. And though she pulled the covers up around his shoulders and neck, his body continued to shiver and his teeth to rattle.

"I'm cold too, dammit," she muttered irritably as she piled still more wood on the fire. If the wind blew the flames any higher, they would escape the gully and set the pines above on fire. Of course they wouldn't burn long in this thick snowfall.

"Kate!" Flint whined. "I'm freezing."

"So am I," Lauren called back irritably, "and I'm going to do something about it."

She flipped back the blankets and working as fast as she could, stripped Flint down to his long underwear. She couldn't believe what she was about to do as she scrambled out of her jacket, shirt, and denims. But when she dived between the blankets and felt the warmth of Flint's long body, she was glad that she hadn't acted like a prim old maid who would have sat before the fire and frozen to death before she would lay her body next to that of a man who wasn't her husband.

The combination of their body heat and the roaring fire soon had their bodies relaxed, and as warm as they would have been at home in their beds.

It was still dark when Lauren felt a chill on her shoulders and came awake. During her exhausted sleep the fire had almost gone out. Flint had curled his body around hers, and it took a while to free herself from the arm he had flung across her waist so that she could go replenish the fire.

As she hurriedly tossed wood on the embers she became aware that it had stopped snowing. She told herself that was all well and good, except that the wind was blowing harder.

"I hope we won't have to climb through snow-drifts when we leave here," she muttered as she climbed back under the covers.

Chapter Seventeen

Lauren stretched her slender body in euphoria. Keeping her eyes closed, she clung to the dream she'd been having. To help her hang on to it, she moved closer to the male form that she had dreamed was making love to her and lifted her fingers to curl in his thick hair. This brought on a sharp intake of breath and a tightening of the arm lying across her waist.

When Lauren snuggled yet closer, she became aware that her head rested on a broad shoulder. How neatly she fit there, she was thinking when lean fingers began to slowly unbutton the top of her underwear. She gave a little moan of pleasure when her breast was covered by a callused palm and gentle fingers began to caress and knead the firm mound and roll her hardened nipple.

She grew warm, and trembling, and sighed her acceptance when her breast was gently freed and warm lips drew half of it into a warm mouth.

Then teeth began to tease her nipple, and a tongue laved the swollen tip a moment before drawing it into the mouth again to slowly suckle it.

Flint had a woken to find all his dreams come true. Lauren was lying beside him, snuggling up to him and seeming to encourage his every move.

When he had her so worked up that she was thrashing her head about, he slid his palm inside the bottom of her underwear and cupped the soft mound between her legs. With his middle finger he probed the tender lips apart. After toying with the little hard nub there a moment, he slid his finger inside her.

Lord, she's small, he thought. I wonder if she can take me. He took her hand and slid it down the front of his long underwear. When she made no move to take his member into her hand, he curled her fingers around his largeness. She had a right to know how big he was, that he might hurt her.

His size didn't seem to bother her, for which Flint was thankful. He wanted to make love to her so badly he didn't know what he would do if she said no. Deep down he knew that he wouldn't take her against her will, but he would be one aching man.

When he whispered huskily, "Let's get out of our underwear," Lauren readily agreed, and was out of hers before he was half finished getting rid of his.

They both sighed and went into each other's arms. They began then to lave wet kisses all over each other's bodies. When it came time to consummate what they had started half an hour ago, each carried a large love bite on one inner thigh, close to where they would make their connection.

"It will hurt a little," Flint said as he hung over Lauren. "But only for a moment. I will be as careful as I can."

Lauren's answer was to lift her arms and place them around his neck.

Flint watched her in the firelight, and saw the pain that came over her face as he slid slowly into her. Halfway inside her, he paused to let her get used to the probe of his manhood. After a moment her legs tightened around his buttocks, signaling for him to continue.

Cupping her small rear in his hands, he rocked slowly against her, each thrust of his body going in a little deeper. It took about five minutes before blond hair and black were meshed together. Flint paused again for Lauren to rest, and experienced something that had never happened to him before.

Even though they were lying quietly, Lauren's slick, warm sheath was pulling at his manhood, milking him. He lay quietly, and soon he was convulsing in relief. A relief such as he had never had before.

"How did you do that?" he asked, raising himself up on an elbow.

"Do what?" Lauren looked puzzled.

"You know . . . milk me."

"I didn't know that I did." Lauren looked embarrassed. "I couldn't help it. It just happened."

Flint gave her a crooked grin. "Do you think you could do it again?"

"I can try," Lauren said, and lifted her breasts to him.

As soon as his lips closed over a nipple, Lauren's sheath began to tighten, then release. This time he made sure Lauren found release too, and several long minutes later they were both moaning as they climbed the peak of ecstasy together. Later, Flint moved off Lauren, and pulling on his underclothing, helped her to get dressed in hers. The fire was still burning brightly, so he wrapped her in his arms and pulled the blankets up around their shoulders. It was mere seconds before they fell into an exhausted sleep.

Dud sat on the porch, sipping at his third cup of coffee. The snow had stopped during the night and he was sure Lauren would be coming home any minute. His eyes seldom left the trail that led to the Mahone ranch. When the storm had struck yesterday afternoon, he hadn't worried too much. Surely Kate would convince Lauren that it would be safer to spend the night there. But where was Lauren now?

"I'm not going to wait any longer," Dud grumbled, standing and carrying his cup inside the kitchen. He would ride down to the Mahone place and see to it that Lauren was safe.

He pulled jacket on and slapped his old hat on his head. "You can't go with me," he said to Wolf. "Stay in here by the fire." The dog wagged his tail as if he understood, and Dud added, "As if you want to go out anyway."

Dud ran toward the barn through the snow that had accumulated during the night. He saddled his horse, Jingle, and led him outside. The stallion snorted. He had no desire to leave the warm, dry barn. But when Dud touched him lightly with spurs, the stallion sprang away.

Twenty minutes later Kate spotted a determined figure galloping toward the house. A worried frown creased her forehead when she recognized Dud. Had something happened to Lauren on her way home?

She opened the door as Dud dismounted. "Dud," she called out. "Is anything wrong?"

"You tell me. Is Lauren still here with you?"

"No, she's not. She left yesterday during the storm. I thought she had plenty of time to get home before the snow got too deep."

"Is Flint home? Maybe he'll go with me to find her."

"I'm sorry, Dud, but he left early yesterday morning to hunt deer. I'm concerned about him too. Of course, he can take care of himself."

"I've got to get moving. God, only knows what's happened to her." Dud lifted Jingle's reins and nudged him to move out.

"As soon as Flint gets home I'll send him out to look for Lauren too," Kate called after Dud's retreating back.

Dud didn't stay long on the river road. He would not find Lauren there. He would have seen her before if she'd been on it. By hunch alone, he steered the stallion off the beaten way and entered the timberline on his left.

It was a little easier traveling. The thick pines had blocked much of the snow and it wasn't deep in there.

With his attention always on the ground, his pulse gave a leap when he spotted a ghost of a trail winding through a stand of bare aspen.

After a while, when the trees became more sparse, there would be spaces of several yards where the snow was windswept, leaving Dud no hint of what direction to take next. Dud had never felt so hopeless or helpless in his life. He had never before felt like sitting down and willing himself to die.

But Lauren was out there somewhere in that cold white hell, and dead or alive, he must find her. Jingle was plodding wearily now, but he responded to Dud's nudging him on the flanks.

A throbbing pain in his head awakened Flint. He gingerly touched his fingers to the bandage on the front part of his head. The events of the past twenty-four hours rushed back to him. Someone had tried to bushwhack him. Who and why? he wondered.

He remembered being lost and finally finding the gully where he had taken shelter and had been shot. He thought that perhaps he had been unconscious for some time for the next thing he remembered was seeing Lauren's face. She had bandaged his head and later crawled into bed with him to keep him warm.

A wide smile curved his lips. Man, oh, man, had she kept him warm.

What would her attitude be toward him now? he wondered with a crooked smile. Would she still hold herself aloof, look down her nose at him? Surely not. She had done none of those things last night as she lifted her slender body to receive each thrust of his hips.

But maybe she would be ashamed. Maybe she would prefer to pretend that nothing had happened. He frowned. What kind of attitude should he take with her? He had no experience dealing with virgins.

Flint decided he would follow her example. If she didn't acknowledge what had gone on between them, than he would act as though everything was the same as it had always been between them.

In case he had to do that, he thought, he'd best get out from under the covers and put his clothes on. After that he would attend to the horses, making enough noise to awaken her. She would be less embarrassed if he wasn't around when she woke up and found herself naked.

When Flint had pulled on his clothes and added wood to the fire, it struck him that there was no more wind and that the snow had stopped falling. He would have no trouble finding his way home now. He knew the area well. In fact, he now recognized the gully that he and Lauren had taken shelter in.

Lauren awakened to the sound of Flint talking to his mustang. She lay still a moment, wrestling with the confusion in her mind. Where was she? She turned over on her side, and her gaze fell on the campfire and the tarpaulin stretched over her head.

She began to remember: being lost in a blizzard, spotting Flint Mahone's fire. Someone had shot him in the head. She had done what she could for him, even getting into bed to warm him up.

This last remembrance made her aware of her naked state, and what that had led to. She felt her whole body go hot from embarrassment. What must Flint Mahone think of her?

She grasped at the hope that he might not

remember anything that had gone on between them. After all, he had a long bullet gash in his head. He could very well not remember any of it.

Lauren sat up and reached for her clothes. If he caught her naked, that could very well trigger a memory that might never occur otherwise.

She was sitting in front of the fire, combing her fingers through her tangled hair, when Flint walked up to the fire, leading the two horses. He slid her a fast, hooded look. "They seemed to have weathered the storm all right," he said.

"Yes, they look fine," Lauren agreed. "I imagine they are hungry, though. I sure am."

"Yeah, me too," Flint said. "Now that I can see the area, I recognize where we are. We'll be home in less than an hour."

Lauren averted her face to hide the disappointment that swept across it. If Flint did remember anything that had gone on between them last night, it hadn't meant much to him. She hadn't meant any more to him than the whores he visited in the pleasure house.

"I guess we'd better get going," Flint said. "We've got people plenty worried about us."

He was putting out the fire by pulling all the unburned sticks and shoving them into the ground when Dud came riding down the gully.

"I knew I'd find you two together." His hand went to the pistol at his waist.

"Now hold on, you old goat," Flint said angrily. "Don't start imagining things in that thick head of yours."

"Imagining? You think I'm imagining things? Tell me why it is that every time Lauren is missing I find her with you."

"Dud," Lauren said sharply, "it hasn't happened all that often. It was always coincidence when it did. If I hadn't stumbled onto his campfire last night, I would have frozen to death before morning."

"All right," Dud said grumpily. "Maybe I did jump the gun a little." He looked at Flint, but instead of apologizing to him he said in the same tone of voice he had been using, "Well, if you're going to show us the way home, let's get going. I'm sure Lauren is hungry and would like to get in bed and sleep the rest of the day."

Flint gave Lauren a sly look. "Are you sleepy, Lauren?" he asked.

Lauren gave him a suspicious look. Had she caught innuendo in his question? She couldn't be sure what he remembered of last night. After all, he had been out of his head, calling her Kate all the time.

She decided to give him the benefit of the doubt and answered with cool dignity, "Yes, I am."

Flint buried his head in his coat collar so that she wouldn't hear his chuckle of amusement.

"What happened to your head, Mahone?" Dud asked as they mounted up.

"Someone tried to dry-gulch me yesterday."

Flint turned the mustang around and headed him in the direction of his ranch.

They rode single file in silence for a few minutes, Flint leading, Lauren coming next, and Dud following her. Then Dud, being a garrulous fellow, called to Lauren, "Did Miss Kate learn you anything about cookin' vittles?"

"Yes, she did. You're going to be surprised."

"I hope you know how to make stew."

"I do. And I also know how to make bread."

"You want to stop by for supper tonight," Dud invited Flint, "try out Lauren's braggin'?"

Flint waited a moment for Lauren to echo the invitation.

When it didn't come he said, "Some other time. The youngsters will be expecting to eat with me."

"Yeah, I expect so," Dud said, and followed Lauren's horse when she reined him onto the fork that would take them home.

Chapter Eighteen

As Flint had claimed, three little people, flanked by Kate and Asher, stood on the porch waiting for him. As soon as he dismounted, Mercy flew into his arms. The boys were right behind her, picking at his sleeve for attention. Although Kate frowned at the bandage around his head, it was Asher who asked, "What happened to your head?"

"Some idiot shot at me a couple times." Flint handed the mustang's reins over to a young stable boy who had appeared.

"Are you shot bad? Should you go to the doctor in town?" Kate asked anxiously.

Flint shook his head. "It's just a crease. Parted

my hair a little and gave me one hell of a headache for a while."

"I don't suppose you know who shot you?"
Asher walked along beside Flint as they went
into the house.

"Naw. He was shooting at me in the middle
of a heavy blizzard. I couldn't see more than a
couple yards ahead of me."

"Who bandaged your head?" Kate asked,
leading the way into the kitchen.

Flint wished that Asher wasn't here. He'd ask
all kinds of questions when he heard that Lauren had found him, make sly remarks.

And Flint didn't want anything of a deroga-
tory nature said about Lauren spending the
night with him. He felt that their lovemaking
had been almost spiritual.

He set Mercy on her feet, and without any
hesitation said, "An old Indian found me and
tied this cloth around my head. He built a fire
in a gully and that's where I slept. He was gone
when I woke up this morning."

"As soon as you have something to eat, I'll
take a look at your head," Kate said as she
started several strips of bacon to frying.

Asher filled a cup with coffee for Flint, then
refreshed his own cup. "How about going into
town tonight and raising a little hell?" he suggested, sitting down across from Flint.

Flint's first instinct was to refuse the invitation. After making love to Lauren he had no desire even to look at another woman. But Lauren

did not seem to share his realization that something extraordinary had happened between them.

On second thought Flint wondered if perhaps it would be a good idea to go into town. A night out with the boys would distract him from thinking about the enigmatic Miss Hart. And maybe being around the whores would bring him to his senses. With such women you never had to worry how they felt about you. You never had to be careful how you talked, what you said, how coarsely you spoke in front of them.

He looked at Asher and grinned. "That's not a bad idea. I'm going to go easy on the drinking, though, and I don't want to get into any fights."

"I can understand that," Asher said; then a devilish grin spread across his handsome face. "And don't forget to let your bed partner do all the work."

Both men blushed and Asher let out a sharp cry as Kate whacked him on the back of the head. "From now on you two idiots look around before you start mouthing off. We don't live here alone anymore."

"We forgot, Kate," Flint said as Kate slapped eggs and bacon in front of him. "It won't happen again."

"What won't happen again, Uncle Flint?" Tommy asked.

"Uncle Asher and I forgot to buy sugar for

Kate. We'll be riding into town later to pick some up."

At the look of disappointment that spread over the children's faces, he explained, "We probably won't be going until it's time for you youngsters to go to bed."

Relief washed over the children's faces, but when Flint glanced at Kate, there was disappointment as well as disapproval on her face. He turned even redder and looked away from her. She knew why he and Asher were going into Jackson Hole.

I'm damned if I'll feel guilty, Flint thought, straightening his shoulders and refilling his coffee cup. I just want to have a night out with my friends.

Sighing heavily, Kate pushed her chair away from the table and entered her room, which was right off the kitchen.

"What's wrong with Kate?" Asher asked. "She looks put out about something."

"Dammed if I know, but she's got something in her craw."

"Maybe it's a woman thing," Asher said solemnly.

"What's a woman thing?" Henry asked.

"Dammed if I know, kid. I've just heard that excuse given for women's strange ways."

Flint didn't say anything about Asher's explanation, only rolled his eyes at the ceiling.

When Asher had no luck engaging Flint in conversation, he griped, "I'm going back to the ranch now to talk to a fence post. I'll be back after supper and I hope that by then you'll be in a more talkative mood."

"Sorry, Ash, but I got something of a headache. I'm gonna take a nap after Kate changes the bandage on my head."

When Asher left, Flint knocked softly on Kate's door. "Kate, I've finished eating breakfast. You can change the dressing on my wound now, if you want to."

Kate walked back into the kitchen carrying a flat, tin box that she always kept handy. It held various salves, antiseptics, a small bottle of laudanum, needles and catgut thread, and strips of clean white cloth. Flint had seen the box many times before.

She poured warm water from a big black tea kettle into a basin and dropped a cloth into it. Then, with the children watching, she began to unwrap the cloth from around Flint's wound. As she peeled the dressing away she wondered where an old Indian would have gotten such fine material. She came to the conclusion that she hadn't heard the real story of who had taken care of Flint's head and who had tended him through the night. She sighed inwardly. She probably never would get the whole truth of it.

"Did you happen to see Lauren Hart or Dud on your way home?" she asked. "She was missing last night too, and Dud was real worried this morning."

"He found her," Flint replied uncomfortably.

"I saw them heading toward their ranch."

Hoping to escape further questioning, Flint went to his room, stretched out on his bed, and slept until darkness settled in and Asher was shaking him awake.

"Come on, man, let's get going."

Flint was sorry he had agreed to go to town with Asher. He didn't feel like getting drunk, and he didn't plan to end up in bed with one of the whores. But when you promised Asher something, he never let up on you until you kept your word.

Flint crawled out of bed, got dressed in clean clothes, then shaved and combed his hair. "Come on, you wild coyote, let's go," he said, slapping his hat on his head.

As they left the house and walked to the barn, Flint was thankful the children were in bed. He wouldn't have to see them watching him with their big sad eyes.

As Flint and Asher rode at a trot, the forest was still and lonely. There was the sharp tang of spruce and pine. They tucked their chins into the collars of their mackinaws as a cold wind came down the slopes of the mountains.

The wind seemed to have followed them as they entered the single street of Jackson Hole. A pale lemon-colored moon made the town of false-fronted buildings look all the more weather-beaten, like the face of an old man or woman, trying to hang on to a life that really wasn't worth the effort.

The wavering lights came from three places of business: the Trail's End Saloon, the cafe, and Maudie's House of Pleasure.

Maudie's light, shining through the red chimney of the lantern that hung over the door, didn't do much to show a customer the way to her door. The other two businesses didn't help much either. The repeated shoveling of snow from the boardwalk in front of their establishments had left piles higher than a man's head in some places. And the street was mostly fetlock-deep in mud and dirty, trampled snow.

Flint cursed himself as a damn fool for listening to Asher. He was cold, his head was hurting again, and he had no desire to bed one of Maudie's whores.

Flint heaved a sigh of relief when Asher, leading the way, rode past Maudie's place and continued on to the saloon. Maybe his friend didn't desire a woman tonight.

But when Asher turned down an alley that led to the livery, Flint knew that had been a foolish thought. Asher wanted to make a night of it in Jackson Hole. Probably he planned to spend most of the time at Maudie's place of business.

A boy in his teens came from a small room in back of the place, and Flint and Asher handed over their horses along with a good-sized tip and the order to cover the animals with a heavy blanket.

The young man would have done this without an order. Flint Mahone was his idol.

As Flint stepped from the cold to the warmth of the saloon, his eyes watered. He paused a moment just inside the door, wiping away the tears so that he could see. Now that he'd been shot, he was more careful about walking into a place where a gun might be pulled on him by a stranger. Or someone he knew and had always thought of as a friend.

But there were only three men at the bar, older men that he had known all his life. They gave him and Asher a friendly smile, asked if it was cold enough for them, then returned to whatever conversation they were having.

"What happened to your head?" Hank Jones asked as he poured Flint a glass of whiskey.

"Some bastard is out to kill me, Hank." Flint took a swallow of his drink. "Whoever he is, he took a couple shots at me last night. He missed twice, but the last one gave me a gash across the head, just above my ear."

"Do you have any idea who it is? White or Indian?"

"No." Flint shook his head. "I've racked my brain and I can't come up with anybody who would hate me so much he'd want to kill me."

"Well, one thing's for sure." Hank laughed and wiped at the bar with a cloth that didn't look too clean. "It's no husband who is after you. I give you credit for staying away from married women. Especially since you could have most any one of them you wanted."

"Another man's wife never appealed to me,"

Flint lied. After all, he couldn't very well admit to his affair with Ruth Spencer.

"What about you, Asher?" Hank grinned at the tall, lean cowpuncher.

Asher shook his head. "Not this old cowboy," he said. But from the way he blushed, Hank and Flint knew he was lying. The bartender suspected that Asher had fooled around, and Flint knew for a fact that his friend had visited a lot of wives when their husbands were at work. A little light went on in his head. He'd bet anything that Asher was the man Ruth Spencer was sleeping with these days.

Before Flint and Hank could rag him more about wives, Asher finished his drink and said as he set the glass down, "Come on, Flint, let's go visit Ole Maudie for a while."

"Yeah," Hank said solemnly, "I imagine all the wives are in bed with their husbands by now."

"Why don't you go to hell, Hank!" Asher headed for the door, buttoning his jacket as he stomped away.

Flint grinned and winked at the bartender before he followed his friend.

As Asher knocked on the door of the pleasure house, Flint said to him, "Asher, my head is hurting pretty bad. I'm going home."

"Aw, come on, Flint. You don't want to do that," Asher argued. "Take one of the women to bed. She'll take care of your headache."

"Hah!" Flint snorted. "A woman would only make it hurt worse."

As they exchanged words, the door opened and a half-dressed young woman stepped outside and stood under the red light. It was Tillie, the girl Flint usually asked for. "What are you two doing, standing out here in the cold?" she asked.

"Flint wants to go home, and I'm not ready yet," Asher replied.

Tillie gave Asher a push toward the door. "You go on in and pick yourself a companion for the night," she said. "I'll convince Flint to stay."

Then she turned to Flint and batted her lashes up at him. Before Flint knew what she was up to, she grabbed his hand and plunged it inside her low-cut neckline.

"What in the hell do you think you're doing?" Flint tried to extract his hand without hurting her. "I hear a buggy coming down the street. Whoever is in it is going to see everything."

"I don't care." The woman laughed louder and longer.

"Well, dammit, I care." Flint finally managed to pull his hand away from her breast. As he flung her grasping fingers away in disgust, the buggy wheeled past, leaving him staring after it in dismay.

Colly King handled the reins of the high-stepping filly and Lauren Hart sat beside him.

Flint flinched at the contemptuous look she gave him.

Tillie laughed again. "Don't tell me you're sweet on Lauren Hart?"

"Tell Asher that I've gone home," he said grimly, refusing to answer her. Stepping off the small porch, he walked toward the livery stable.

Chapter Nineteen

Lauren sighed in vexation as she had to walk around Dud yet again. It seemed as if every time she turned around he was in her way.

She knew he was doing it on purpose. She had risen from bed when first light was just coming over the mountains. As soon as she had built up the fire in the fireplace and started one in the kitchen stove, he had come out of his bedroom. She had been surprised at that. What was he doing up at this early hour? Ever since they had taken possession of the ranch, he had slept late, claiming there was no reason to get out of bed before the sun was fully up.

As she turned strips of breaded salt pork in

the cast-iron skillet, Lauren was thinking of different things she could have said to him about that. He could feed the dozen or more hens and one rooster that had come out of the woods a day after she and Dud had settled in. And it would be a big help if he would gather the eggs some of them were laying. She was half afraid of the fussy old hens. They pecked her hands with their hard old beaks when she attempted to take their eggs. Then there was the milch cow who showed up one morning, now tied fast to a stall in the barn.

But of course it was beneath Dud to milk her. She'd had to ask her new friend, Janice Summers, how to milk the little Jersey, which she called Daisy. Daisy's rich milk was highly appreciated. Kate had taught her how to churn butter from the thick yellow cream she skimmed off the milk. And the chickens fought over the milk that she and Dud didn't consume in a day.

No, she thought, today Dud was up to needle her about going into Jackson Hole to help her Aunt Lillie put up the stock in her new dress shop.

Lauren wondered, as she had many times, what exactly was the reason that Dud and her aunt didn't get along together. She had asked both of them, at seperate times, why they disliked each other so.

Dud answered that he didn't want to talk

about it, and that as far as he was concerned that was the end of it.

But what did Dud have against Colly? she asked herself as she placed meat and eggs on the table. He didn't even know Lillie's stepson, but still he treated him coolly, saying very little to him.

She hoped Dud wouldn't be his usual crabby self toward Colly when he came to drive her to town in a rented buggy, Lauren thought as she took the coffeepot from the stove and set it on the table.

When Lauren called that breakfast was ready, Dud came clumping to the table. He took his usual seat at the head of the table and reached for a slice of sourdough. Lauren looked at his face and sighed. His features were cold and stony. She decided that if he didn't speak first, it would be a silent breakfast. She was tired of coaxing him out of his snits. He might as well get used to the idea that Aunt Lillie was going to be a part of her life.

Only the sound of flatware clicking against plates broke the silence as Lauren and Dud ate their breakfast. Lauren was filling their cups with coffee the second time when Dud cleared his voice and growled, "When is that greenhorn Colly King coming after you?"

"Somewhere between ten and eleven."

"Why are you up so early?" Dud asked spooning sugar into his coffee.

"Because I have things to do around here before I can leave. I have to feed the chickens, milk Daisy, and tend to the horses. I'm sure the water in their pails is frozen solid by now."

When Dud didn't offer to see to any of the animals, Lauren didn't continue with the rest of the things she had to do. Dud would think those chores were foolish.

But she had learned from visiting Janice and Kate that keeping one's home neat and clean was very satisfactory and enjoyable. The once-grimy windows that the sun could hardly penetrate now sparkled, shining brightly on the floors she scrubbed at least once a week. The kitchen floor was scrubbed every evening when she was sure Dud wouldn't be tracking any more mud in until the next day.

Dud did make a halfhearted effort to wipe his feet on the rug she had placed in front of the kitchen door, she thought with a half smile. And if she was to be honest, Wolf tracked in as much mud as Dud did.

"I don't know why I couldn't drive you to town," Dud said, breaking in on Lauren's thoughts.

"For one thing it's cold, bouncing around in that wagon, and besides that, you'd want to leave after an hour."

"Hell's bells, how long do you plan on staying?" Dud's voice rose.

"I'll be there several hours. There's a lot of work stocking shelves, hanging up dresses and bonnets, and putting ladies' fancies away."

"What in the hell is ladies' fancies?" Dud demanded.

"You know, women's underwear."

"Why don't you call them what they are? Bloomers and petticoats."

"Fancy ladies don't call the silks and satins by those names."

"What a bunch of hogwash," Dud snorted peevishly. "You'll be tellin' me next that you want to wear such frippery."

Mischief sparked in Lauren's eyes. "I've been thinking about it."

Dud slammed his empty cup back into its saucer, grabbed up his jacket from the hook beside the door, and stomped outside.

Lauren grinned and sipped her coffee. He wouldn't be gone long. It was too cold out there.

Her thoughts went back to ladies' lingerie. How would it feel to have silk and satin underclothing next to her skin? She had never worn anything except rough muslin petticoats and plain bloomers.

She sighed and, standing, began to gather up the dishes she and Dud had used. By the time she tended her livestock and swept the floors, dusted and polished the furniture, it would be time for Colly to come fetch her.

She liked Colly well enough. He was pleasant and very handsome, Lauren thought as she stacked the plates and cups and saucers into the dishpan in the sink, but it made her nervous the way he looked at her sometimes. It wasn't the kind of look a man should give to a female related to him.

Actually, they weren't kin, she reminded herself as she lifted a tea kettle from the stove and poured its hot contents over the dirty dishes. He was Aunt Lillie's stepson. There would be nothing wrong if he wanted to court her.

But Colly didn't interest her in the least. She dropped a bar of lye soap into the dishwater. Her hands paused as she ran a dishcloth over a plate. Flint Mahone had entered her mind. She tried to push him away, but he stubbornly remained.

He is so handsome, she thought. And so wild. Just the other night she'd seen him in town with one of the girls from the pleasure house. Apparently, their lovemaking had meant nothing to him, for he'd run right into the arms of another woman.

Could a woman ever tame him . . . a wife? she wondered bitterly. Their time together had been heaven to her. But Flint had made no move to court her since. Either he didn't remember, or he simply didn't care.

Lauren gave a bleak sigh. Stop daydreaming, you foolish woman, she thought. It was doubtful Flint Mahone would ever settle down with one woman. And if by some miracle he did, it wouldn't be with a woman like herself. It would be one with wealth equal to his own. He would never tie himself to the ragtag daughter of an outlaw who had been shot down by a posse.

The old clock on the mantel, the only item she and Dud had brought with them when they ran from the law, struck nine. She rinsed the plate and picked up another one. Colly would be here soon.

The clock had been in the family for as long as Lauren could remember. It was the only thing of importance they owned. It had been her mother's, passed down to her by *her* mother. Every time they'd had to run from the law the clock had gone with them. It had been such a comfort to her to hear its familar striking when they settled into a new hideout.

Lauren had the four rooms swept, the furniture dusted, and the kitchen put to rights and was waiting for Colly when the clock struck ten. Ten minutes later Colly was driving a rented buggy up to the cabin. She pulled on her new jacket, tied a scarf around her head and neck, and rushed outside. She wanted to leave before Dud came in from the barn. She was afraid he might say something to Colly that would hurt his feelings.

"I understand there's going to be a dance at the town hall this Saturday," Colly said as the buggy wheels whirred along. "Will you attend it with me?"

Lauren was so surprised by Colly's invitation, she couldn't answer him for a full fifteen seconds. She had never been to a dance before. She wouldn't know how to act, how to talk with anyone who might strike up a conversation with her. And she didn't have a fancy dress to wear either.

The only thing in her favor was that she could dance. Her father and the outlaws who lived with them had taught her many different steps. She knew mountain dances, the Scottish fling, not to mention the Irish jig.

But the last two couldn't be danced in Western boots.

"Well," Colly urged, "what is your answer?"

"Thanks, but I don't think so, Colly. I don't think Dud would want me to." She knew that Dud wouldn't want her to go with Colly, but she also knew that if she had wanted to go, her old friend's wishes wouldn't make any difference.

"Why do you have to listen to that cantankerous old goat?" Colly asked irritably. "He can't keep you to himself forever. He's got to know that someday you're going to get married and leave him."

His words and tone regarding Dud didn't sit at all well with Lauren. She loved the gruff old fellow with all her heart. Although she might get aggravated with him sometimes and say unkind things, she didn't want anyone else doing it.

When she made no response to Colly's outburst, he knew he had said too much, and so he tempered his words and voice when he spoke again. "Your Aunt Lillie is really hoping that you will attend the dance and then stay all night with her when it's over. She's already put aside one of the shop's new dresses for you to wear."

Colly took her hand, and squeezing it gently, urged softly, "Please say you'll come to the dance with me."

The thought of a fancy dress was very enticing. It would be her first one, and she had never before danced to any musical instruments other than a Jew's harp and spoons being struck together for rhythm.

She decided that maybe she would go to the dance, but she knew Dud would raise the devil if she tried to spend the night with Aunt Lillie.

A tiny frown creased her forehead. What if Dud decided to drive her to the dance himself? She cringed at the thought of him sitting on the sidelines, keeping an eagle eye on any young man who asked her to dance. She would be embarrassed to death.

Lauren became aware that Colly was waiting for her answer. "Thank you for the invitation, Colly," she said gently. "I'll try to convince Dud to let me go with you."

"Has someone else already asked you?" There was an undertone of jealously in Colly's voice.

Lauren smiled thinly. "Now who would be asking me to a dance? I haven't been here long enough to get acquainted with any men."

"There's that rough Flint Mahone. He's always eyeing you. And so is his rowdy friend, Asher Davis. He'd kill to take you dancing."

At first Lauren wanted to laugh at Colly's ridiculous idea of Flint Mahone taking her dancing. Then she became angry that Colly thought she would be willing to go anywhere with that whoremonger.

"I should punch you in the nose, Colly King, for even suggesting that I would go anywhere with either one of those men," she snapped angrily.

"Well, you'd be the only female within fifty miles of Jackson Hole who wouldn't. The women around here are loco about Mahone."

"Don't they know what kind of women he prefers? Every time I see him it seems he's in a compromising position with a prostitute."

Colly turned his head so that Lauren wouldn't see his tickled grin. "I shouldn't be taking up for him," he said finally, "but he is single and he probably wants to stay that way for a while. If he only dallied with nice girls, their fathers would be after him to get married. He's safe from that if he sticks to whores."

Lauren's response to that statement was an indifferent shrug of her shoulders. It was just a male taking up for a male.

They rode on for a minute; then Colly asked impatiently, "Why wouldn't Dud let you go with me?"

"I'll just have to ask him, won't I?" Lauren decided that if Dud's arguments made sense, then she would do as he wished. If he was only being ornery because he didn't like Aunt Lillie, she would go with Colly. It was out of the question, of course, that she would sleep over at her aunt's house. Colly would have to be prepared to drive her home after the festivities.

The weathered buildings of Jackson Hole loomed ahead, and the subject was dropped. When the buggy rolled to a stop in front of Lillie's Dress Shop, Lauren was impressed by what her aunt had done to the building. It had never had a coat of paint applied to it, but the years of winter blizzards and summer storms had turned the boards a silvery gray. It boasted a big plate-glass window in which, Lauren imagined, dresses and bonnets would be displayed.

Lillie welcomed her with a kiss and a hug. Inside, everything seemed a shambles. Boxes were strewn all over the floor, some large, some small. The long glass counter had its share of unpacked merchandise also.

"Colly," Lillie ordered, "take the horse and buggy back to the livery, then come back here and open these boxes for me. And go to the mercantile and buy a hammer and some nails. I need some racks put up and a few more shelves."

When Colly left, grumbling to himself, Lillie gave Lauren a wide smile and said, "While we wait for Colly to return, come into the back and see my living quarters."

There were two rooms, each a good size. Lauren was awestruck by the grandeur and luxury of the bedroom and parlor. Where had her aunt found such fancy furniture, such a lovely bedspread and pillows, such beautiful lamps, in the small town of Jackson Hole?

"Everything is beautiful, Aunt Lillie," she exclaimed when they had finished touring the living quarters and were sitting on a satin-covered sofa of blue damask. "I am surprised that you found all these lovely things in this rough hole of a town."

Lilly's merry laughter rang out. "I'm sure they could not be found here," she said. "I brought all my finery with me. It traveled here by wagon train. It arrived day before yesterday. I found a young couple who wanted to come west and homestead. They didn't have the money to purchase a wagon and outfit it for the long trek. I struck a deal with them. I would provide the wagon and supplies and they would bring my furniture to me.

"They are a nice, honest couple so I gave them the wagon and two horses."

"That was awfully sweet of you, Aunt Lillie."

Lilly shrugged. "What was I going to do with a wagon and two horses?"

Lauren started to say, "You could have sold them," but didn't. Her father, Lilly's brother, would have done the same thing. And maybe she would be the same if she ever had anything to give away.

"Did I tell you that they also brought along our riding horses? I have a pretty little mare and Colly has a splendid roan stallion."

Lauren was anxious to talk more about horses, but just then Colly arrived.

There wasn't much time for conversation after Colly opened the boxes, then started hammering and sawing, constructing dress racks and shelves for fancy underwear and gowns.

As Lauren handled the silks and satins, she vowed that someday she would own a camisole and a pair of pantaloons of such smooth material. They wouldn't be for everyday wear, just for when she went to town. It would be wonderful, she thought, if she could wear something like that when she went to the dance Saturday night.

She sighed, thinking how unlikely that would be.

The sun was high overhead when Lillie took off her duster and said, "I don't know about you two, but I'm hungry for some lunch. Let's get a bite to eat at the cafe."

"Sounds good to me." Colly pulled on his heavy jacket, then helped Lauren into hers. When he had helped Lillie on with her coat, he followed them outside. They waited while he locked the shop door.

He grinned at Lillie and said, "Maudie's girls have been walking up and down the boardwalk eyeing the dresses and bonnets in the window. They would rob you blind if they could get in here alone."

When they entered the cafe, Lauren immediately felt ill at ease. Unlike her previous visits, there were a number of women there today. They were all neatly dressed in woolen skirts and starched blouses. There were mothers and daughters, and girls in their teens together, having lunch. She must look a fright in her worn denims and down-at-the-heels boots. She hadn't worn her new boots and pants because she had figured that she would only be in the shop helping to put stock away.

A few minutes later, after they had been seated at a table by a friendly waitress, Lauren felt better. A rancher had entered the eatery, along with his wife and four daughters. The females didn't look at all stylish in their drab skirts and cotton blouses. But their appearance didn't seem to bother them in the least.

And surprisingly, many of the other customers smiled and greeted them warmly. She noted that the girls weren't exceptionally pretty, but their sunny smiles and genial greetings made them very attractive.

Lauren noticed then how the cowboys in the cafe smiled and made eyes at the young ladies, and how they flirted back. She wondered for a moment why the young men weren't giving her any attention. She happened then to look at Colly.

No wonder they are not flirting with me, she thought, seeing the threatening look in Colly's eyes, the way his fists were clenched. She felt like sticking her foot out under the table and kicking him hard in the ankle. Why did he think he had the right to scowl at any man who looked at her? She was quite capable of doing that herself.

The waitress came to take their order. They each ordered a bowl of chili. When the young woman had left them, Lauren said, "She is very pretty, isn't she, Colly?"

"Is she? I never noticed," Colly answered, smoothing his mustache, something he did often, Lauren had noticed.

"The hell you didn't," Lauren said coolly, making her aunt and Colly look at her in surprise. She had never sworn in front of them before.

Colly's face grew red and he squirmed in his chair. Lillie threw back her head and let out a loud burst of laughter. The girl had some of her aunt in her after all.

"Look," Lauren said, "I don't care how many women you look at, but you extend me the same freedom. I don't want you giving threatening looks to every man who glances my way."

"I'm not aware that I gave anybody threatening looks," Colly muttered.

His denial was greeted with hoots of laughter from Lauren and Lillie.

"Every man in here knows better than that," Lillie said. "Now keep your looks to yourself before they all gang up on you and mess up your pretty face."

A pouty, sullen look came over Colly's face, and when their chili was served, he gave it all his attention. Lauren and Lillie grinned at each other, then ignored him as they began talking about the dress shop.

By the time they had finished their lunch, Colly had decided that his long face wasn't having any effect on his female companions. As they drank their coffee he became his usual genial self, acting as though he hadn't made an ass of himself. He pretended not to see the covert looks the men kept sliding at Lauren. When Colly finished smoking his cigarette, one he had rolled in the brown tobacco paper he preferred, they returned to the shop. There they worked until the last of the twilight had faded into darkness.

"What do you think, Lauren and Colly, does the shop look grand?" Lillie asked as she fussed with one of her bonnet creations.

"It's lovely, Aunt Lillie." Lauren turned slowly around, taking in the rows of evening gowns and day dresses and walking suits, the bonnets and and shelves of fancy shoes and boots. Her gaze rested finally on the glass counter that held scarves and fine leather gloves, as well as white ones for summer. There were also purses of all sizes and colors, and a selection of beads, rings, and pins.

Lauren thought of the women she had met, and knew that they could never afford to buy such splendid-looking clothing. "Aunt Lillie, do you think the women of Jackson Hole will buy your lovely things?"

A bit of sadness entered Lilly's voice when she answered, "Jackson Hole's women won't be buying much, but the wives and daughters of the area's wealthy ranchers will be in for the dance. They'll be fighting over my gowns and bonnets."

Lauren didn't argue. She knew nothing about wealthy women, probably never would.

"What do you say we go home," Lillie said. "I'm tired and hungry and I need a bath."

"I'm more than ready to leave," Colly said, "What about you, Lauren?"

Lauren nodded. "Dud will be raising Cain about now, wanting his supper."

"That old rascal can cook," Lillie grumbled. "Let him cook his supper."

Lauren smiled proudly before saying, "I'm a fair cook these days, Aunt Lillie. He likes my cooking now."

"Who taught you, honey?" Lillie asked.

"Kate Allen, Flint Mahone's housekeeper."

A suspicious scowl came over Colly's face. "Does she come to your place, or do you go to the Mahone ranch?"

"Mostly she comes to my place. She's an awfully nice woman. You would like her, Aunt Lillie."

"I'm sure I would. I would like to meet her sometime."

"Now, you know you wouldn't have anything in common with a housekeeper," Colly declared.

Lauren was ready to fly at him, but Lillie beat her to it. Her eyes shooting sparks, she threw her stepson a deprecatory look and said icily, "Before I met your father and we made money with the saloon, my closest friends were housekeepers, cooks, waitresses, and even a couple prostitutes.

"They were all honest, hardworking women who would give a friend their last dime if the man or woman needed it. I wouldn't trade one of them for all the so-called ladies in Jackson Hole."

Running out of breath, Lillie said quietly, "Bring the buggy around, Colly, while Lauren and I get our coats on."

"Yes, ma'am," Colly answered in a small voice, properly chastised, and quietly closed the door behind him when he left the shop.

When Lauren and Lillie had pulled on their wraps, Lauren closed the damper on the fancy little wood stove and Lillie lowered the wick in the equally fancy lamp, then blew out the flame.

As they waited inside for Colly to arrive with the buggy, Lillie asked, "Will you be coming to the dance with Colly Saturday night?"

"Yes, if Dud allows it, but I can't stay all night with you. As much as I would like to, I'm afraid Dud would throw a fit."

Lillie laughed softly. "He would indeed. I want Colly to bring you here before you go to the dance. I have a dress I would like for you to wear."

"Thank you very much, Aunt Lillie. I imagine you know that I don't have any fancy duds."

"Dear girl—" Lillie stroked a finger down Lauren's cheek—"one so beautiful as you has no need of fancy clothes. But every young lady craves them, and you shall have them too."

With wet eyes Lauren started to thank her aunt; then Colly pulled up in front of the shop. The lighted lantern hanging from the roof of the vehicle illuminated the vapor streaming from the horse's nostrils.

Colly jumped to the ground and helped first Lauren, then Lillie into the lightweight buggy. When he had wrapped lap blankets around them, he hopped back into the vehicle and picked up the reins.

It took but a couple minutes to arrive at the hotel and help Lillie onto the boardwalk. "Don't linger coming home," she ordered Colly. "It's too cold for the horse to stand around."

"I'll send him straight home, Aunt Lillie," Lauren called as the little mare began to trot down the frozen street.

The air was brisk, the stars just coming out in the clear sky. Lauren tucked her chin into her scarf and sighed softly. She had enjoyed the time spent with Aunt Lillie. She had never before spent time with women, conversed with them. And Aunt Lillie had such a sense of humor. Lauren hadn't laughed so much in a long time.

When the buggy pulled up in front of the

ranch house, Colly swore under his breath. Dud sat in one of the chairs, obviously waiting for Lauren to come home. There would be no time for him and Lauren to have a little chat, maybe do a little hand-holding. The old man didn't like him.

Dud came down the porch steps, the dog, Wolf, right behind him. "It's about time you got home," he griped. "Me and the dog was gettin' ready to come lookin' for you."

When he raised his hands to help her down, Lauren said, "It's not late, Dud."

"It's plenty late to be out in a freezing night like this," he retorted, taking her by the arm and hurrying her up the porch steps. Lauren barely had time to call "Good night" to Colly.

As soon as they got into the house Lauren spun around, anger sparking her eyes. "Why were you so rude to Colly?" she asked as she took off her mackinaw. "He's a very nice man. He's polite and very kind to Aunt Lillie. He's nothing like that Flint Mahone you're so fond of. He's a real gentleman."

"Gentleman, my butt," Dud snapped, picking up a poker and jabbing at the fire in the fireplace. "He's not a gentleman at all. He's just a good pretender. He don't meet a feller's eyes when he's talkin' to him.

"As for my liking Mahone, I know he's hard-bitten and tough, but there's nothing false about him. What you see is what he is."

Dud studied Lauren with old and wise eyes.

"Don't you like Mahone a little bit? I bet he likes you."

"Hah!" Lauren snorted. "I hope not, for I have no time for womanizers."

"What if I told you Colly King visits the whorehouse every night? The only difference between him and Flint is that Colly sneaks in the back way."

Lauren gave Dud a hard look, then said sharply, "I wouldn't believe it." She left the room with her boot heels clicking sharply on the floor.

"You ever try to marry that four-flusher and I'll shoot him," he ground out.

Chapter Twenty

Colly hurried the livery horse along, the buggy bumping over the frozen ridges in the dirt road. His unsuccessful visit with Lauren had started a throbbing in his loins. He wanted to get back to Maudie's Pleasure House to hire a whore for the night.

Colly scowled into the night and brought the short whip down on the mare's rump, urging her to go faster. Tillie, his favorite whore, never welcomed him with open arms. She complained that he was too rough, that he demanded things she wasn't willing to do.

A wolfish smile bared his teeth. Tillie had a child to support; though she was reluctant, she did everything he demanded of her because he paid her well to do it.

In just a short time Colly turned the livery horse and buggy over to the kid in his teens who stepped out of the long, low building. If only things had gone better with Lauren, he was thinking. If only Mahone wasn't sniffing after her too.

Flint was riding home with supper on his mind. He'd been out on the range all day, making repairs to his line shacks. He was passing just below the summit of a ridge when a bullet struck the snow a couple feet in front of him. He swung Shadow behind a large pine and watched the stallion, for its senses were keener than his. He drew his Colt and waited.

Five minutes went by and all was quiet. Shadow's ears settled down, leaving Flint to think that whoever had taken a shot at him had traveled on.

He lifted the reins. He was only about ten minutes from home. He kicked the stallion into a hard gallop. Somebody wanted him dead, and he couldn't imagine who it could be.

Morning came over the mountains, bringing a pale light to the eastern sky. Flint lay quietly, in no hurry to leave the warm nest of the feather bed. His thoughts were on the man who had bushwhacked him. As he had done so often, he racked his brain for someone who would want him dead. As usual no one came to mind.

He decided that after he had breakfast and spent some time with the children, he would go to the spot where he had been shot at. Maybe he could find some kind of evidence that would lead him to the shooter.

Kate decided that it was too cold for the children, especially Mercy, to make the short trip to the cookhouse, so she would make breakfast for the family.

"I suppose you're going to the dance tomorrow night," she asked Flint as she stirred up a bowl of pancake batter.

"Yeah, I can't disappoint the ladies," Flint grinned, taking a long swallow of the coffee Kate had poured him.

"Can we come too?" the boys chorused while Mercy looked hopefully at him.

"I don't know." Flint looked serious. "Can you boys dance?"

"I can!" Henry exclaimed.

"You cannot," Tommy declared. "All you do is jump up and down like a toy monkey on a stick."

When the heated argument that followed looked like it might lead to fisticuffs, Flint interrupted the pair by saying, "Don't waste your breath arguing, boys. You'll be in bed by the time I leave for the dance. In the meantime, while you're getting older, maybe you can talk Kate into teaching you how to dance. She taught me and your father."

"Was our pa a good dancer?" Henry wanted to know.

Flint realized the boys were hungry to hear about their father.

"Yes, he was, Henry. One of these nights when it's too cold to do anything but sit in front of the fire, I'll tell you all about your father. It will be a long story and I don't want to be hurried through it."

When Flint finished eating, he looked at Kate and said, "A fellow was shot at again last night." He waited for her to figure out that he was talking about himself. When she nodded her understanding, he added, "I'm going to mosey out to that patch of pines and look for cows."

Kate nodded again that she understood where he was going and why. He would not be looking for cows.

"You be careful." A worried frown creased her forehead. "Some of those old bulls are meaner than sidewinders."

"I'll be careful," Flint said, then looking at his nephews, warned, "When I get back I don't want to hear that you two have been fighting. Your father and I never fought." His last words made Kate turn her head so the kids wouldn't see her laughing. Flint and Jake had fought like cougar cubs.

Along the hillsides and the mountain draws the aspens had lost their leaves. Nothing stopped the cold wind that whipped through the trunks, giving their full force to Flint. He was chilled when he came to the spot where he'd been shot at the night before.

He swung out of the saddle and, leaving Shadow ground-hitched, began a slow tour of the ground, his eyes searching closely for anything that would help him find the man who was out to kill him.

He had half come to the conclusion that a renegade Indian was shooting at him, though he couldn't remember ever having harsh words with one.

But Flint knew it was no Indian when he discovered the pine where the gunman had waited to shoot him. The tracks there were revealing. An Indian mounted from the left side and a white man from the right. So who was the white bastard who wanted him dead?

As he reined Shadow around and headed back toward the ranch, he went through every male he knew, from kids in their teens to old men who couldn't sit a horse anymore. It was worrisome being the target of some gun-happy man. It was also disturbing to think that any man of his acquaintance held such antipathy toward him. He mostly liked the folks he knew, and had until now thought that they liked him also.

The ranch house came in sight, and Flint pushed the shooting out of his mind and began to think of the dance coming up tomorrow night. Would Lauren be there? he wondered. If she was, and he asked her to dance, would she let him hold her in his arms again, or would she give him a contemptuous look and turn her back on him?

She would probably come with that Colly King, her aunt's stepson. The man was handsome, and it was plain by his actions that he knew how to treat a lady. Flint had seen how he helped Lauren into the small buggy, helped her to mount her horse. Of course he could do those things too, if he made himself remember. He just wasn't used to being a gentleman. A man didn't have to mind his manners when associating with whores. Those women didn't expect it of him.

But against his will he was so attracted to the cold beauty, he wanted to show her that when it came to being a gentleman, he could outdo the handsome Colly.

Flint wondered if King showed the whores he visited the same respect he showed Lauren and his stepmother. As he stripped the gear off Shadow, he decided that the next time he was in town he would question the girls about King's treatment of them.

The corners of Flint's lips twisted in a grin as he walked up to the house. His friend Asher Davis's horse stood at the hitching post at the end of the porch. If he was not mistaken, he would be seeing Maudie's girls sooner than he'd expected. He felt sure Asher would suggest a trip to the pleasure house.

When he opened the kitchen door and the

children came running from the front room, Flint knew he wouldn't be going with his friend. He had promised to spend the day with them and it was important to keep his promises to them. They'd had too many broken promises in their young lives. He wanted them to know that they could depend on his word.

He found that it wasn't hard to keep his word to them. The boys were entertaining little fellows with their quarrels and questions. And little Mercy felt so soft and warm curled up in his lap as she played with the doll that seldom left her arms.

"Where have you been?" Asher asked as Flint caught Mercy under the arms and tossed her in the air.

"I'll tell you later." He gave a significant look at the children.

Asher nodded, then asked, "Are you about ready to ride into town?"

"I can't go with you today. I promised the young'uns I'd spend the day with them." Flint kissed Mercy on top of the head, then set her down.

"But it's Friday," Asher protested. "We always go to town then."

"I don't think it will kill us if we miss this one time," Flint said as he went to the sideboard and poured out two glasses of whiskey. "There's the dance tomorrow night," he said, handing one of the glasses to Asher. "We've got that to look forward to."

"Hell, that's no fun. You can't get fall-down drunk; them ladies will throw you out if you do. And it's no fun dancin' with their daughters either.

"If you pull them up against your"—He paused as Flint nudged his foot under the table—"feet, they squeal. And everybody frowns at you if you dance with Maudie's girls."

"Since when did that bother you?" Flint grinned at his longtime friend.

"It don't bother me exactly. I feel bad that the girls get their feelin's hurt. Some people forget that they're human."

"I don't think Maudie's girls expect to be treated like ranchers' daughters. Take Tillie, for instance. Would you take her home and introduce her to your ma?"

"Introduce a whore to my ma?" Asher snorted laughter. "She'd take a stick to both of us."

Asher cast a devilish look at Flint. "Are you gonna ask Miss Hart to dance with you? It would be a perfect chance to rub your . . . knees against her . . . knees. It's what you've been dying to do."

Flint didn't like Asher talking that way about Lauren. They had both talked about women in that way before, and it hadn't bothered him in the least.

He hurriedly switched subjects. "Someone took a shot at me last night. I'm getting damned tired of it," he said when the children left the room.

"That's the second time," Asher said, concern on his face. "Do you have any idea who is trying to dry-gulch you?"

Flint shook his head. "I only know that it's a white man."

"Oh?" Asher gave Flint a questioning look.

"I rode up to the stand of pines where the bastard had hidden and waited for me. I found his tracks where he had mounted his horse after shooting at me. He mounted from the right side."

"Maybe you shouldn't ride out alone for a while," Asher suggested. "Always have someone with you to watch your back trail."

"I'll be damned if I act like some old woman who's afraid of her shadow."

"Better that than take a bullet in the back."

"I'll get the coward if he tries to gun me down again," Flint said grimly.

"I hope so," Asher said, picking his jacket off the floor and shrugging into it. He grinned at Flint as he slapped his hat on his head, "I don't want to break in a new sidekick." He walked toward the door. "You sure you don't want to come into town with me?" he asked, his hand on the doorknob.

"I'm sure," Flint answered. "Hurry up and close the door. You're letting the heat out."

"Sure thing," Asher readily agreed. But with the grin of Satan he opened the door as wide as he could and fanned it back and forth, letting the cold air rush in. He scooted through it only when Flint stood and took a threatening step toward him and Kate came at him, a stove lid lifter in her hand.

"Damn fool yahoo," Flint said goodnaturedly when Asher slammed the door behind him.

Putting another log on the fire, Flint sat back down, and crossing his long legs at the ankles, he began dreaming of Lauren, of the night they'd spent together during the blizzard.

He hadn't really looked forward to going to the dance, but Asher's remarks about what could happen if he danced with Lauren had changed his mind.

But what if she refused to dance with him? He wouldn't put it past her. Hell, she was too stubborn to let on what had happened between them that night. She had gone up in flames in his arms that night, but come morning she was the same haughty ice queen she had always been.

He had thought at first that maybe their lovemaking hadn't affected her as much as it had him.

"No," he said silently. "It got to her. She's just too proud and stubborn to admit it."

Twenty-one

"You can just keep sayin' no until your tongue drops off." Dud dried the last of their lunch dishes. "I'm taking you to that shindig or you're not goin'."

Lauren asked for the third time, "Why can't Colly take me? There's no call for you to go out in this freezing weather and get your rheumatism stirred up."

"Don't worry about my rheumatiz. I'll dress plenty warm for the ride. And as for Colly King, I don't trust him for a second. He never looks me square in the eyes when he's talking to me. You know why that is?" Lauren shook her head.

"It's because he don't have respectable intentions toward you."

"Come on, Dud." Lauren laughed. "We're practically relatives."

"But you ain't, and that thought has entered his mind many times."

"I guess I'd have something to say about it," Lauren snapped, becoming angry that Dud thought she would let any man take advantage of her. "Anyway, Aunt Lillie would have something to say about it too."

"I agree that she would if she knows what kind of man he is. You gotta remember, she raised him since he was five. She may be blind to his faults."

"I've found she's a very savvy woman. If Colly is a scoundrel, she knows it and she'll protect me from him."

"To be on the safe side," Dud snorted, "I'm gonna protect you too."

Her hands on her hips, Lauren demanded, "What are you going to be doing while I'm at the dance? I hope you don't plan on sitting there, keeping an eye on any man who asks me to dance."

"Not exactly," Dud answered after a moment. "But I'll be lookin' in on the goings-on every once in a while." He added with a sardonic laugh, "Maybe I'll sit on the sidelines with your Aunt Lillie. We can keep an eye on the young men while we snap and snarl at each other."

"I'm sure she'll like that." Lauren sniffed contemptuously. "You're always so pleasant to her."

When Lauren had hung up the dish towel and removed her apron, she said, "You might as well get used to seeing her. She's going to be coming out to the ranch a lot."

Dud stared after Lauren as she left the kitchen, a thoughtful look on his face.

The sun was sinking behind the mountain when Lauren and Dud left the ranch and headed toward Jackson Hole and the annual barn dance. The sky was low and gray, clouds heavy with moisture. Snow or rain? A wild wind scattered leaves along the ground and whipped tree limbs with savage force.

"We oughtn't to be goin'," Dud said, worry in his voice. "We're in for some bad weather."

"We've got to go on," Lauren insisted. "There will be people expecting us. Aunt Lillie, for instance."

"It's against my better judgment," he said testily, and touched spurs to the stallion.

Lauren couldn't remember ever before being so chilly when she and Dud drew rein in front of her aunt's shop and living quarters. She practically fell into Colly's arms when he hurried outside to assist her to dismount.

A frown on his craggy face, Dud stomped after them as they entered the shop. He followed them into Lillie's comfortable little parlor, and sneered at the knickknacks sitting on top of lacy doilies. She always was one for cluttering up a place, he griped to himself.

Lillie bustled out of her bedroom and exclaimed, "Lauren, honey, you look half frozen. Bring her over here by the stove, Colly."

As she helped Lauren off with her jacket, she gave Dud a cool look and said brusquely, "I expect you're cold too, you old reprobate. Come over here and sit beside Lauren," she added as she moved aside, making room for him.

It looked for a minute as if Dud would refuse Lillie's offer of a seat. The women exchanged amused looks as he started nervously making his way around tables, a plush sofa, and two rocking chairs. Both were feeling sorry for him. With the exception of visiting the gaudy waiting room in a house of prostitution, the poor fellow had never been around such finery before.

Dud frowned when Lillie helped him off with his coat, but made no cutting remark to her. He gratefully took the glass of whiskey Colly handed him, but offered no thanks. He pretended not to see Lauren's warning look.

"Well, Lauren," Lillie said after a few minutes of uneasy silence, "if you're warm now, I think it's time we got you all gussied up."

"Hold on there a minute." Dud sat forward. "I don't want her all rigged out in a fancy dress like the whores wear." He threw Lillie's beautiful and modest dress of navy blue satin a contemptuous look. "And I don't want you painting her face either."

"Who cares what you don't want, you old devil? I'm her kin, not you."

"By blood, but that's all," Dud retorted. "Who reared her when you took off when she was just a little tyke. Who took care of her when she was sick? Who carved her wooden toys when she didn't have any to play with? Who—"

"All right, all right!" Lillie interrupted his tirade. "Whether you believe it or not, I thank God every night that Lauren had you. I shouldn't have said what I did. You are more a relative than I am, Dud."

"I didn't have to mouth off the way I did either," Dud said quietly. It was the nearest thing to an apology he had ever made. "It's just that I reared her to be a lady the best way I knew how. And"—he smiled proudly at Lauren—"I think I done a good job."

Tears jumped into Lauren's eyes. She rose and rushed to her old friend. "Oh, Dud"—she wrapped her arms around his shoulders—"you have been like a parent to me all these years."

She wiped at her wet eyes and looked at Lillie. "Not once did this old grouch lay an angry hand on me. And there were times when he should have."

"All right now, that's enough." Dud pulled away from Lauren. "Don't go slobberin' on me."

"Come on, Lauren." Lillie took her by the arm. "Let's go put that paint on your face."

"Now hold on." Dud half rose from his chair. "I told you I don't want her painted up."

"You old loco rooster!" Lillie turned on him. "Do you honestly think that I want my niece to look like a tavern woman?"

Dud hesitated a minute, then muttered, "I guess not."

Fifteen minutes later the rough old man's eyes gleamed with pride and love when Lauren walked from Lillie's bedroom into the fancy little parlor. She positively glowed in an exquisite gown of lush blue velvet.

"You're pretty as a picture, honey," he said, his voice wavering. "Your dad would be so proud if he could see you now."

It was at that moment Colly decided that maybe he would marry Lauren Hart. She would make any man proud to have her for a wife. She was too spirited for his liking, of course, but a few good beatings would curb her stubbornness and sharp tongue. They would have to live somewhere else, though. That Dud would shoot him if he ever heard that a rough hand had been laid on his precious Lauren.

Lillie entered the room, her coat over her arm. She handed it to Dud. When he just looked at it in some confusion, she snapped, "Help me on with it, you big dolt."

Dud grunted something, then grabbing her by an arm, roughly shoved it into a sleeve.

Lillie wheeled around and kicked him as hard as she could in a shin with the sharp toe of her laced shoes. When he yelled "Ouch!" and grabbed at his leg, Lillie sailed toward the door, calling over her shoulder, "Come on, children, we're late."

Dud hobbled along behind them, cursing like a cowpuncher until he stepped outside and the wind took his breath away.

The dance was in full swing when the four of them arrived. The dance floor was crowded with couples hopping and jumping around. The long bench on one side of the room was taken up with mostly older women. Groups of men stood around discussing cows and feed, no doubt. Children ran around, laughing and darting between the couples on the dance floor.

There was a stir when Lauren and Lillie entered the room. The young men gaped and stared at Lauren when Colly helped her off with her coat. Lillie got her share of looks from the older generation, a fact that Dud didn't miss. He hurried and helped her with her coat, telling himself that if he didn't, she might kick him in the shin again, and he was still limping from the first time.

Some of the young men started toward Lauren, plainly intending to ask her to dance. They looked into Colly's threatening eyes, then down to where his hand hovered over his pistol. They moved on then to another group of girls.

Lauren looked around the room and waved to a few people she knew: Baldy Jenkins, the livery stable owner; Bob and Esther Thomason, her favorite store owners: Janice and Ty Summers, her new neighbors and friends. She gave

Kate Allen, Flint's housekeeper, a wide smile. Then she saw Asher Davis, Flint's sidekick. He gave her a wide wink and started across the floor toward her. Would Colly scare him away? she wondered. Somehow she doubted it.

She was right. Asher walked right up to her, and ignoring Colly, asked with twinkling eyes, "May I have this dance, Miss Lauren?"

"You certainly may," she answered, her own eyes twinkling. They swept out onto the floor, leaving Colly glowering after them.

They had circled the room twice when she saw Flint leaning in the doorway. He gave her a lazy, taunting grin and she felt her face growing warm. Why was he smiling like he knew something that she didn't?

A thought came to her that made her blush all the more. Was it possible that he had known what was going on between them that night, even though he'd called her Kate?

She tilted her chin and looked away from him. She would ignore the long-legged wolf.

That wasn't going to be easy to do, she found out a minute later. Devilish Asher finished circling the room and halted beside Flint. "I wasn't sure you were gonna make it to the dance, Flint." He grinned.

"Now why would I miss dancing with the prettiest girl in three counties?" Flint asked, and before either Lauren or Asher knew what he was about, he had pulled Lauren from his friend and clasped her in his arms. Without

313

missing a beat of the music, he swung her out onto the dance floor.

Flint had taken her from Asher so swiftly, so smoothly, Lauren was too surprised to do anything for a moment. When she got her wits about her, she pushed both palms against his broad shoulders. "Turn me loose," she panted.

"Don't make a scene," he growled in her ear. "People are watching us. Especially that self-important Colly King. You wouldn't want me to put my fist in his handsome face, would you?"

"Why would you want to do that?" Lauren glared up at him.

"Because I'd be forced to protect myself. He's working up his nerve to accost me. I'm shaking in my boots."

"Hah!" Lauren snorted. "I can't see that happening. You're probably hoping that he will say something to you, give you an excuse to start a fight."

"Now where did you get such an idea about me?" Flint whirled her around the dance floor, making her head spin.

"I hear people talk." Lauren stopped pushing at his broad chest.

"Maybe you've been listening to the wrong people." Flint pulled her up so tight against him, their hipbones pressed together. Lauren gasped her outrage when she felt his hard throbbing maleness between her thighs.

"Turn me loose," she hissed, trying to squirm away from the insistent probing.

"Not yet," he whispered hoarsely. "I'd be too embarrassed for everyone to see the shape I'm in."

"You devil, I hate you," Lauren grated, but stopped squirming against him, realizing that she was only working him up all the more.

Finally Flint put some inches between them and motioned to one of the young men who was watching them from the sidelines. When the cowpuncher came eagerly forward, Flint said, "I've got some business to tend to. You and your friends see to it that Miss Lauren has dancing partners."

Lauren was about to object to Flint's handing her over as if she was a toy he had grown tired of. Then she happened to look across the room and changed her mind. Colly was leaning against the wall, sullen and pouting. That changed her mind. If she refused to dance with Flint's friends, she would be stuck with Colly all night. When the young cowpuncher swung her onto the dance floor, she sighed with relief. Her aunt's stepson stalked out of the room. She relaxed and had the best time of her life as she was passed from man to man.

Colly, who watched from outside, clenched his fists helplessly. He couldn't take them all on. Actually, he told himself, it was Mahone he worried about the most. He wondered suddenly if Flint would be all that interested in Lauren if he knew that her father had been an outlaw and had been killed by a posse's bullet. Tonight he was going to test the wealthy rancher's feelings about that, he thought with a humorless smile as he started walking down the street to locate Flint.

Flint left the dance and stood a minute on the boardwalk fronting the building, sniffing the air like a wolf. An icy cold had descended on the silent town. They were in for one hell of a blizzard.

Flint continued on down the boardwalk, heading toward the hotel. When the folks inside left the dance and discovered how the temperature had dropped while they were inside enjoying themselves, most of them would rent a room for the night. Everyone knew the dangers of being caught in a freezing, blinding snowstorm.

He must talk to Lauren's Aunt Lillie and her old friend, Dud. He must warn the old man to leave for his ranch right away, and tell him that it would be best if Lauren spent the night in the hotel.

A grimace passed over Flint's face. He'd rather ride a wild bucking bronco than try to convince that old wolf that Lauren should stay in town. The old man did not trust him. The corners of his lips twitched. And well he shouldn't.

Flint walked into the lobby of the hotel, and was surprised to see Dud sitting beside Lillie on one of the blue velvet-covered sofas there. They were laughing and talking together like a pair of kids in their teens on a date. If he remembered correctly, those two usually got on like cats and dogs. Now they were acting like lovers.

When he approached the pair, Lillie gave him a wide friendly smile, but Dud only scowled at him.

"Won't you join us, Flint?" Lillie asked. "Dud and I were just remembering old times."

"Thank you, Lillie. I don't have time to sit and chat, but I do want to talk to Dud."

Dud's scowl deepened. "What do you want to talk to me about?" he growled.

Flint gave the old man a stony stare, thinking that he would punch him in the mouth if he wasn't old enough to be his father.

"It's about the weather. In the past hour it has changed dangerously. When the dance is over and everyone comes outside and discovers how cold it is, everyone is going to make a beeline over here to rent lodgings for the night. The women will, at any rate. Most of the men may try to outrun the blizzard that's on the way. I know that I will. I'm heading for home shortly. If you like, I'll make arrangements for Lauren to stay here at the hotel."

"Well, now, I don't know about that." Dud frowned. "She might not like that. She's never spent a night away from me." He gave Flint a suspicious look. "Are you sure you're goin' home tonight?"

"I've got to. I have a special mare ready to foal

317

any day now. I can't risk being stuck here in town. My cowhands will probably sleep in the livery tonight, so they won't be there to help the mare if she needs it."

"I'd stay in the livery too," Dud said, "but there's been a couple cougars hanging around our barn. I don't dare leave our stock unprotected."

Flint nodded. "Shall I fetch Lauren home tomorrow, or will you be riding in?"

Dud hesitated a minute, thinking how cold it was going to be tomorrow, and that his bones didn't take to freezing weather anymore.

Flint broke the silence. "Why don't I ride in and pick her up. You stay home and keep the house warm for when she gets back. And if I were you, Dud, I'd leave for home right now before the blizzard blows in."

"Yes, I think you should, Dud," Lillie said, standing and reaching her hand down to him. She gave him a coy smile. "First, though, you can see me home."

A blush and a smile lit Dud's face. "I'll sure do that. Let's get our coats on."

Flint grinned and shook his head as they headed for the cloak room. As he walked over to the desk to rent Lauren a room, he asked himself with a chuckle if old Dud could still get it up.

When Flint stepped outside the hotel, he pulled the collar of his mackinaw up over his ears and tugged his flat-crowned hat down so the cold and piercing wind wouldn't blow it off his head. He started to step off the porch, thinking that he must warn the dancers that a storm was brewing and that they should head for home as soon as possible, when Tillie came running up to him.

"Tillie!" he exclaimed. "What are you doing out on a night like this?" He noted that she was shivering, and wasn't surprised when he saw that she wore no gloves or scarf over her head. And that the material of her jacket wasn't very heavy.

"Go on back to Maudie's," he said when Tillie grabbed hold of his arm.

"I will," Tillie agreed, clinging to him fiercely, "if you will come with me."

"Can't you wait to get to her room, Mahone?" a voice behind them sneered.

Flint flung Tillie's hand off his arm and spun around to face Colly King.

"What's it to you, King, whether I do or not?"

His eyes narrowed to slits, and his hand flaying his leg with the short quirt he carried, Colly lashed out, "It's my business because I just paid that Maudie woman so I could spend a couple hours with the little slut." He grabbed Tillie and jerked her to his side. Grasping her chin, he grated, "We're going to have us a high old time, ain't we, little bitch?"

The way Tillie flinched away from Colly made Flint look down at the quirt in the man's hand.

He's a vile-tempered man, Flint thought, and he wouldn't hesitate to take that whip to Tillie if she angered him. He wondered if she had already felt the sting of it. Was that why she wanted him to go to Maudie's with her?

He gave Colly a threatening look. "I'm going to be seeing Tillie tomorrow night. If I see any marks on her, I'll be coming after you. I'll take that quirt away from you and flog you to ribbons."

Flint stepped out into the street, and as he crossed it he could feel King's eyes boring into his back.

His face white with anger, Colly shoved Tillie toward the pleasure house. "I'll join you in a minute. I've got something to say to that bastard."

"Hold up, Mahone," Colly called as he hurried after Flint. "I have something to say that might interest you."

"I can't imagine that anything you could say would interest me," Flint said when they faced each other.

"Oh, I'm sure this will. I think you should know before you get more involved with Lauren Hart, she's the daughter of Red Hart, the outlaw that was shot and killed by the law a little while back."

Colly's words jarred Flint, and it was only grim determination that allowed him to say calmly, "Is that all?"

"My stepmother told me that Lauren's staying

in town tonight. I just wanted you to know that I've got a room at the hotel too." He gave a suggestive smile that turned Flint's stomach. "I'll be happy to look in on her for you."

Flint had no intention of doing what he did next. He doubled up his fist and punched Colly hard in the mouth. Colly, bleeding from a cut lip and smashed nose, gaped at him a moment. Then his knees buckled and he fell forward in the street's frozen mud.

"Lie there, you bastard," Flint said harshly, then turned and retraced his steps toward the hotel. Without hesitation he strode up to the desk and reserved the room next to Lauren's for himself. It had a connecting door.

The clerk looked down at the names, raised an eyebrow, but didn't say anything. He reached behind him and took two keys from among the others and handed them to Flint. Flint gave him a look that dared him to say anything. The young man didn't make eye contact with him. He knew that if he did he would burst out laughing, and that wild Mahone might shoot him. He contained himself until Flint walked out into the night.

Flint hurried through the darkness toward the laughing, dancing people who had no idea of the terrible threat building up in the mountains.

He stepped into the room of carefree merrymakers. He edged his way around the dancing couples until he stood behind the musicians. He tapped the fiddle player on the shoulder and motioned to him that he had something to announce. The music dwindled away and Flint stepped forward to look down at the faces staring up at him. Their expressions said that they feared he was going to say something very serious.

"Folks," he began, "there's been a sudden drop in temperature and there's one hell of a storm brewing up in the mountains. If you people want to get home tonight before the blizzard strikes, I advise you to go right now. If you don't want to chance it, you can put up at the hotel."

As soon as Flint said the word blizzard, those couples with children at home were out the door and running toward the livery stables. Others, mostly cowhands who had a long ride to their ranches, hurried across the street to the hotel. They didn't want to sleep in a pile of hay in the livery if they could help it.

The big room was soon empty, with only Lauren and Asher standing undecided beside the door.

"Lauren," Flint called, walking toward her, "Dud left for home about half an hour ago. He and your aunt asked me to rent a room for you over at the hotel." He turned to Asher. "Asher, if you light out of here right now you can get to the ranch before the snow hits."

"I'll see you tomorrow then," Asher said, and hurried away.

The wind had become so fierce, so icy cold,

that when Flint and Lauren stepped outside neither talked for fear their lungs might freeze.

Flint had reserved the hotel's best room for Lauren, and when they entered, she was impressed. Flint only glanced at the big bed and the few pieces of plain furniture. The furnishings couldn't hold a candle to those in his bedroom at the ranch.

"It's very nice, isn't it?" Lauren said as Flint closed the door behind them.

Lauren gave him a surprised, suspicious look. "Shouldn't you be heading home if you want to beat the storm?"

"My plans have changed," he said, adding to himself, "Thanks to your friend Colly King." As he slowly pushed the scarf off her head and unwound it from around her shoulders, he said, "I'm staying in town also. I have the room next to yours."

Lauren caught at his fingers when he started to unbutton her jacket. "I'll do that," she said nervously. Just the touch of his hand on her throat had her areolas puckering with desire. "You go on to your room. I'm tired and I want to go to bed."

Flint slid her a lazy smile. "You're not as unmoved by me as you pretend, Lauren. Why did you act as though nothing happened between us in the woods?"

"I . . . I don't know what you mean," she stammered. What was it about Flint Mahone? When she was near him commonsense flew out the window. She made no protest when he pushed the neckline of her blue velvet gown down over her shoulders.

She was like a small bird hypnotized by a cobra, unable to move as he untied the ribbons of her camisole and slowly pushed it down to her waist.

He gazed at the twin mounds of her breasts, surmounted by pink puckered tips. "You are a wonder," he breathed, then lowering his head, opened his mouth and covered most of one.

The roughness of his coat pressing into her tender flesh, the working of his teeth and tongue on her breast brought Lauren near to fainting.

Flint groaned his pain. His hunger for her was bone-deep. He had to remind himself not to tear the dress as he practically ripped it off Lauren.

When she finally stood naked before him, Flint had only removed his hat. In his eagerness to possess her he wasn't even aware of that fact as he sank to his knees and cupped both of her breasts in his hands.

Lauren gasped her delight as he began to nibble and suck at her pebble-hard nipples. She groaned and clutched her fingers in his raven-dark hair as she was grasped in the throes of sexual release.

Lauren was weak as a kitten as Flint finished undressing her, then slid her between the bedcovers. She watched with dreamy eyes as he undressed before her, letting her see his arousal, its length and thickness, his desire for her.

When he bucked his hips at her, she flipped back the blanket and held out her arms to him.

It was like coming home when he slid his throbbing length inside her. She gasped her pleasure and wrapped her legs around his waist.

"Oh, Lord," he whispered hoarsely as she lifted her hips to meet his slow rhythmic driving ones. As he rocked back and forth in the well of her smooth hips, the headboard slapped against the wall, keeping time with the drive of his body. He thought wryly that it was a good thing he and Lauren shared the wall. If somebody else was in there, they would complain to the management about the noise they were making.

After about an hour of whirlwind passion, they stopped to rest and realized that the blizzard had arrived. The wind beat at the building, making Flint fear that the roof might come off. He slid out of bed and peered through the window. He couldn't see much through the curtain of blowing snow. The street was empty. When he didn't see any roofs tumbling down, he felt better and went back to bed. Lauren was waiting for him with open arms.

It was near dawn when Flint came awake. He lay a moment. All was quiet outside. The wind had died down. He carefully removed Lauren's leg from around his waist, and leaning upon an elbow, gazed through the wide gap of the drapes, which had not been tightly drawn.

Snow no longer fell. The blizzard had rushed in, then left as quickly.

Flint shifted his gaze to Lauren's sleeping face. She looked so beautiful, so innocent.

With an inward groan, guilt washed over Flint. The night before he had convinced himself he was staying at the hotel to protect Lauren from King. But no sooner had he been alone in the room with her than he'd been overcome by the lust that seemed to consume him whenever she was concerned.

The faint purple smudges under her eyes made it evident that he had possessed her many times during the night.

He laid his head back down on the pillow. Flinging an arm across his eyes, he gave serious thought to Lauren. She was in his blood, there was no doubt about that. Even now he longed to pull her slender body beneath him and ease his throbbing hardness inside her warmth.

But he must never do that again, he told himself. He was afraid he had already loved her too well and too often. What if she was pregnant after last night?

He hoped not. He still wasn't sure what kind of a father he would make. Besides, he had his niece and nephews to think about, to raise.

So what could he say to Lauren when she woke up? If she gave him that sleepy smile of hers, he wouldn't say anything to her. He'd roll on top of her and wear them both out.

No, he must leave her now while she still slept. It was the coward's way, he knew, but it would be the best way in the long run.

Flint quietly got dressed, then rummaged through all his pockets until he found a wrinkled piece of paper and the stub of a pencil.

"Lauren," he wrote, "I had to leave early. My mare is foaling. I will send Asher after you."

He laid the note on his pillow where she would see it, then lowered the wick in the lamp and blew out the flame.

He felt like the worst kind of coyote as he stepped out into the hall and closed the door behind him.

Chapter Twenty-two

The last stars were fading as Flint rode into the barnyard of the ranch where Asher worked. For all the fierceness of the blizzard, it had only dropped a few inches of snow on the area. He drew rein, dismounted, and leaving the stallion ground-hitched, quietly entered the bunkhouse. The long room was filled with the odor of dirty socks and the noise of different-sounding snores. In the gray semi-darkness he made his way to Asher's bunk. He laid his hand on the tall man's shoulder and shook him awake.

"What in the hell are you doin' here at this hour?" Asher whispered, frowning up at Flint.

In a low voice Flint told his friend the same

lie he had written to Lauren, then added, "I told her that you would come and see her home sometime this morning. Will you do it?"

"Are you trying to make a joke?" Asher sat up and swung his feet to the floor. "That old Dud person won't sic their wolf-dog on me, will he?" he asked as he pulled a pair of pants up his long legs.

"No, he won't do that. He'll be surprised, though, that you're bringing Lauren home. I told him that *I* would. I'll see you later today," Flint said as he walked toward the door. He paused there a moment, then opened the door and walked outside.

A gray dawn had entered the room when Lauren awakened with cold shoulders. She fumbled the covers up around her neck, then reached a hand to Flint's pillow. His head was not there. A piece of paper lay there instead. She noted that the light in the kerosene lamp had been blown out, and decided that Flint had gone to his own room.

She picked up the note, brushed the hair out of her eyes, and peered at the writing in the dim light. She was a little disappointed in its wording. It didn't in any way resemble what she thought a love note might be. The words were plain and to the point. Of course, he could be worried about his mare.

She rolled over on her back and stared up at the rough board ceiling, remembering every moment of the past several hours. Other than his lovemaking, which she thought must be the best in all Wyoming, what kind of husband would he make? Would he be considerate, stay home with her nights, or would he want to continue his wild ways to some extent?

Her soft lips firmed to a tight line. If he so much as looked in the direction of that whorehouse, she would fill his behind with buckshot.

Her lips curved in a smile. There would be no reason for him to look beyond his home. She would keep him quite happy in bed.

She sat up and stretched, then gave a little moan. She was stiff and sore in every muscle. She scooted out of bed, thinking that was a small price to pay, considering all the loving she'd had.

The pitcher on the washstand was full of water. She filled the matching basin from it and dropped in the cloth and bar of soap provided. Asher would be knocking on her door any minute.

Lauren had just finished brushing the tangles out of her hair when the rap she was waiting for sounded. Asher called out, "I've come to fetch you home, prettiest girl in Jackson Hole."

"Just a minute, most handsome man," Lauren called back gaily. "I'm putting my coat on now."

When she opened the door to Asher, he held his hand over his eyes. "Your beauty blinds me, lady," he said, and Lauren's laughter floated down the hall.

"You're loco, you know that, don't you, Asher Davis." She laughed as he helped her into a light sleigh that belonged to his boss. It didn't bother him in the least that he hadn't asked permission to use it.

"Only about you." Asher seated himself beside her and picked up the reins. He snapped them against the trim little mare's rump and they were off down the street. "Flint is the loco one. Preferring the company of a mare to you."

Asher roared with laughter when Lauren said, with tongue in cheek, "Maybe his mare has sleeker lines than I do. Maybe her eyelashes are silkier and longer than mine."

They were still engaged in tomfoolery when they pulled into the yard of the Hart ranch.

The cabin door opened immediately and Dud came thumping down the three porch steps. As he lifted his arms to help Lauren to the ground, he demanded, "How come this long drink of coffee is bringin' you home? I thought that Mahone was going to do that."

"He has a mare that is foaling and he's with her," Asher answered for Lauren.

Dud's response to that was a grunt that could mean anything. "Come in and warm up before you start back," Lauren said to Asher.

Asher wanted to do that in the worst way. He was chilled to the bone. Still, he looked at Dud as though for permission. If the old reprobate didn't want him inside his home, he might very well sic the wolf-dog on him.

Dud grudgingly nodded his head and led the way up the steps. Inside the living room he laid a fresh log on the fire, then poured glasses of whiskey for Asher and himself.

That act surprised Asher, and he thought to himself that maybe the old fellow was not as ornery as he'd thought. He had a right to look after Lauren, to be leery of any man who came around such a beauty. He smiled a wry smile to himself. Dud Carton should be especially wary of him and Mahone.

Flint could barely keep his eyes open. He had been sitting with the children ever since breakfast, answering the boys' questions about their father. He told them of their youth, the things he and Jake did while growing up. How they had fished in the Snake River, hunted deer and rabbit up in the mountains. He promised that he would take them hunting and fishing too.

Mercy, curled up in his lap, asked no questions. She didn't remember the father they were talking about. Flint wondered again why the boys didn't bring up their mother, ask about her. He supposed it was understandable that they would want to forget about the woman who had abandoned them.

Flint frowned. He saw Asher pull up in a light sleigh. Though it had been his idea, he didn't

like the thought that his friend had just escorted
Lauren home.

Get used to the idea of men courting her, he
ordered himself. *Maybe Asher will be one of
those men.* How would he like that, he wondered, then answered honestly that he wouldn't
like it at all.

*Then make up your mind, bucko, whether you
want the girl or not.*

Flint was saved from his tormenting thoughts
by Asher stepping inside the big, warm room.
He looked so pleased with himself that Flint
wanted to hit him.

"I made some headway with that old Dud today," Asher said, discarding his jacket and holding his hands out to the flames in the fireplace.
"He actually let me come into the house and
gave me a glass of whiskey to warm me up. We
talked about cows for a while before he told me
it was time I was getting on home. Said it was
too cold to keep the horse standing in the cold."

A soft lazy smile parted Asher's lips. "I think
I made a little headway with Lauren too."

"Oh? In what way was that?" Flint asked, a
coolness creeping into his voice.

"It's hard to explain. It was the way she
smiled and thanked me so sweetly for bringing
her home when she walked with me to the
door."

"Did she invite you to come visit sometime?"
Flint sat forward to hear his friend's answer.

"Well, no, she didn't. She could hardly do that

with the old man sitting there, watching us like a hawk. But come spring I'll be courtin' her. You'll see."

"Sure you will," Flint scoffed. "I'm sure she's just dying to be escorted around by a long-legged cowboy."

"Laugh all you want to"—Asher gave him a sheepish grin—"but you'll see."

Flint laughed out loud when Asher looked at him and said, "Let's go to town and get ourselves a poke."

"If you're so in love with Lauren Hart, I'm surprised you'd want to visit a whore," Flint said to Asher.

"One has nothing to do with the other," Asher said defensively. "I wouldn't expect anything from Lauren until we were married. But in the meantime a man has to have his release regular."

"My friend, you don't know what you're talking about," Flint said to himself, remembering last night and the lovemaking he and Lauren had enjoyed, how she had given herself totally to him.

When Asher pressed him for an answer, he shook his head. "I'm too beat and it's too cold to ride to town."

"You're getting old, Mahone," Asher griped, pulling on his jacket. "I'll see you tomorrow," he said as he opened the door and walked outside.

Flint yawned. He was ready for some sleep.

He'd had very little last night. He slipped away from the children and went to his room. He'd catch a few winks before lunch.

It seemed to Flint that he had barely closed his eyes when Asher was shaking him awake. "What in the hell do you want?" he growled, turning over on his back and glaring up at Asher.

"A terrible thing has happened, Flint!"

Flint sat up. He had never seen his friend so upset. "What has happened, Asher?" he asked, reaching for his boots.

"Tillie from down at the whorehouse has been killed. Doc says her neck was broken. And there's lash marks all over her body."

A single image entered Flint's mind: the memory of a quirt lashing against Colly King's trouser-clad leg.

As Flint shoved his feet into his boots, he told himself that King was the kind of man who could do such a thing. And who better to torment than a weak woman who couldn't fight back.

Seeing the look of purpose in Flint's eyes, Asher asked, "What are you planning to do?"

"I plan to find out who killed Tillie. But first I'm going to make a call on a party in Jackson Hole."

It was bitterly cold as Flint and Asher guided their horses as quickly as they could through the fetlock-deep snow. The tears that the icy wind brought to their eyes froze as soon as they rolled down their cheeks.

Asher wanted to ask why they were going to Jackson Hole, but didn't want to move the warm scarf tied around his neck and mouth. He figured that he would find out eventually.

Asher found out fifteen minutes later when Flint pulled rein in front of the Frontier Hotel. When he slid from the saddle and ground-hitched his horse, Asher followed suit. It wasn't until they stepped up on the snow-swept porch that Asher asked, "Do you think whoever killed Tillie will be holed up in here?"

"You never know where a cur dog will seek a hiding place," Flint said crisply as he strode to the desk and turned the register around to face him. Running a finger down the list of names, he gave a grunt of satisfaction when he found the one he was looking for. "Come on to room number three," he said, taking the stairs two at a time.

Number three was locked, so instead of knocking he kicked the door in.

There was no one inside. The bed had not been slept in. It was neatly made up, but a few pieces of clothing were scattered about on top of it. Someone had packed his clothes in a hurry for there were three odd socks lying on top of the quilt and one on the floor.

Where had Colly King run? Flint wondered. He stood a moment, staring down at the floor, thinking. Could he be with Lillie, his step-mother?

"There's nothing here," he told Asher. "You may as well head on home. I'm going to call on a lady friend."

Lillie was talking to two customers when he entered her shop. She excused herself from the ladies and walked over to where he stood. She gave him a mischievous smile and said, "Now, Flint Mahone, what could you be wanting in a ladies' shop? I wonder which young woman has caught your eye?"

"Well, now, Lillie, do you mean some pretty lady besides yourself?"

Lillie slapped his hand playfully. "Don't go flattering me, you handsome wolf. Why are you really here?"

"I wanted to have a word with Colly, but he's not at the hotel. I thought he might be down here with you."

"No, he's not. I haven't seen him since early yesterday evening." Lillie paused a moment. "Our riding horses arrived a few days ago. You might find him at the livery looking after his roan stallion."

Flint nodded his head. "I'll check there." He pushed away from the counter. "Nice talking to you, Lillie," he said, and left the shop.

Outside, he climbed onto the stallion's back and turned the animal's head in the direction of the livery.

Flint rode up to the wide double doors of the

stable and leaning out of the saddle gave a strong tug on the rope tied to the bell that was attached to the wall.

A kid in his teens rushed from inside to pull open one of the doors. When Flint had entered the warm interior of the barn, the young man hurriedly closed the door behind him.

Flint climbed down to the straw-covered floor and handed the reins to the young man. "Stable my horse, will you? But be careful. He bites and kicks." The boy gave Shadow a wary look but led him away.

Flint walked down the wide aisle, going to Baldy Jenkins's tack room and office. "How are you, Flint?" Baldy greeted him warmly and reached down behind him to pull up a bottle of whiskey. He blew the dust out of two glasses and filled them with a liquid the color of strong tea. "Put that under your belt and warm your gizzard." He handed a glass to Flint.

"Thank you, Baldy, I needed that," Flint said, and sat down in the only other chair in the small room.

"What brings you out on such a miserably cold day?" Baldy asked as he opened the stove door and fed a small log to the fire burning there.

"I'm looking for Colly King. I understand he's been keeping a roan stallion here."

"Yes, for the last few days. But it's not here now. Sometime after the dance ended he came storming in here and ordered the kid to saddle his horse. He took off then, riding like the devil was on his tail. Ain't seen him since. To tell you the truth, I don't care if I never see him again. He's a mean bastard. He treats that stallion of his awful. I've heard stories that he tries to treat Maudie's girls the same way, but she won't put up with it."

Apparently Baldy hadn't yet heard about Tillie, Flint thought, or he might have his own suspicions. Flint sat with Baldy another five or ten minutes, then said he had to get back to the ranch. His ranch was the last place he intended to go. He was going to track down Colly King. He would get the truth out of the bastard. And if that truth turned out to be what he thought, he would then beat the man half to death before taking him to the sheriff.

As Flint rode down the only road that led out of Jackson Hole, tears smarted his eyes. When he came to the spot where several roads branched off the main one, he drew Shadow in. Which one of them should he take? he asked himself.

Following his gut instinct, he turned the stallion's head in the direction of the mountain. Sometimes it was slow going because of snowdrifts. There were times Flint had to dismount and lead the stallion through snow that was past his knees. But he kept on going. Something told him that he was on Colly's trail.

Once, as the wind moved through the passes, he thought he heard the angry nicker of a horse.

He pulled Shadow in and listened. He heard nothing but tree limbs rubbing against each other. He decided that was the noise he'd heard, and rode on.

He was beginning to climb now and the horse was tiring some. Flint noted also that it was growing late, that the sun would be going behind the mountains before long. He had no desire to be caught up here in the wilds after dark.

Flint was about to turn the stallion around and head for home when he definitely heard the snort of an angry horse and the stamping of hooves. He cautiously urged Shadow up what was now a narrow path.

He sucked in his breath when he rounded a bend and saw what lay before him. A crumpled body was flung on the path. Above it stood a horse, its nostrils distended, its eyes rolling.

This must be the roan that Lillie had mentioned. Blood streamed freely over its head and down its face. There were deep whiplashes all over its smooth hide. Flint dismounted, and talking softly and soothingly to the animal, began to slowly advance on him.

The stallion snorted and pawed the snow-covered ground a moment, then decided to trust the gentle-talking man. When he backed away from the prostrate figure, Flint, still talking soothingly, walked up and squatted on his heels to look down on Colly King. The man lay in dead silence, staring sightlessly up at the sky.

He had been dead for sometime Flint saw

from the evidence surrounding King. There were drifts of snow on some parts of his body. His face was a mask of hoofprints.

Flint shook his head, knowing what had happened. The ruthless man had tried to make the stallion climb through a slippery snowdrift. When the animal couldn't make it, Colly had taken the whip to him. When the stallion could endure no more torture, he had turned on Colly with all the rage that had festered in him for so long.

Flint could only guess at how many times the poor abused animal had slashed his hoofs into the man who had treated him so cruelly. He had no doubt in his mind that Colly had killed Tillie. The bastard still had the quirt clenched in his hand.

Now, he thought, standing up and staring down at the crumpled body, how was he to get Colly back to Jackson Hole? Shadow hated the scent of blood and would never allow the body to be put on his back. And the poor trembling roan might go crazy if he was forced to carry the man who had nearly killed him.

"For sure the wolves will get him if I leave him here."

Flint pondered the dilemma he found himself in. Colly didn't deserve any better than to be torn apart by hungry wolves, but he was a human being, and Lillie would be even more devastated if she couldn't provide a decent burial for her stepson.

He remembered then how the Indians and the mountain men kept the animals away from their kills, summer and winter. They hung everything high in a tree. He would do that with Colly. The body would be safe there from wolves and other varmints until he could get back with the sheriff.

Chapter Twenty-three

Lauren turned from the shop window and walked into Lillie's living quarters. Her aunt lay curled up in the center of the big fancy bed, crying softly. Dud sat in a chair at the bedside, trying to console her.

Lauren gazed down at the grieving woman, her own eyes damp for her aunt's sorrow. She had learned to truly love the kind, good-humored woman.

Lillie had been in a state of shock ever since Flint had returned to town two hours ago, leading Colly's roan stallion. The horse was nervous and skittish until Flint gentled him down. He looked at the crowd that had gathered around him and said, "I want you people to take a good look at this animal. I want you to see how he's been almost whipped to death, that it's a miracle he's still alive. I want you to say then that you don't blame this poor dumb animal for trying to kill Colly King."

The toughest men in the group had wet eyes when they gazed at the red welts that crisscrossed the beautiful hide. Even the horse's proud, beautiful head hadn't been spared.

"Colly King carries a quirt," someone in the crowd said. "Do you think he was the one who killed Tillie?"

"It was him," Mahone said quietly, rubbing the soft spot between the horse's ears.

"Come on, men, let's go after him," the same voice called out.

"But it's too late to punish him for his crimes," Flint said. "I came upon his dead body about an hour ago. This poor devil was still standing over him, striking him again and again with his front feet. I had a hard time dragging him away from King's broken body."

"What did you do with the bastard's body?" someone asked. "Left it for the wolves, I hope."

"I was tempted," Flint answered, "but because of Lillie, his stepmother, I managed to hang him up in a tree. For her sake I wish some of you men would cut him down and bring him to the undertaker's."

"He don't deserve that kind of treatment, but

Lillie seems like a good sort, so I guess we could do it for her," they agreed.

Now Lauren approached the bed and patted Lillie's shoulder. Her aunt had nearly fainted when she'd heard the news of Colly's death. Luckily, Lauren and Dud had been visiting her in town when Flint brought word of what had happened.

Lauren looked across at Dud now. He held Lillie's hand, slowly stroking it as he softly spoke words unintelligible to Lauren. But her aunt seemed to understand. She nodded and pressed her cheek lovingly against Dud's hand.

Lauren could only stand and stare for a moment. When had this all come about? As far as she knew, there had never been a tender moment between these two. Now they looked like they had spent a lifetime together.

She quietly backed out of the room. She wasn't needed, nor wanted, here.

As Lauren walked into Lillie's tiny kitchen, she experienced an emotion she had never known before. Was she being replaced in Dud's affections? Ever since she could remember he had always been the mainstay of her life. She knew that her father had loved her dearly, but it was Dud who was always there for her. He was as dependable as the rising sun. But she had this awful feeling now that things were going to change. She felt deep inside her that Lillie was going to upsurp her place in Dud's heart. She knew, of course, that Dud would always look out for her, as would Aunt Lillie. But it would be different. Their life would not be hers.

She sighed. She should have a husband and children, make a home of her own. Lauren walked to the kitchen window and looked out onto the street. Daylight was gone. In another half hour services would begin for Colly. Would anybody attend other than herself, Aunt Lillie, and Dud? She doubted it. The whole town was in an uproar over the beating death of Tillie. The whores went around with empty eyes, knowing that such an end could be waiting for them. The townspeople wouldn't venture out on such a cold night to pray for the soul of Colly King.

There would be a few who would show up, she knew, who would come out of respect and liking for Lillie King, and she felt that Flint would attend, seeing as how he had discovered Colly's body. And Asher always did whatever Flint did, so he would be there.

The church wouldn't be crowded, that was for sure, Lauren thought. And there would be still fewer people going to the cave where Colly's body would be kept with others waiting to be buried. Come spring, when the ground thawed, there would be burials for all of them.

Lauren saw lamplight glow in the church window across the street, four buildings down. The preacher was preparing to start services. It was time she roused Aunt Lillie and got her ready for the ordeal ahead.

Lauren didn't think she could have gotten Lillie ready if not for the help to Dud. It was he who coaxed the almost fainting woman out of bed, and talked to her gently so that her hair could be combed. It was Dud who helped her into her coat and placed the black velvet hat on her head.

It rested slightly askew on her yellow curls, and after Lauren straightened it, they left the shop. Lillie leaned heavily on Dud's arm. As Lauren walked behind her aunt and Dud, she wondered how her aunt could grieve so for Colly after the dastardly thing he had done. Were there many loves like that? she wondered. Could she love someone so strongly?

Her answer came readily. Yes, she could. If it were Dud who was going to be sealed away in a cave for months, she would be crying her eyes out, regardless of what he had done. And what about her feelings for Flint Mahone? It seemed her love for him could overlook all kinds of transgression on his part.

By the time the small entourage following the two men carrying the coffin arrived at the church, Dud had to put a supporting arm around Lillie's waist. No one had built a fire in the potbelly stove and the breaths of the nine people gathered there puffed from their mouths and nostrils like small clouds of steam.

The service was short, for which everyone

seemed thankful, Lauren thought, considering how rapidly the church emptied. Flint and Asher paused long enough to give Lillie their condolences. Asher gave Lauren a big smile, but Flint only darted her a sidelong look.

They were walking toward the livery and Lillie's shop when Dud spoke. "Asher," he said, "would you mind seeing Lauren home? I don't think Lillie should be left alone tonight."

Flint wanted to hit his friend in the mouth when Asher almost tripped over his tongue in agreeing. Lauren wanted to hit Dud. Already it was starting: his drawing away from her, his getting closer to Lillie. The crazy old idiot. Did he plan on courting her aunt? And at their age? Ridiculous.

"Lauren," Asher said, interrupting her thoughts, "why don't you have a cup of coffee at the cafe while I get our horses from the livery? That stable is no place for a lady like you."

Lauren nodded her agreement and parted ways with Asher and Flint. She was making her way through the snowy ruts of the street, her head down, when she felt a hand on her arm. Surprised, she looked up to see a heavily rouged woman, dressed in red.

"My name is Maudie, maybe you've heard of my place? Tillie was one of my girls.

"Miss Hart," she went on, "I have watched you and you seem like a very caring woman. I have to tell this to someone."

"What is it, Maudie?" Lauren asked when the

madam paused and looked uncertain whether or not to go on. "You can tell me what is bothering you. I promise I won't tell a soul what you say."

Maudie spoke then, all in a rush, as though to get it out and done with. "Tillie left behind a little boy. He's not even a year old."

Lauren looked at the big woman, speechless. When she regained her composure she asked, "Where is the child?"

"A farmer's wife a few miles out of town has been taking care of the little one ever since he was born. The woman has a brood of her own, and the money Tillie paid her every week helped the woman to put beans and potatoes on the table."

Maudie sighed. "As soon as she hears that Tillie is dead and will no longer come every week to pay for the little one's care, she will bring the baby to my place and leave him there."

Maudie laid a gloved hand on Lauren's arm. "You know that a whorehouse is not a fittin' place to raise a child, don't you, Miss Hart?"

"I agree with you, Maudie. However, I feel that you and your girls would do your best for him." Lauren took Maudie by the arm and they started walking. "I was on my way to the cafe. Let's get a cup of hot chocolate and discuss this in warmer quarters," she said.

Maudie held back. "Are you sure you want me to go in there with you?"

"If I didn't want you to, I wouldn't have asked

you to accompany me. Now come on in where we can talk in peace."

When Lauren and Maudie stepped into the warmth of the cafe, the young waitress there looked the madam up and down with a curl of her lip.

Lauren matched her look for look and demanded, "What is wrong with your lip, young lady? Is it a permanent grimace, or do you only use it on certain occasions? In case you don't know it, it makes you look uglier than hell."

The waitress snorted her anger, and Maudie giggled her pleasure as she and Lauren were left to choose their own table.

It was plain from the scowl on her face that the young miss did not want to wait on her two new customers. But a cold, cutting look from Lauren kept her from being openly rude to them.

When she had brought their drinks and flounced away, Lauren leaned toward Maudie and asked, "Did Tillie know who the father of the child is?"

"Oh, yes, she knew, but she would never say. Me and my girls have our opinions, but that's all they are. Some of the girls think it's one of the rich uppity men who used to sneak up the back way to sleep with her.

"The rest of us are split. Half think Mahone is the father, and the other half think it's Asher."

"Do you think the father knows?"

"It's doubtful," Maudie said. "Tillie wasn't the

kind to try and pin something on a man when she was just as guilty as he was."

"There's one other thing," Maudie said after a lengthy silence had settled between them. "Tillie would never let us go with her to visit the little one. She said that one look at the child would tell anyone who his daddy is. And she made us promise not to go nosin' round, trying to see the little one."

"Why are you telling me all this?" Lauren asked.

"Tillie told me Flint Mahone was sweet on you." Maudie hesitated a minute. "I just thought you had a right to know."

After begging Lauren again not to mention what she'd revealed, the madam left, her bright red skirt dragging in the dirty snow. She walked with her head lifted high. Hadn't she just sat in the cafe and enjoyed a hot drink with a young woman who owned a ranch?

When Maudie left, Lauren ordered another hot drink. She needed to think. To think about the father of Tillie's child.

There was a bleak, hopeless look in her eyes and an empty feeling in her heart. Why should she care if Flint Mahone was the child's father?

But she knew that she would, and the emptiness seem to grow. Why did she have to fall in love with a man who didn't seem to have any morals?

Lauren leaned forward and looked out the

cafe window. She caught sight of Asher leading her stallion down the street.

A frown creased her forehead. Why was Flint Mahone riding with him?

Asher had asked Flint the same question.

"Don't you trust me to get the girl home unharmed?" Asher asked curtly.

"Can a buffalo fly?" Flint smiled thinly.

"I resent that, Flint," Asher answered, somewhat testily. "I have never gone beyond what a woman wants."

"Yeah, but that slick tongue of yours and those smooth hands have made a lot of them do more than they had counted on."

"And you've never done that, have you?" Asher asked sardonically. "Remember who you're talking to."

Flint turned a dull red. What Asher said was true. He had coaxed Lauren into giving herself to him last night at the hotel, and he felt like a dirty dog for doing it. He knew it must have hurt her feelings the way he'd abruptly left her, with only a note for explanation, but he also knew that if he kept seeing her he wouldn't be able to keep from loving her again and again.

However, the thought of Asher, or any other man, making love to her was something he didn't think he could bear. If he didn't have the children to think of, he would go up into the mountain wilderness. There he would spend the winter in solitude, get Lauren Hart out of his system.

But there were the children to think of and he would have to tough it out. Every man in the country might come courting her and he couldn't do diddly about it. He did not have his brand on her. And maybe that was a mistake, he thought.

It was too late to think of that now, he told himself. He wasn't the right man for her. He just wasn't the marrying kind, and Lauren deserved nothing less.

"Remember, she's a lady and you treat her that way," he told Asher. "That old Dud person will carve your heart out if you don't."

"Don't I know it." Asher laughed. "That old codger scares the hell out of me. But seriously, I won't treat Lauren any way except as a lady."

They had stopped in front of the cafe, and Asher said, "I'll see you tomorrow."

"Why tomorrow?" Flint looked at Asher with dry amusement. "I'm not going anywhere."

"I hope you don't think you're going to tag along with me and Lauren," Asher asked incredulously.

There was a hint of laughter in Flint's eyes when he answered, "I thought I might. I haven't got anything else to do. I can't see any harm in me riding along with you."

"All right, you long-legged wolf," Asher exploded, "you can ride along with us, but keep your damn mouth shut."

That I will, Flint said to himself. After I make sure that Lauren understands I'm not the right kind of man for her.

Chapter Twenty-four

"What's *he* doing here?" Lauren demanded of Asher, looking daggers at Flint. "I thought Dud asked *you* to take me home."

After learning this latest bit of damning evidence against Flint's character, she was in no mood to spend any time with him.

Flint looked taken aback at her rudeness; Asher just grinned. Apparently Lauren preferred him as an escort over his friend.

As they mounted their horses, Asher made an attempt to get a conversation going.

"Are you going to the Cattleman's dance Saturday night?" he asked Lauren.

"I'm not sure," she answered. The only man

she'd want to go with was Flint, but she was too mad at him to let him take her.

"How about you?" Asher asked, looking at Flint.

"Naw," Flint said. "That's the same night Maudie and her girls are giving their yearly party." He winked at Asher. "Everything is free, if you know what I mean."

Lauren was sure she would choke on the tears that rose in her throat. The night of lovemaking that she had thought so special had meant nothing to Flint Mahone. He probably hadn't enjoyed himself. After all, she knew none of the tricks girls like Tillie used on the men. She mentally swore at the tear that threatened to slip down her cheek. She bit her tongue, gathered up the reins, and as she kneed her stallion into motion, said in a stone-cold voice, "You certainly wouldn't want to miss all that free bed-shaking."

Flint stared after her narrow, straight back. He had done what he had started out to do. So why did he feel like a yellow cur? He feared he would never feel whole again. His shoulders sagged like those of an old man.

The moon was coming up when they rode into Lauren's barnyard. "You go on home, Flint," Asher said, dismounting. "I'm going to build a fire in the house and put a pot of coffee on for Lauren."

It looked for a moment as though Flint was going to dismount also. But he seemed to think better of it. Saying good-bye, he gathered up his reins and rode on.

Moments later, Lauren sat shivering, watching Asher snap small sticks between his hands, making kindling for the fire in the fireplace. She hadn't removed any of her outerwear, not even the scarf tied around her head. She was sure she would never be warm again. And that not only because of the weather. Flint's behavior today and Maudie's revelation had practically dealt her a death blow. She would never be the same, and she would never trust a man again. They would take all they could from a woman, then toss her aside as though she were a broken toy. And come to think of it, that was the way she felt.

In no time Asher had a fire burning brightly, its smoke flying up the chimney. Lauren untied her scarf, removed it from her head, then shrugged out of her jacket.

She was beginning to thaw out when Asher reentered the room with two cups of steaming coffee in his hands. He handed one to her, and as he sat down in a chair opposite her, he said, "I don't know what has got into Flint lately. He's not his old self. He's moody, edgy. He never has a decent word to say to a fellow."

"Maybe his love life isn't going smoothly," Lauren offered bitterly, not knowing what to say.

"Love life, hah!" Asher's lips twisted wryly. "What love life? He ain't got one and what's more, he don't want any. He likes the females, all right, but he'd never tie himself down to one. He's got all he can handle now, what with his little relatives."

"He doesn't seem to mind having them around," Lauren said after taking a cautious sip of the hot coffee.

"He sure don't. He's crazy about them little scutters. Especially the little Mercy. He told me last week that he was going to raise her to be a lady. Just like you, he said."

"Me, a lady?" Lauren exclaimed in surprise. "Where did he get the idea that I'm a lady? The other night at the dance was the first time that I can remember ever wearing a dress."

"What you wear doesn't make you a lady, Lauren," Asher scolded. "Look how fancy Maudie and her girls dress." Asher gave a short laugh. "You certainly wouldn't call them ladies."

"I guess not," Lauren agreed, "but . . ."

"And you know something else?" Asher cut in before she could finish her sentence. "More than half them heifers whose daddies own the biggest ranches are no better than the whores, but they're considered ladies by most of the people in town.

"But me and Flint and a few other of our friends know that those girls can outdo Maudie's whores in the bed. Do you get my meaning, Lauren?" he asked, then took a long swallow of his coffee.

"Yes, I think I do," Lauren answered sadly.

Would Asher think her a lady if her knew how she had so wildly given herself to Flint?

Lauren stared into the fireplace, asking herself if that was why Flint had lost interest in her. She turned her head and looked at Asher. "When did Flint remark that I was a lady?" she asked.

"He brought it up again today."

Well, then, Lauren thought with relief, he isn't holding my actions against me. But what caused him to change so? she wondered.

Perhaps he had found her performance lacking. She grew angry at the thought and almost said aloud, To hell with you, Flint Mahone, if I didn't act the whore with you. I haven't had much experience, you know.

Lauren contained her anger, however, and when Asher said, "I'm not going to Maudie's party. Would you go with me to the dance?" she hesitated only a moment before accepting his invitation.

Asher was so surprised at her answer he could only gawk at her for a minute. Finally he managed to croak, "That's fine. Shall I pick you up here or will you be in town with your Aunt Lillie?"

"I think maybe here," Lauren said after a thoughtful pause. She didn't know when Dud would be coming home. Probably he would stay in town until he was sure Aunt Lillie no longer needed him.

Asher, a big smile on his face, stood up and

began to button his mackinaw. "I'll be here around seven then."

When Lauren had walked him to the door and returned to the fire, she told herself that she mustn't give Asher any hope that they would be close. He was a nice enough man, but he was cut from the same cloth as Flint. And though he might settle down someday and make a fine husband, she wasn't attracted to him romantically. It was her bad luck to feel that way about only one man: Flint Mahone.

She roused herself from thoughts of Flint. It was time to feed and water the animals. She also wanted to get wood in for the night. All kinds of varmints came nosing around in the dark. It was the cougars she feared most. They were vicious creatures, ready to attack humans and animals. Every night they came around the barn, causing a rukus with the stallions.

She told herself she didn't fear the wolves. They were afraid of her dog, Wolf. Wolf had killed a couple of them since she and Dud had settled in. But where was Wolf? She hadn't seen him since Asher had brought her home.

Working by the light of a lantern, Lauren carried water to the horses and pitched fresh-smelling hay into their mangers. She made three trips to the back porch where Dud had stacked cords of wood. She then dusted off her hands and the front of her jacket and entered the house. The fire was dying down and she added more wood to the coals, then before removing her jacket, she lit the lamp on the table beside her chair, then went into the kitchen and lit the one sitting on the table and another hanging on the wall. She hoped the lamplight and warmth would comfort her, make her feel less alone in the night.

Flint was almost half a mile from home when the stallion's head lifted sharply, his ears pricked. Flint reached for the Colt that was holstered by his leg. Something had startled Shadow.

As Flint scanned a stand of leafless cottonwood trees, a bullet struck the snow near him. He searched the tree trunks, looking for one large enough to hide a man. Suddenly he saw a figure, bent over, running among the trees. He snapped off a shot, but missed.

While he was filling the empty chamber of his gun, Flint got a full view of the man who wanted him dead. As he gaped in surprise a bullet slammed into his left shoulder, knocking him out of the saddle. As he hit the ground, his head struck a rock and he knew no more.

Chapter Twenty-five

When Asher left Lauren's home he was so caught up in fantasies about going to the dance with her, he didn't notice the cold or the dark. He had never attended the Cattleman's dances before. They were too tame for him. But attending one with Lauren would be something to remember.

Asher was wondering and worrying a little, whether he would know how to act around the class of people who would be attending the dance when a bullet whipped sharply against a tree he was passing under. He pulled his Winchester from its scabbard and whipped it to his shoulder. When he saw the shadowy figure of a horse and rider moving among the bare trunks, he squeezed the trigger.

He missed his target. Swearing, he put the Winchester back in place and kicked his horse into a gallop. He was going to catch the sneak who would shoot at a man without any warning.

Asher gave up after about fifteen minutes. It was no use. The man had disappeared among the trees. He pulled his horse in and sat quietly for a moment, getting his bearings.

He had tightened his grip on the reins and was ready to go on when he heard a groaning off to his right. His pulse jumped. Had his bullet hit the man after all?

Asher would have trampled Flint if his horse hadn't suddenly snorted and reared backward. "What is it, boy?" Asher pulled his gun as he dismounted.

He approached the still figure cautiously. The man could be playing dead. He nudged the big body with his foot and when it didn't move, he knelt down and turned the man over.

"My God, Flint!" he exclaimed. "Are you alive?" He tore the glove off Flint's hand and felt for his pulse, his frightened gaze on the large patch of blood on the front of his friend's mackinaw.

He sighed in relief when he finally felt a faint, but steady pulse beat. He heard the heavy stamp of horse hooves then, and peering through the trees saw Flint's stallion, Shadow, standing in a patch of moonlight.

He knew the horse would allow him to approach as long as he didn't have the odor of blood on him. He knew also the horse would go wild if Flint tried to mount him with all this blood.

Asher, still kneeling beside his friend, studied on the problem a minute. He had to get Flint home, see how seriously he was wounded, get him warmed up before he froze to death.

He suddenly began to scoop up handfuls of snow and to pack it on Flint's chest. When he had completely covered the patch of blood, he scrubbed his hands with snow. Hoping then that all scent of blood was gone, he approached the stallion, speaking calmly to him all the time.

The stallion was skittish, but allowed Asher to rub the soft spot between his ears. Holding his breath, Asher give the reins a gentle tug, and Shadow followed him to his master.

Asher's only problem then was to get Flint's heavy, unconscious body onto Shadow's back.

He was sweating profusely when he finally had Flint lying belly-down across the stallion's back.

Ever since night had fallen, Kate had been making trips to the kitchen window to stare out into the darkness. It was long past supper time now.

When Asher had come hurrying back to the house before lunch, insisting that he had to see

Flint, Kate had wondered what he was up to. Flint had already refused to go into town with him earlier. But suddenly, Flint was rushing out the door, calling that he'd be back in time for supper. She wondered if Asher had coaxed him into going to Jackson Hole after all. She hoped not. Flint had more or less stopped going to the saloon there since his niece and nephews had come to live with them. The young ones were turning this big old house into a lively family home filled with laughter . . . and some spats, she admitted with a wry grin. She could hear the two boys arguing about something in the front room now.

She had given them their supper, made them wash up and put on their nightclothes. When Flint got home he would be tired and she could send them to bed quickly.

Kate was looking out the window when she spotted Asher riding up. She frowned when she saw that he was leading Shadow, a body lying across his back. She hurried out onto the porch, the cold wind catching her breath.

"Oh, Asher," she cried, "is he alive?"

"Yes, he is, Kate." Asher grunted with the effort of pulling Flint's limp body into his arms. "But he's wounded and half frozen."

"We must get him thawed out, then examine his wound," Asher added, puffing as he carried his friend up the steps and onto the porch. Kate ran ahead and ushered the children away from the fireplace.

"Your uncle has been shot, children. We are going to need all the room we can get in here."

She glanced at the children, saw their frightened faces, and said softly, "He's going to be all right. We just have to doctor him a little. Go sit at the end of the hearth and be real quiet." She patted the boys' backs and kissed Mercy on the cheek.

The snow that Asher had packed onto Flint's chest was melting, running down his chest in pink rivulets as it mixed with the blood that still oozed from his wound.

"Let's get him out of this mackinaw so that we can see what's going on in there," Asher said, concern on his face.

No matter how careful Kate and Asher were in trying to get the mackinaw off him, the slightest movement made Flint groan. In the end Asher cut the garment off him, as well as his blood-soaked shirt.

Asher unbuttoned the top piece of Flint's underwear and pulled back the two edges, revealing the wound. "It doesn't look as bad as I thought it would," Asher said, gently pressing the flesh around the wound, "but the bullet is still in him. Let me have a cup of coffee with a hefty shot of whiskey in it, Kate. Then I'll try to dig that bullet out."

Kate brought him a full glass of Flint's best whiskey, and as Asher sipped it, he said quietly for her ears alone, "You'd better put the young'uns to bed. Flint is going to do some yelling when I start probing around. I hope the bullet isn't in too deep."

"You can do it," Kate said, ushering the children down the hall to their rooms.

"Pray God I can," Asher whispered as he scrubbed his hands with yellow lye soap.

Meanwhile Kate had torn strips of cloth from a clean sheet, and had scrubbed a poker clean and laid it on the hearth.

Asher took his bowie knife from its sheath and uncorking the whiskey bottle, he poured a good amount over the sharp blade, then poured more on the wound. Flint moaned as the fiery liquid hit his open flesh. Asher sighed, then bent over his friend.

He moved the knife slowly and carefully, trying not to hurt Flint more than necessary. After about three minutes he gave a thankful grunt and looked up at Kate, a pleased smile on his face. "I've found it. It's not deep at all."

Another few seconds and the bullet was making a pinging sound as Asher dropped it into the basin of water.

"He's gonna yell bloody hell now," Asher said, picking up the poker Kate had stuck in the coals. "I've got to do it. It's the only way I can stop the bleeding. Grab his shoulder and hold him down the best you can."

Kate nodded, and climbing onto the couch, put her knee against Flint's good shoulder and pressed hard. With sweat streaming down his face, Asher lifted the poker.

Just before he pressed the glowing end to the wound, Kate placed her hand firmly over Flint's mouth.

Her action muted his cry of agony, but it still rang out. Kate, however, had closed the children's doors. They knew nothing of the torture their uncle was enduring.

Dud rose from his cozy spot in front of the fire and crossed the room to close the shutters against the wind that seemed determined to invade the small shop. When he returned to his spot he did not sit down, but rather paced back and forth in front of the fire.

"Are you worried about Lauren, Dud?" Lillie asked.

"Yes, I am, Lillie. I've never left her alone before. I just can't settle down, knowing she's all by herself out there."

Lillie grabbed Dud's hand as he passed by her. "What are you going to do?"

Dud caught her hand and held it. "You know there's only one thing I can do." Dud gazed solemnly down at her. "I must get back to the ranch tonight."

Lillie nodded agreeably. "But, Dud, do be careful. I don't want to lose you after finally finding you."

Lillie drew a long, calming breath and, walking to the door, took Dud's jacket off a hook and held it for him. Before he went out into the cold and dark he planted a swift kiss on her cheek.

"Don't worry about me," he said. "I'll be back in the morning."

Half asleep, Kate sat nodding beside Flint. She wished that he was in his own bed. He would be much more comfortable there. But he was a big man, and Asher had done well to get him inside and onto the leather couch.

She looked down on Flint's face, calm and so handsome in repose, then gazed into the fire. Would he ever get married and settle down? And who was it that was determined to kill him? Or what if it was a woman? A woman Flint had spurned perhaps.

Kate suddenly felt eyes gazing at her. She turned her head and looked into Flint's dark gray eyes.

"Flint!" She went down on her knees beside the sofa. "How are you feeling, honey?"

Flint gave her a weak smile. "You haven't called me that for a long time."

"I know. You made me stop calling you baby names when you were around nine years old."

"I was sorry about that the next day, but I was too stubborn to tell you."

Kate stroked a hand over his unruly raven-black hair. "You always were a stubborn little scutter. Now tell me how you're feeling."

"I feel a little dizzy, but I'm so hungry I could fight a wolf over a bone."

Kate's happy laughter rang out. If Flint was hungry, he was going to be all right. She jumped to her feet and headed for the kitchen. A steak was what her boy needed. As she walked past Asher, who sat snoring in a rocker, she whacked him on the shoulder. "Wake up, you lazy hound dog, and talk to your friend."

"What do you want to talk about, you old buzzard?" Asher laid his palm on Flint's forehead. "It's good to see you don't have a fever. Do you feel like talking about who shot you?"

Flint's expression darkened. "You'd never guess in a million years who that dry-gulching varmint is. But first, I've got to sit up. This piece of furniture is hurting me more than my wound. I'll tell you all about it."

Just then, Kate came sailing into the room, a large tray in her hands. As she placed the tray on a low table beside the sofa, she explained, "I made two steaks. I figured you'd be hungry too, Asher."

"Thanks, Kate, I am hungry, but Flint was about to tell me who shot at him."

"That can wait." Flint picked up his knife and sliced into the juicy steak.

"I guess so," Asher agreed brusquely, and cut into his own steak.

When their plates were wiped clean of every morsel of food and Kate had poured coffee, Asher pinned Flint with narrowed eyes. "You're gonna tell us now who tried to dry-gulch you or I'll shoot you in your other shoulder."

Flint laughed and said, "Hold on to your

boots. It's been old Jonas Kile who has been trying to kill me."

"How could that be?" Kate exclaimed. "Everybody knows that the Indians killed him and his sons."

"Well, he got away from them somehow. It was that old devil shooting at me tonight. I saw him as plain as I'm seeing you now."

Asher shook his head doubtfully. "Tomorrow morning I'll go up to the Indian village and find out what happened when the Kiles were brought there. It's plain Jonas got away. I'm wondering now if some of the others escaped too. Nobody will be safe if they are still free to roam around."

Asher slapped his hand hard on the chair arm when he remembered something very important.

"What is it, Asher?" Flint asked when he saw the alarm that he had come over his friend's face.

"It's Lauren," Asher answered, his voice shaken. "She's at her place alone. I left her there not more than an hour ago."

"My God!" Flint exploded, getting to his feet. "Kile probably hates her as much as me."

"What do you think you're doing?" Asher jumped to his feet, alarmed.

"What do you think I'm doing? I'm going to see how Lauren is getting along."

"You can't do that!" Asher and Kate called out in unison.

"I've got to protect her." Flint's voice was like steel. "Asher, you ride to town and get Dud. I'm going straight to the Hart ranch to make sure she's all right."

Lauren stood in front of the kitchen window, gazing out into the night as she drank her coffee.

She had reheated a piece of beef for supper, but had no appetite for it. She had never been alone like this before. The freezing wind that blew across the windows moaned and howled, making her feel even more lonesome.

"Wolf, where are you?" she cried. He should have been home a long time ago. Had he tangled with a pack of wolves? Was he out there in the cold, dead or dying?

Lauren finished her coffee and placed the empty cup on the table. She went to the door then and opened it wide enough to stick her head out. Taking a deep breath, she whistled as loud as she could. She felt like crying when the wind blew it back in her mouth.

Closing the door, she went back to the kitchen window. As she wiped away the vapor of her breath that clouded the windowpane, the clock on the mantel struck midnight.

There was a menacing silence gripping the cabin now. She peered out the window and a cold chill came over her. In the dim light of the lamp on the table she made out the long slinking shape of a cougar. As she watched, terrified, fearing the large animal could rip away the shutters and enter the house, it started running toward the cabin. When it was only feet away from the porch it gathered its legs together and gave a great leap.

She barely repressed a scream when she heard its paws hit the roof. Would it come down the chimney? She hurried to the fireplace and added a couple small logs to the fire. The new flames should deter if from trying to get inside that way.

Lauren remembered then stories she had heard about the big cats climbing onto a roof and curling around the chimney to keep warm. She prayed silently that warmth was all the cougar was after. She remained quiet, making no noise that might alert him to her presence.

She was returning to the kitchen when a movement on the porch caught her eye. Was there another one out there? She almost panicked. She crept quietly to the window and peered outside, then gave a small cry of relief and joy. Wolf was on the porch, his nose quivering delicately as he tested the air. He was sniffing the scent of the cougar, Lauren thought, and hurriedly opened the door and called for him to come in.

She had never been so happy to see the big dog. She felt safe now. If the cat decided to come down the chimney, Wolf would attack him. She offered the dog some of the beef she had kept warm on the stove, and smiled when he refused it. He had made a kill while he was out roaming around. She decided that she might as well go to bed now. Nothing was going to hurt her with Wolf curled up on the floor beside her bed.

Lauren was in her nightgown and slippers and getting ready to blow out the light when she heard heavy footsteps on the porch. She froze, her heart pounding with terror.

Chapter Twenty-six

It's probably someone lost in the storm, she tried to convince herself; then she wondered why Wolf wasn't raising a ruckus. He had lifted his head at the sound of feet outside, but then laid his head back down.

Lauren let loose a glad cry when a male voice called, "Lauren, girl, open the door. I'm about froze."

Lauren unlatched the door, pulled Dud inside, and gave him such a hug, he grunted. "Come by the fire and take off your jacket and boots and I'll get you a glass of whiskey. You'll be toasty warm before you know it.

"And then I'll tell you everything that has happened to me."

Dud paused in unbuttoning his jacket. "That damn Asher didn't pull any of his stunts on you, did he?"

"No, of course not," she said from the small cabinet where Dud kept his liquor supply. "Asher is always the gentleman."

"I bet you can't say that about his long-legged friend Mahone." Dud pinned Lauren with narrowed eyes.

"I don't know," Lauren lied, "but I'm sure I could handle him if he ever did."

"You're probably right," Dud replied as though reluctant to admit it. "He don't strike me as the type of man who would ever force himself on a female."

No, he wouldn't do that, Lauren thought. He'd charm himself into her bed. And then forget all about her.

"How is aunt Lillie?" Lauren asked, handing Dud his whiskey.

"She's still crying over him." Dud shook his head as if he couldn't understand anyone grieving for a man like Colly King.

As if she had been reading his mind, Lauren said, "She seemed to love him very much. He was like a son to her."

"I guess," Dud grunted. "But couldn't she see what a weak character he was?"

"I guess love blinds you, Dud." Lauren gave such a long sigh, Dud shot her a curious look.

"Why the sad sigh?" Dud asked.

"Oh, I didn't mean to sigh," Lauren answered swiftly, her face going a little pink. "I was just wondering what Aunt Lillie will do now, with no man to help her."

"Hah!" Dud snorted. "That wastrel was never no help to her. He lived off her. She'll be better off without him."

"I wasn't thinking that she would need him for money, just that she'd miss having a man to lean on emotionally. Like I have you."

Dud was silent for a while before saying, "My shoulders are big enough for two women."

Lauren looked at him, then gave a wide smile. "Are you saying that you're going to take on the job of caring for Aunt Lillie?"

Dud's face reddened. "I reckon that's what I'm trying to say."

"But I thought you two always hated each other."

"Naw." Dud shook his head. "It was always just the opposite. We was crazy wild about each other. It was my fault Lillie rode away and left us. She wanted me to quit the outlaw gang. Said she wouldn't marry me unless I did.

"I was older than she was, thought I knew best. I told her if she really loved me she wouldn't care what I did for a living. The last thing she ever said to me was that she hoped I enjoyed living without her."

Dud stared into the flames, the glass forgotten in his hands. "It was my foolish pride that wouldn't let me go after her when she rode away an hour or so later." He sighed. "It was my pride again that made me talk mean about her afterward."

"You're very lucky to have gotten back together again after all this time." Lauren looked gravely at Dud. "When are you getting married?"

"As soon as possible."

"Will you and Aunt Lillie be living in town or out here on the ranch?"

"We haven't talked about that yet. Where would you rather live?"

"You mean you want me to live with you?" Lauren's expression showed her surprise.

"I shouldn't even answer that," Dud half shouted. "Where in the hell did you think you'd live?"

"I wouldn't want to be in the way of a couple newlyweds," Lauren tried to explain. "I'm sure you wouldn't want me underfoot all the time."

"Gol darn it, Lauren, me and Lillie ain't a couple kids who will be crawling all over each other all the time."

"I guess not." Lauren blushed. She smiled at the man who had been like a second father to her for as long as she could remember. "I'm glad you and Aunt Lillie want me to live with you."

Dud yawned. "I'm ready for bed. What about you?"

"Yes. It's been a long hard day for everybody."

"That's for sure," Dud said as his boots hit the floor.

Lauren had just brushed out her hair and braided it, preparatory to retiring, when she thought she heard a creaking noise at her bedroom window. She twisted her head in that direction and listened intently. She only heard the roar and whistle of the wind. The shutter must be loose, she decided. She turned down the wick in the lamp, then blew out the flame.

Just as the light was extinguished, she saw a movement from the corner of her eyes. She gasped and spun around, but she was too late to avoid the rough hands that grasped her by the arms. "Turn me loose!" she gasped, kicking backward at her assailant's legs. The man swore harshly and clapped a rough palm over her mouth.

"Shut up, bitch," he whispered harshly, "or I'll slice your throat with my huntin' knife. Now, if you promise to keep your yap shut, I'll move my hand so that you can get dressed and put on a jacket so that you won't freeze."

She nodded and the man released her. When she realized that he wasn't going to give her any privacy, she jerked a woolen dress from her wardrobe and pulled it on over her nightgown.

"Shy, ain't you," he sneered. "You'll get over that by the time I'm through with you. I intend to keep you naked most of the time."

Lauren took the boots he thrust at her and

grabbed the coat that was flung in her face. "Hurry up and get into these or you'll go as you are."

Who was this awful man? she wondered, but she couldn't get a good look at him in the dark room. And then she was being forced out her bedroom window and tossed onto a horse that looked half starved.

The man sprang up behind Lauren and clamped an arm across her waist so tightly she cried out. Worse still, his clawlike fingers moved up her midriff and cruelly grasped her breasts.

I will not scream, she told herself through the almost unbearable pain. That is what he wants me to do. I will not give him the satisfaction. As the horse plodded through the snow for nearly an hour, Lauren realized that she might never see Dud and Lillie again . . . or Flint Mahone.

Half frozen and numb with cold, she grasped the saddle horn as the horse lurched to a stop. She no longer felt the pinching of her tormentor's bony fingers on her breasts. Feeling had left them a long time ago.

"About time we got here," her tormentor grumbled, jerking Lauren to the ground. She was so stiff she stumbled and fell against the old horse. With an ugly oath the man grabbed her arm and sent her reeling toward a porch that looked like it wouldn't survive the winter.

Following her, he threw open a door whose rusty hinges groaned. Another push sent Lauren stumbling through the dark into what must be a disgustingly filthy room if the smell was anything to go by.

"You damn well better know how to cook," her abductor growled. "I'm so hungry I gotta eat before I can bed you." With that, he struck a match and lit the stove.

"You!" Lauren cried, getting her first good look at him. It was the beast who still haunted her nightmares. Jonas Kile.

A fuzzy white moon gave Flint enough light to show the way to Lauren's house, "Pray God I find her safe at home," he whispered as he urged his little mountain horse through the snow.

It felt like his heart had stopped beating when Flint arrived at Lauren's ranch. Lauren's bedroom window stood open, and outside in the snow were the marks of a scuffle and the hoofprints of a horse leading toward the mountain.

"Oh, dear Lord," Flint groaned. "The bastard has her." He wheeled his horse around, unmindful that the wind was blowing snow into Lauren's open window, and urged the animal forward.

The tracks of Jonas Kile's horse were easy to follow in the moonlight and Flint wasn't surprised that they led toward his run-down place. As he urged the horse on, a refrain like that of a song ran through his mind.

"Please, God, let her be all right. She is my heartbeat. If any harm comes to her, I don't know what I'll do."

The horse was plodding when the faint outline of Kile's shack came into view. Flint intended to slip up on the dilapidated building, but a piercing scream had him flying out of the saddle and bursting through the flimsy door.

Jonas had Lauren in his grip, her clothing opened to her waist. As the door slammed open, Jonas spun around and stared. His face grew white and dread looked out of his eyes. He seemed to know he was looking into the eyes of death.

"Damn you, Mahone," he grated, pushing Lauren away from him. "I'll get you this time."

He grabbed for the gun lying on the table. His fingers had barely touched it when Flint's Colt roared. Jonas screamed and grabbed between his legs. Flint had deliberately shot him in the crotch.

"Dammit, man," he groaned, "that's an awful place to shoot a man."

"I agree," Flint said coldly as he hurried to catch the fainting Lauren. "But you aren't a man. You will suffer now for all the women you've put through hell in your lifetime."

Flint was tempted to shoot Jonas again as he helped the trembling Lauren fasten up her clothes and saw the long, angry-looking marks of the man's clawlike fingers on her white breasts. Only the need to get her to a dry, warm place kept him from taking the time to pump lead into Kile again.

Jonas's cries of pain followed him and Lauren down the mountain. Jonas would be a long time dying.

The mountain horse walked up to Flint's ranch house just shy of daylight. Kate, who had just started breakfast, looked out of the window, and almost dropped a bowl of eggs in relief when she saw Flint slide off his horse with Lauren in his arms.

She hurried to fling open the door. "Thank God, Flint, you found her," she cried, pulling a chair away from the table and motioning him to place Lauren in it.

Panting slightly, Flint lowered her gently, then turned to Kate. "Kile had her, all right," he explained. "When I got to her place, she was gone. I followed the tracks of Kile's horse up to his old shack. He was about to rape her when I shot him . . . in the crotch. I feel satisfied that by now the bastard is dead."

"Are you all right, honey?" Kate asked Lauren as she helped her out of her jacket. "He didn't do anything to you, did he?"

"No. Flint came just in time," Lauren said weakly. "I'm just so tired."

"Come on," Flint said gently. "You can lie down in Kate's room."

He took her up in his arms again and carried her into Kate's small room behind the kitchen. Laying her down on the bed, he brushed strands of hair away from her face. His eyes met hers.

"Thank God I got to you in time. I would never have forgiven myself if that bastard had hurt you."

"You don't have to pretend you care, Flint," Lauren said tiredly. "You made it pretty clear last night that you're just interested in one thing from a woman. And the girls at Maudie's will be giving it away for free next Saturday."

"Lauren—" Flint protested, but she turned her head to the wall.

I'll let her sleep, he thought, tell her how I feel when she wakes up.

It was late afternoon as Flint sat gazing somberly into the leaping flames of the fireplace. Lauren was still sleeping in Kate's room. He had spent the last hours thinking how he could convince her that he'd changed his wild ways. When was the last time he'd lain with one of Maudie's girls? He couldn't even remember. Certainly none of them had appealed to him since he'd met Lauren. He hadn't noticed the change himself, hadn't realized the depth of his own feelings until last night, when he'd risked losing her.

He was about to go wake Lauren up when he saw, coming up the drive, a farm wagon pulled by a bony old mule. He recognized the middle-aged man handling the reins, as well as the woman sitting beside him. They had a farm a short distance outside of Jackson Hole and sold the produce they raised to the town's citizens. He knew that poor Tillie had gone often to visit the couple. He imagined they were related somehow.

He wondered what they were doing out so late in the day, and in such cold weather. Especially cold for the baby the farm woman was holding in her arms.

"Howdy, Mr. Mahone," the man said as he hopped out of the wagon, then turned to help his wife climb to the ground.

"Howdy, Ben," Flint replied. "Come on in the house and warm up."

"We can't stay long." Ben pushed his wife ahead of him. "Actually, we're here on business."

"Oh?" Flint said, wondering what kind of business the farmer would want to discuss with him.

Ben Harper remained standing as his wife sat down and began undoing the wraps around a small infant. "It's like this, Mr. Mahone," the farmer began. "About a year ago one of Maudie's girls came to us and made a bargain with my wife. If Hessie here would care for her newborn baby and never tell who its father was, she would pay her a goodly sum every week.

"Hessie kept her word. It has never crossed our lips who the father is. But now the mother is dead—it was Tillie, you see—and with Tillie dead and all, we feel that the father should pay for the baby's care." Ben looked at Flint and asked somberly, "Don't you agree, Mr. Mahone?"

"Yes, I do," Flint answered honestly. "If a man fathers a child, he should support it."

The farmer's lips spread in a wide smile. "Didn't I tell you, Hessie, that he would feel that way?" Ben looked at his wife.

"Yes, you did," the woman smilingly answered, and removed the last blanket from around the baby.

"Meet your son, Mr. Mahone." She smiled widely.

Flint couldn't stop staring. He was gazing at a tiny replica of himself. The baby had deep gray eyes, and raven-black curls clung to his small head.

"Do you want to hold him?" Mrs. Harper asked.

Flint couldn't speak over the lump in his throat. When he only nodded with a soft smile on his lips, Hessie held the baby out to him. "Be careful of him. He doesn't walk yet."

Flint reached for his son, and the little one chortled and grabbed his nose with a chubby hand. Flint buried his face in the soft black curls.

A low gasp from the kitchen doorway brought his head up abruptly. Lauren was standing there, sleep-touseled and pale, with bright tears in her eyes. "So it's true. You are the father of Tillie's baby. Maudie tried to tell me—" She broke off, whirling back into the kitchen. She grabbed her jacket and ran out the door toward the barn.

Flint took a step after her, then realized he still held the baby in his arms. When he tried to hand the little one back to Hessie, her husband broke in.

"Now see here, Mr. Mahone. We'll need more money if we're to go on caring for the boy. Anyone can see he's your child."

"Of course he's my child," Flint said impatiently. "And I'm going to raise him. I don't know why Tillie never told me about him herself."

"I suppose he was all she had," Hessie said.

"Well, I'll be caring for him from now on," Flint said. "How much money do I owe you?" he asked, wanting to conclude his business with the Harpers so he could go after Lauren.

"You don't owe us anything. Tillie had paid for the month before she was killed.

"I think we'd better get goin' now. Dark will be here soon." Ben patted the baby's fat little cheek and Hessie kissed it.

"I would be pleased if you would bring him to the farm once in a while," she said. "Me and Ben have grown awfully fond of the little feller."

As he saw the couple to the door, Flint caught sight of Lauren galloping out of the yard on a borrowed horse.

What must she think of him? he wondered grimly, turning back to the front room. He would never convince her that he'd changed his ways now. How could he when the proof of his carousing with whores was right before her eyes? How could he ask her to marry him and take on the job of raising not only his niece and nephews, but also his illegitimate son? What woman would put up with that? He thought of Dud's description of the man he had in mind for Lauren's husband, and gave a bitter laugh. Flint was about as different from that man as he could be.

Sadly, Flint sat down in a rocker and gazed at his little son, who waved his arms and mouthed words that only he knew the meaning of. "None of this is your fault, Jakie," he whispered, deciding on the spot that he would call the child after his dead brother.

Flint came out of his trancelike state when Kate bustled into the room, unwinding a scarf from around her throat. "Wasn't that Farmer Harper and his wife who just left?" she asked, taking off her jacket and hanging it on the wall. "What did they want?"

"They brought me something that is mine."

"And what was that—" Kate began, then stopped to stare at the infant in Flint's lap. She grabbed the back of a chair, then eased herself into it. "That baby is yours," she finally said in amazement.

"Yes," Flint answered, a wide smile on his lips. "Did you ever see a more handsome little feller?" he asked proudly.

Dusk had fallen and the lamps were lit by the

time Flint told Kate all that he knew about the birth of the baby, and how he was puzzled that Tillie had never told him about the child.

Little Jake had fallen asleep in Flint's lap when the boys and Mercy came running in. They stopped short and stared when they saw the infant curled up in their uncle's arms.

"Did you buy me a dollie, Unca Flint?" Mercy came and leaned against her uncle's knee and touched a finger to the baby's cheek.

When Baby Jake frowned and squirmed, she jumped as if she had been hit. Flint explained that he wasn't holding a doll, but a real live baby who would be living with them. At this, Mercy began to cry.

"Mercy, why are you crying?" Flint put an arm around her.

"Because I won't be your little girl anymore," she hiccuped. "I can't sit in your lap anymore."

"That's not true, honey," Flint said gently, and to prove it he lifted the little girl up to sit on his knee. "I was hoping that you would help Aunt Kate take care of him. He can't even walk yet."

"Hand the little fellow over to me," Kate said to Flint. "Then you go up in the attic and look in the north corner under a canvas sheet. You'll find a crib that you and Jake used. I never dreamed that you would have anything to do with filling it again. At least not this way." She gave Flint a teasing grin.

"Neither did I." Flint grinned back. "You can bet it was an accident."

"You know that you're going to take a lot of razzing, don't you?"

"I know," Flint agreed, "but I don't care. He's worth it."

"He might stand in the way of some woman marrying you someday." Kate said seriously. "Maybe a woman you will really care for."

"That's not likely to happen," Flint said gruffly. The only woman he could care for was Lauren, and the damage had already been done. "I'll go bring down the crib. Should I put it in your room?"

Kate gave him a look as though to say, "Where else, you idiot."

All was quiet in the house. The children had finally settled down and were asleep. Baby Jake slept peacefully in the crib where his father and uncle had slept years ago. Kate had also retired. Only, Flint, restless, paced back and forth between the kitchen and the front room.

He loved Lauren, loved her desperately. It wasn't only her body he wanted. He wanted her in the way a man wants a woman when he hopes to spend the rest of his life with her.

It was a bitter discovery that nothing could ever come of his love. Lauren knew too much about his wild ways, his carousing, his lying with prostitutes. And by tomorrow morning, if not already, everyone in and around Jackson Hole would know about little Jake.

Flint laid his head back against the chair. He

would never regret his little son. His innocent little son.

Flint suddenly came to a decision. Perhaps nothing would come of it, but nothing was happening anyhow. He was going to the Hart ranch and have a talk with Lauren. He was going to tell her honestly how he felt about her, that he wanted to marry her and settle down. He would also tell her about his son.

Should he tell Kate where he was going? he asked himself. He decided he would leave her a note. There was no point in disturbing her.

He scribbled her a few lines, saying that he was going to the Hart ranch and would not be back until Lauren had agreed to be his wife. He propped it on the mantel where she was bound to see it, then slipped out the back door.

Flint tucked his chin into his jacket collar as he rode the stallion out into the barnyard. It was icy cold. All was silent except the crunch of snow under the horse's great hoofs.

But the clean night air was like medicine to him. His head was clear and his resolve firm when the stallion climbed the bluff that looked down on what was now called the Hart ranch.

The door was opened almost immediately to Flint's knock. It was hard to say who was the more startled. Lauren spoke first. Giving him a sharp look, she asked icily, "What are you doing here?"

Flint smiled and looked her in the eyes. "We've got to talk, Lauren."

Norah Hess

Lauren started to close the door. "I don't want to talk to you."

Flint slid his foot in the crack of the door. "Couldn't I at least get warmed up before I have to turn around and ride back home?"

His voice was soft and coaxing and Lauren knew she would be unable to turn him away.

"All right," she snapped. "Ten minutes by the fire and then you have to leave."

Before she could open the door wider Flint stepped inside, his body pressing snugly against hers. "Where's Dud?" he asked.

"He decided to spend the night in town with Aunt Lillie. Since I didn't expect you, I told him I'd be perfectly safe." He ignored her innuendo.

"What about a glass of whiskey," he asked as he sat down in a big rocker. "It would help me warm up."

Lauren gave an aggravated sigh, but went to the sideboard and half filled a glass with Dud's whiskey. When she handed the drink to him, she let loose a little squeal. Flint had grabbed her wrist and pulled her into his lap.

"Turn me loose right now," she ordered. "I don't want to sit in your lap."

"But you're going to sit here until you hear me out," Flint said. "Lauren, honey, I'm not the man I used to be. I know all the folks around talk about Flint Mahone, about my wild ways, but I swear that's in the past now. I haven't even had the desire to bed another woman since I laid eyes on you. I didn't understand it myself until last night when I thought I might lose you. Then it hit me like a load of bricks. You're the only one for me."

"But Tillie's baby—"

"I didn't even know she was pregnant. She left town for a while, never said a word about him when she came back. I would have helped her if I'd known." He smiled down at her. "Since my brother's kids arrived, I've found I like being a family man. Only thing my brood's missing is a mama." He looked at her expectantly.

"Is that your idea of a marriage proposal?" she asked, acting offended. She squirmed on his hard thighs, trying to escape his hold.

"I love you, little girl," he murmured, then asked teasingly, "Is that any better?"

"Oh, Flint," she laughed, "you are an idiot."

Flint urged her head down so that he could capture her lips with his mouth. As his tongue moved in and out between her lips, he unbuttoned her bodice. He freed a plump, firm breast and transferred his lips to bring as much of the white mound as he could into his mouth.

It was but seconds before she was threading her fingers through his black hair and urging his head closer to her breast. Flint obliged her, at the same time undoing his trousers. As she moaned his name, he took her hand and gently curled her fingers around his length.

The stroking and suckling soon had them both sweating. Flint rose and carried Lauren into a bedroom. He didn't know whose bedroom it was, nor did he care. He only knew that he must join his body with Lauren's, unite their souls now and for all time.

Long into the night, the bed rocked and the walls shook as they gave themselves to each other with lips and hands and heart. Flint was sure he would never get enough of Lauren.

And evidently she felt the same. An hour before Dud returned the next morning, she promised Flint that she would be his wife.

Two weeks later a double wedding took place in the little log church in Jackson Hole.

When Lauren delivered their first baby, a girl, before the year was out, people smiled when they counted the days on their fingers. The couple was short three weeks. But what else could you expect of a hell-raiser like Flint Mahone?

SNOW FIRE

NORAH HESS

She is lost. Blinded by the swirling storm, Flame knows that she cannot give up if she is to survive. Her memory gone, the lovely firebrand awakes to find that the strong arms encircling her belong to a devilishly handsome stranger. And one look at his blazing eyes tells her that the haven she has found promises a passion that will burn for a lifetime. She is the most lovely thing he has ever seen. From the moment he takes Flame in his arms and gazes into her sparkling eyes, Stone knows that the red-headed virgin has captured his heart. The very sight of her smile stokes fiery desires in him that only her touch can extinguish. To protect her he'll claim her as his wife, and pray that he can win her heart before she discovers the truth.

___4691-1 $5.99 US/$6.99 CAN

WINTER LOVE

NORAH HESS

As fresh and enchanting as a new snowfall, Laura always adored Fletcher Thomas. Yet she fears she will never win the trapper's heart—until one passion-filled night in his father's barn. Lost in his heated caresses, the innocent beauty succumbs to a desire as strong and unpredictable as a Michigan blizzard. But Laura has barely cleared her head of Fletch's musk scent and the sweet smell of hay before circumstances separate them and threaten to end their winter love.

___52365-5 $5.50 US/$6.50 CAN

Dorchester Publishing Co., Inc.
P.O. Box 6640
Wayne, PA 19087-8640

Please add $1.75 for shipping and handling for the first book and $.50 for each book thereafter. NY, NYC, and PA residents, please add appropriate sales tax. No cash, stamps, or C.O.D.s. All orders shipped within 6 weeks via postal service book rate. Canadian orders require $2.00 extra postage and must be paid in U.S. dollars through a U.S. banking facility.

Name_____
Address_____
City_____State_____Zip_____
I have enclosed $ _____ in payment for the checked book(s).
Payment <u>must</u> accompany all orders. ❑ Please send a free catalog.

Raven
Norah Hess

When Raven's two-bit gambler husband orders her to entertain a handsome cowboy at dinner, she has no idea of the double dealings involved. How is she to know that he has promised the good-looking stranger a night in her bed for $1,000, or that he has no intention of keeping his word? Cheated of his night of passion, Chance McGruder can't get the dark-haired little beauty out of his mind. So he is both tantalized and tormented when she shows up at the neighboring ranch, newly widowed but no less desirable. What kind of a wife will agree to sell herself to another man? What kind of a woman will run off with $1,000 that isn't hers? What kind of a widow can make him burn to possess her? And what kind of man is he to ignore his doubts and gamble his heart that when she gives her body, it will be for love.

___4611-3 $5.99 US/$6.99 CAN

Dorchester Publishing Co., Inc.
P.O. Box 6640
Wayne, PA 19087-8640

Please add $1.75 for shipping and handling for the first book and $.50 for each book thereafter. NY, NYC, and PA residents, please add appropriate sales tax. No cash, stamps, or C.O.D.s. All orders shipped within 6 weeks via postal service book rate. Canadian orders require $2.00 extra postage and must be paid in U.S. dollars through a U.S. banking facility.

Name_____/_____
Address_____
City_____ State_____ Zip_____
I have enclosed $_____ in payment for the checked book(s).
Payment <u>must</u> accompany all orders. ❑ Please send a free catalog.
CHECK OUT OUR WEBSITE! www.dorchesterpub.com

Velvet & Steel

Sylvie Sommerfield

Commanded to marry a Saxon heiress in order to secure her lands for his king, Norman knight Royce, Sword of William, does not expect to find the lovely creature who stands before him. Her defiant eyes the color of cornflowers on a summer day reveal intelligence and gentleness. For once, Royce is struck speechless—and he knows that he will be the one to spark the fire that will set this maid aflame with desire. He is the largest, most intense man she has ever encountered. But it is his gaze that both unnerves her and touches her soul: His golden eyes glance over her body and heat her to the very core of her being. For though he is the Sword of William—a knight so passionate and powerful on the battlefield, legends tell his tale—Lynette sees the pain behind his handsome visage, and knows that she will be the one to heal the wounds of his tormented past.

___4576-1 $5.99 US/$6.99 CAN

Dorchester Publishing Co., Inc.
P.O. Box 6640
Wayne, PA 19087-8640

Please add $1.75 for shipping and handling for the first book and $.50 for each book thereafter. NY, NYC, and PA residents, please add appropriate sales tax. No cash, stamps, or C.O.D.s. All orders shipped within 6 weeks via postal service book rate. Canadian orders require $2.00 extra postage and must be paid in U.S. dollars through a U.S. banking facility.

Name_____
Address_____
City_____ State_____ Zip_____
I have enclosed $_____ in payment for the checked book(s).
Payment <u>must</u> accompany all orders. ❑ Please send a free catalog.
CHECK OUT OUR WEBSITE! www.dorchesterpub.com

Lacey
Norah Hess

Norah Hess's historical romances are "delightful, tender and heartwarming reads from a special storyteller!"

—Romantic Times

Stranded on the Western frontier, Lacey Stewart suddenly has to depend on the kindness of strangers. And no one shows her more generosity than the rancher who offers to marry her. But shortly after Trey Saunders and Lacey are pronounced husband and wife, he is off to a cattle drive—and another woman's bed. Shocked to discover that the dashing groom wants her to be a pawn in a vicious game of revenge, the young firebrand refuses to obey her vows. Only when Trey proves that he loves, honors, and cherishes his blushing bride will Lacey forsake all others and unite with him in wedded bliss.

_3941-9 $5.99 US/$7.99 CAN